THE DEAD KIDS CLUB
Rich Hosek

nifni
PRESS
Sherman Oaks, California

Visit **www.RichHosek.com** and
Facebook.com/WrittenByRichHosek
for more information about
a free audio version of this book,
special editions and offers,
and future stories From the Files of Eddie Horne.

Copyright © 2021 Rich Hosek
All rights reserved.

No part of this book may be reproduced in any form whatsoever
without written permission from the publisher.
The characters and events in this book are fictitious.
Any similarity to real persons, living or dead,
is coincidental and not intended.

Nifni Press
a division of
Paraphrase, LLC
P.O. Box 56508
Sherman Oaks, CA 91413

Read a Book, Read a Mind

ISBN: 1-953566-02-2
ISBN-13: 978-1-953566-02-7

Printed in the United States of America
First Printing: January 2021

For everyone who has been with me on this journey,
especially my family and friends.

There are too many to list by name.

But if you have the slightest suspicion
that I mean you,

I do.

Also by Rich Hosek

A Raney/Daye Investigation series,
with Arnold Rudnick and Loyd Auerbach

Near Death
After Life

Anthologies:

Beyond the Levee and Other Ghostly Tales
(contributor, edited by Peter Talley)

The Dead Kids Club

NICK

The Dead Kids Club

one

I pull into the drop-off lane of the elementary school. Ahead of me are bright blue skies, but as I look in the rearview mirror to check on my six-year-old son, Nick, I can see dark, roiling clouds out the back window.

Nick, as usual, is staring out the side window as he sits perched in his booster. "We're here," I tell him.

He unbuckles his seatbelt as one of the drop-off lane volunteers opens the door for him.

"Have a good day!" I say.

"You, too," he replies. He grabs his backpack, jumps out of the car and rushes off to join the other first graders as they funnel into the school.

I pull away and check my watch. Late again, but if I make a couple of lights on the way, I should get to the office in time for my first meeting.

A familiar voice shouts, "Dad! Dad!"

I check my rearview mirror and see Nick running toward me. I turn around and notice the lunch bag sitting on the back seat next to his booster. I pull over.

An engine roars.

A car horn blares.

A woman screams.

There is a sickening thud.

I get out of my car, looking around to see what the commotion is all about.

I don't see Nick.

There's a car on the sidewalk, the driver stands beside it, confused. Something is wrong. Where is Nick? He was just there.

I walk toward the school, scanning the kids for his bright red shirt. Then I see it. He's curled up on the grass.

A yellow-vested crossing guard leans over him, a look of horror on her face.

I rush over.

Sounds flood in.

Screams, shouts, crying.

Nick lies on his side. I turn him over. Blood trickles out from the corner of his mouth. His eyes open for a moment and look at me. "I want my mom…" he manages to say with his last breath.

Someone screams, a wail of anguish that overpowers the approaching sirens.

That someone is me.

two

Rebecca bursts into the emergency department. She spots me sitting across the room.

I look at her and mouth the words, "I'm sorry."

She shakes her head as she walks toward me. "No, no," she says, "where is he? I want to see him. Where is my son?"

I stand and walk toward her.

A uniformed police officer standing by the entrance to the treatment area shoots me a glance. I answer with a barely perceptible nod.

Rebecca looks around furtively for someone who can help her. Someone who has answers.

I reach her and awkwardly hold out my arms for an embrace.

She raises her hands in front of her, defensively.

I put a hand on her elbow instead and steer her toward the waiting officer. He opens the doors for us and I lead her down a corridor.

Her breathing grows more labored with each step we take. At the end of the hall is a room. Through a large glass window, she spies the child-shaped lump under a green sheet on a gurney inside.

Rebecca's whole body shakes as she sobs.

A nurse arrives. She opens the door and lets us into the room. We gather around the gurney. Rebecca grabs hold of my arm as the nurse pulls the sheet back.

Nick lies face up, still and peaceful under the green fabric. Someone was thoughtful enough to wipe the blood away from his mouth. But he doesn't look right. He always slept on his side, hugging a stuffed animal.

Rebecca moves to him, places a hand on his cheek. She leans over and kisses him on the forehead.

Then she straightens up and turns to me.

I brace myself for a barrage of accusations and blame. I imagine her fists pounding against my chest as she demands an explanation of how I could let this happen to her son.

Instead, she embraces me and whispers in my ear, "I forgive you."

three

The funeral is a blur.

The burial takes place on a sunny, unseasonably hot day.

Afterward, friends and family and dozens of people I barely know or have never met saunter through my mother's house, offering condolences and food. I see Rebecca only briefly. Neither of us knows the etiquette for how divorced parents should behave at their child's funeral.

A month later, we stand silently at the site of Nick's death while a marble bird bath is dedicated to his memory. His teachers and friends share their remembrances, but neither Rebecca nor I can bring ourselves to say a word.

I don't see or talk with her for another six months, not until the trial begins.

The rookie Assistant District Attorney is confident. Open and shut case, she tells us, he'll take a plea and spend the next ten-plus years behind bars.

Despite her assurances, the case goes to trial.

The driver of the car that killed Nick, Anthony Vitali, sits behind the defendant's table while his slick lawyer dances circles around the Assistant D.A.

We watch him sway the jury with emotional arguments and artful manipulations. The witnesses recount the horror of the day, and then he plants doubt in their minds, questioning their own previously vivid memories that seemed so fresh just moments before.

It's my turn on the stand. I tell the jury what happened. My voice cracks as I describe Nick's last moments.

The Assistant District Attorney thanks me, and Vitali's defense attorney rises to his feet.

I can feel Rebecca's stare burning into me as that slick, charismatic attorney co-opts my grief, telling the gallery and the jury they can't possibly know the outrage and despair I feel. Who can blame me for wanting to hold someone responsible for this senseless accident?

The remainder of the trial feels like a comedy of errors.

The hapless A.D.A. loses motion after motion. The fact that Vitali's blood alcohol was above the legal limit at eight a.m. gets suppressed. His suspended license and previous DUI citations are disallowed from being introduced as evidence. The jury hears only how his politically connected father rallied the community to replace the faulty traffic signals at his personal expense.

The jury is out for less than an hour before arriving at a verdict.

"Not guilty."

Anthony Vitali breathes a sigh of relief. His lawyer slaps him on the back, then he turns around to the gallery and gives a woman, whom I assume is his girlfriend, a kiss and a hug with a smug, satisfied smile on his face.

A smile.

The cocky bastard.

Rebecca squeezes my hand. I look over at the jury. A few of them look our way, pity in their eyes, maybe a touch of empathy, but none of them know what we're feeling. If they did, Vitali would not be walking out of the courtroom, passing us without even a glance, without the slightest bit of remorse or regret.

I can't move.

I can't even breathe.

Is this real?

I close my eyes and the sights and sounds of the courtroom disappear. I hear Nick's musical laugh, hear him talk to his stuffed animals in that funny voice, hear him say, "Goodnight, I love you, pleasant dreams," as I tuck him in.

But that is merely a brief daydream.

There is a coffin not far from this courthouse, buried in the ground, with a marble stone—the same marble as the bird bath—upon which is chiseled his name, and the dates marking his all too short life. And in that coffin is our son.

My heart screams.

Rebecca lays her head on my shoulder, and I can feel her body shaking with sobs.

The divorce several years ago was hard, but through it all I always told myself I had no regrets and would do it all again exactly the same to make sure I had Nick in my life.

Now I didn't know what my life was for. To work for a company that distributed sporting goods? To watch television, barbecue on the weekends and maybe golf once in a while? Was any of that important?

Some people live their lives without children and seem perfectly happy.

I am not one of them.

A kindly bailiff approaches. "You'll need to clear the courtroom. I'm sorry. I'm so very sorry," she tells us.

I look at her and offer a forced smile. I don't think there will ever be another moment of genuine happiness in my life again, but this woman has been kind to us throughout the court proceedings, has always managed to convey a sense of sympathy and caring through her actions and words that no one else in this so-called justice system seems to possess.

I rise and help Rebecca to her feet. Our hands entwine and we walk in silence to the parking lot. Neither one of us can think of a thing to say as I drive her back to her apartment—she has never returned to the house she shared with Nick. I walk her to the door. She turns to me and asks, "Can you stay? I don't want to be alone."

I nod and follow her inside.

We lie together on her bed, not bothering even to remove our shoes. I hold her and let her fall asleep with her head on my chest. Rest does not come for me, however. I stare at the ceiling, fighting the feeling that I'm going to break out into uncontrollable wailing. I remember stories in the bible of people who tear their clothes in mourning.

My grief is so primal, I can imagine shredding my clothes with my teeth and my bare hands, even ripping the flesh from my bones.

What I cannot imagine is a greater pain than what I feel right at this moment.

four

Two months after the end of the trial, my boss calls me into his office. His voice fades as I watch his lips move. I know what he is saying without needing to hear the words. I have not met my deadlines, I come in late and leave early if I show up at all. I don't return coworker's phone calls and emails. They have been patient with me, but it's not working out. There will always be a place for me here, but not now.

I couldn't care less.

It used to be that I worked so I could make money to spend on Nick, tuck away something for his college fund, save up for a house in a better neighborhood. None of that matters now, so what motivation do I have to work? To live?

There is enough money in the bank to last awhile. It's amazing how much of my budget was centered around Nick.

I watch a lot of TV. News channels and television judge shows, mostly. They don't demand my attention and provide a distraction.

I haven't shopped for food in weeks. Whenever I get hungry, I just order a pizza and leave a twenty-dollar bill taped to the door frame with a note for him to ring the bell and leave it.

I haven't showered in days, and the underwear and robe I wear are rank. Flies buzz around the overflowing garbage can. Unopened mail covers the coffee table.

The phone rings. I don't know where it is and am quite frankly amazed that it's warbling at me, I can't remember the last time I bothered to charge it. I try to zero in on where the sound is coming from and find it stuck between the layers of a stack of unread newspapers. I maneuver my thumb to silence the call, but then see that the caller ID is Rebecca.

I answer. "Hi."

"Hi," she replies, with a coarseness to her voice she gets when she's been crying.

"Are you all right?" I immediately want to take that question back. I know the answer. She's like me. Nothing will be all right ever again.

She forgives my careless question and continues. "I saw him today, I saw Vitali. At the store. He... he smiled at me. Like everything was okay."

"God."

"Karen was there. She yelled at him to get out. I couldn't say a word. I was paralyzed."

"I've always liked Karen."

"He gets to shop. He gets to go to the store and buy beer—he was buying beer. Probably the same beer..." Her voice trails off.

"I'm sorry." It's the only thing I can think of saying. It sounds so hollow.

Rebecca ignores my choice of words. She has something else on her mind. "I want to kill him." she says.

"I know."

"No," she says, "I really want to kill him. I want to buy a gun and shoot him. I want him to die."

I don't answer. The thought has crossed my mind. How I might be driving along and see him crossing the street, or walking to his car in a parking lot, and I'd just drive right over him, back up if I needed to.

"Will you help me?"

"Yes," I answer without thinking. Will I really? "Yes, I will."

"I think I know where I can get—"

"No," I interrupt. "not on the phone. Meet me at the trail where we used to go running." I glance at the clock. "Three?"

"Okay," she answers. The tears are gone from her voice.

I hang up.

In the bathroom, my reflection shows matted hair and more than a week's worth of beard with bits of pizza in it. Shaving is difficult, but I scrape my face smooth, strip down and step into a scalding shower. I let the hot water rinse the days of filth from my body before I even attempt to use soap and shampoo. It takes me at least fifteen minutes before I feel clean. Before I feel like I can go back out into the world.

I put on my running clothes and shoes and get in the car. The drive to the running path is short and I'm early, but she's already there. I get out, nod toward the path, and we start off at a medium pace. After a while, we're alone.

"Are you here to talk me out of it?" she asks.

"No. I want to kill him, too. But we can't just do it. We have to have a plan."

"Why? What does it matter? I don't care if I go to jail. I don't care if I die. I just want him dead."

"It matters because then he takes our lives, too. He has to die, has to pay. But it can't come back to us. Whatever happens to us can't be the consequence of his justice. Do you know what I mean?"

She looks at me, quizzically.

I explain. "We have to get away with it like he did. His family has to know his killer is out there unpunished."

She gets it. "How? When?"

"Whenever it happens, we'll be suspects."

"You think so?"

"We do want him dead, don't we?"

A couple of young girls pass us, I can hear the music leaking from their iPhone ear buds. We slow down and allow them to disappear ahead of us.

"We have to assume that everything we say and do will be noticed by someone. We have to live our lives as if we are trying to put the whole thing behind us. Maybe find a support group we can go to. I should try to get my job back."

"We should get back together," she says.

That was on my list, but I was afraid to say it myself. "Yes."

"You can move into my place," she says without an explanation. But I know the reason. Nick's room is untouched in my apartment. A reminder of our loss.

"We can't hide from Nick. People will think it's odd if we don't have pictures or something around."

She nods, knowing exactly what I mean. I know this will be the hardest part for her. Between the funeral and the trial, whenever someone mentioned Nick, or she would see the class photo of him they used in the newspapers, she would have a near breakdown.

"Okay," she concedes. "I think I'm ready for that." But there are tears in the corners of her eyes.

"We can't write any of this down. Not a post-it, not an email, not a text. And we only talk about it in places where we know we are completely alone. But we do need to lay an electronic trail to back up our cover story. Facebook posts, Google searches, purchases on Amazon. We can get started tonight."

"Your mom has been trying to get me to go out with her. I should do that," Rebecca says.

"Good idea."

"Will you come with me?"

"Of course. We can tell her we're back together."

"That'll make her happy."

"Plus, she'll tell everyone she knows. It'll spread faster than Twitter."

She catches herself about to laugh, but stops and looks at her watch. "We should turn around."

"Okay."

The run back is quiet. We don't talk, and besides, there are too many people around now. I walk her to her car.

"Thank you for doing this," she says. "Will you come over tonight? I'll help you move your stuff tomorrow, but I… I want to…"

"Let's go out to dinner. Sushi?"

She nods. I lean in to kiss her. She is surprised by the gesture, but recovers and responds. She gets that everything we do now has an audience, that we are setting the stage and playing roles that will give us the one thing we couldn't get from the police or the courts: justice.

Actually, more than justice.

Revenge.

five

 I have a bag packed with some clothes, my laptop and some things of Nick's I think we should have. When we return from dinner, we turn on Rebecca's computer and start Googling support groups. Surprisingly, there is one not too far away that meets weekly for parents who have lost young children. We print out their flier and put it on the fridge.
 It's late. How far are we going to take living together?
 "I'll sleep on the futon," I say. "Do you have some extra sheets?"
 "You can have the bed," she offers.
 "I'm fine on the futon." It reminds me of the months before the divorce, the nights I spent sleeping on the couch rather than in our bed. I'm sure it reminds her, too, but we have a larger purpose to achieve and neither of us wants to dwell on it.
 "Okay." She grabs some sheets, a blanket and a couple of pillows from a closet as I take my shaving kit and unpack it into her medicine cabinet. As I'm brushing my teeth, she comes into the bathroom and starts her nightly routine.
 Our eyes meet in the mirror in that way that has the illusion of intimacy.
 I wonder if the people in the reflection might still be in love.

six

My old boss is eager to accept my proposition to come back as a contractor. Especially for the ridiculously low rate I quote him. I tell him about getting back together with Rebecca, and he even offers to have us over to his house for dinner. Like in the old days. I promise him we'll do just that.

Resuming work is easy now. I know why I'm doing it. It was never a hard job for me. As a system administrator, I mostly just check logs, push buttons and write reports. Most of it I can automate and spend the rest of my time doing my real work.

The way our data center is set up, I am able to create a virtual machine that only I have access to. I set it up with an anonymous proxy and exclude its activity from the firewall policies and logs. Basically, I can surf the web now without anyone knowing what I'm looking at. I also make sure at the same time to generate web activity for legitimate business purposes so as not to raise any suspicions. I tell my boss I need to download some large virtual machine images to evaluate some new tools and he gives me an approving nod, glad things are back to normal.

At first I think poisons are a good way to go, but the more exotic and untraceable ones are exotic for a reason. They're hard to obtain and even harder to handle. There is no way I can see to suddenly develop a hobby of raising deep water octopuses, or Amazonian tree frogs.

A foray into covert assassination techniques is also fruitless. I have neither the means to acquire the tools necessary, nor the resources to hire a professional. Besides, this is something I am going to do myself. I am going to kill him. I want to watch his life leave his body and make sure he realizes that it is the father of his victim who is taking it from him.

Googling takes me down a few more dead ends, but then I come across a site that captures my attention. It's about a mob killer called The Iceman who, as a hitman, bragged that he never left a target alive. His style was deliberate and decisive.

I return to some research I had done on Vitali. There is a story about how his father is a major player in the mob.

A plan gels in my mind. I'll make it look like a contract killing, focus anyone who looks at it toward organized crime rather than despondent parents.

I shift my queries towards local mob hits, trying to get as many details as I can about the methods they employ. I find a website authored by a local crime writer, Eddie Horne, who has a very comprehensive list of suspected mob related crimes and the people associated with them. I find Vitali's father's name on the site and feel confident I'm on the right track.

One series of murders catches my interest. There is a hitman who has a very specific modus operandi. He kills with an icepick. *That is something I could do*, I think to myself.

At home, I take Rebecca out to a sidewalk cafe in our neighborhood and give her the broad strokes of my plan. She is amazing, throwing in amused giggles and comments about the food to obscure the real subject of our conversation for any passersby.

She is excited. I haven't seen her this way since before Nick's death. And I realize I'm excited, too. We finish our meal with a boisterous conversation about the weather, how mild the winter was and how early spring is.

Nick would've complained about the lack of snow to play in.

seven

The meeting starts in a very somber mood. It reminds me of those support groups you see in movies and TV shows, with coffee and cookies on a table in the back and folding chairs arranged in an incomplete, asymmetric circle.

Most of the people there are couples, but there are a few lone women and a single man, elderly and gaunt with a sadness that visibly weighs on him.

Rebecca and I sit away from everyone else, but the friendly, overweight woman who appears to be in charge guides us to seats within the main circle.

"It's nice to see all of you again this week. Staying connected like this is the only way Brian and I have found that allowed us to make it as far as we have for so long. It's ten years for us next month."

A moment of silence. I wonder if there is some sort of chip you get, like in Alcoholics Anonymous.

She looks to be on the verge of sobbing, but then reaches out for her husband's hand and he gives it a squeeze. (Later I learn her name is Barb, of Barb and Brian, the Browns.) She starts up again with a forced smile that eventually warms into something more natural.

"I'm sorry, I practiced saying that in a mirror a thousand times, and I thought I'd be okay. I don't think I would be if it wasn't for this group."

Encouraging words are offered from some of those sitting in the circle.

Barb acknowledges each of them, then continues. "Thank you. I apologize, I feel like I'm stealing all the attention this evening. But we have some new faces with us tonight, and sad as that makes me to know that they share the loss each of us have experienced..." She pauses, again fighting back tears. She turns to Rebecca and me. "We open our hearts to all newcomers."

Everyone else turns to face us—except the older man. He seems focused on the craggy veins on his hands.

"Welcome," Barb offers. She doesn't appear to expect an answer. "Most people find it takes a while before they're ready to share with the group. We don't require anyone to say anything at all, you're welcome to just listen. But I do hope you, like all of us, find our group..." She searches for just the right word, "... comforting. We all have heard our good-hearted friends and family tell us that they know how we must feel.

"Truth is, they really have no idea, do they? Before I felt this way, I couldn't have imagined just how desperately empty a person could be. Nothing hollows you out like the loss of a child, and I don't expect that any of us will feel... normal, again."

Barb shares a familiar look with her group-mates. They've all heard this before, obviously, but I can see in their eyes that their pain is still there, and I don't expect any amount of sharing and commiseration will ever erase it.

"But that's not why we're here," she says in answer to my unspoken thoughts. "We are here because we know that giving up, that checking out does nothing but tarnish the memories of our children.

"As long as we can go on, as long as we can bear our burdens and make it through another day, a week, a month, another year, they can go on in our hearts. We owe that to them."

I become aware of Rebecca squeezing my arm, I turn and see a tear rolling out of the corner of her eye, and realize that salty drops are trailing down my cheeks as well. I understand the mournful looks on the faces around us and am surprised by how much it affects me. This group is meant to be a cover for our real purpose, killing Vitali. As driven as I am toward that goal, Barb's words cause me to realize that we are not alone.

"We do have a sort of tradition, though," Barb continues, "whenever there is someone new in the group, we all share our stories. It's only fair that you know who we are and why we're here." Now Barb's smile becomes genuine, affectionate, warm as she scans the others in the group.

She turns toward Rebecca and me. "The stories are what helps to keep them alive in our hearts and sometimes..." she casts a gently chastising glance toward one of the older couples, "we get a little carried away. But I hope you'll allow us this chance for you to get to know us and allow us to welcome you into our group."

Rebecca takes my hand, wraps it in her own and pulls it into her lap. We both sit back, relieved at the fact that we aren't expected to share our pain tonight. And that we have found a place that understands it, regardless of the means and motive.

eight

Barb goes first. I notice that she has a locket around her neck, which she opens to reveal a photo of a teenage girl. She stares at it longingly. "Our daughter was the most wonderful girl. An honor student, kind, generous, a true friend to anyone in need. Her one weakness was the boy who lived across the street. They were born only a week apart, so naturally, they became playmates, and we became friends with his parents—despite the fact that we really didn't have much in common with them aside from being neighbors.

"When they were old enough to go to school, they remained friends, and even though as they moved through elementary school, and junior high they had fewer and fewer classes in common, they still walked to school together, and spent time with each other.

"We encouraged her to socialize more with her other friends, even tried to steer her to other boys, but you know how girls are when they're in love. She only saw the good in him, that sweet little boy who protected her on the second grade playground.

"He would get in trouble with the police, small things, Halloween antics, curfew violations, spray painting fences in the alley. And we knew he was one of the kids responsible for the piles of beer cans that littered the park down the street. Probably did drugs, too. But he seemed to insulate her from all that. Maybe he really loved her. Regardless, he couldn't seem to break his ties to the darker part of his life.

"I'm sure she knew all about those things and believed she could fix him. I mean, ladies, haven't we all tried to tame the bad boy? She talked him into going to the prom with her, got him to shave and remove most of the piercings on his face. They were so handsome together, I started to believe that maybe she was right about him."

Barb turns to Rebecca and me. "I'm sure you've guessed that she didn't come home that night. He and some friends had sneaked some liquor into the dance, and they somehow got the limo driver to step out of the car, and then…"

Barb turns away. Brian guides her to her seat, then stands and finishes the story.

"They were going too fast on the expressway on ramp, hit the guard rails at just the right angle, and the car flipped over and fell to the road below. Somehow, by some cruel twist of fate, some cosmic joke, he and one of his friends survived. Everyone else was killed instantly. Our daughter died because she trusted a… scumbag to be a human being."

Barb tries to pull Brian back to his seat. He resists.

"My wife is trying to shut me up. We try not to live in hate. She's much better at it than I am.

"I'm the one who identified her body. We didn't have an open casket."

Barb tugs on Brian's sleeve. "Brian, don't."

"Ten years, Barb." His voice cracks with pain. "We would've had grandchildren by now." He focuses on Rebecca and me. "We try to pretend if we keep the love for our children alive, that's all we need to do." Then he scans the others in the room. "But the truth is—as hard as it is to admit—we need to hate, too.

"Sometimes I think that's really what this group is for—at least for me, and I know a few others here who might not be so willing to admit it—to give us a place to let the hate out, so that when we go home and try to live our lives, it won't get in the way of the love."

He turns back toward Barb, she rises and they embrace. Everyone gives them a moment.

Without any visual or audible cue, the meeting moves on, following an agenda that meets the needs of the moment, the desires of the participants.

nine

A woman to the left of the Browns stands up. She does not have the rosy cheerful facade that Barb has, instead she's quiet yet confident. There is no husband by her side.

"My son and husband were on a vacation, just the two of them. A father and son thing. My boy loved to fish. I never got it. Too boring for me, but my husband was thrilled to have a fishing buddy. They spent two weeks on a remote lake in Canada. It was Todd's dream trip, he was so excited about it.

"Two weeks in the wild, sleeping in a log cabin, all day on a boat. No cell phones, no plumbing. I never thought a ten-year-old could be so enthusiastic about something that didn't involve electricity."

Some in the group laugh.

"I tried to enjoy myself while they were gone. The house was finally clean for more than a day. I had some girlfriends over to watch some chick flicks and I was able to take a bath without worrying about being interrupted.

"When they got back to the base station, Todd called to tell me how many fish he'd caught. Steve emailed me about a hundred photos. They still had a two day drive to get home, but hearing his voice, and seeing how happy he was holding up a two-foot trout..."

She pauses to gather herself. "I got a call two days later from a hospital. They wanted me to come up right away. Steve and Todd had stopped at a little roadside diner for a couple burgers—as much as Todd loved to fish, I don't think he liked eating it every day. The meat they got was tainted. The owner of the restaurant had been cited several times before, but never got around to fixing his freezer.

"Todd hung on until I got there, his last words to me were, 'Did you see my fish, Mom?' Steve's last words were, 'I'm sorry.' The doctors told me if they had gotten help sooner, they might have made it."

She takes a deep breath. "They were so anxious to make it home that they weren't going to let a stomach ache slow them down. Steve tried Pepto Bismal, but at the motel that night, when Todd had bloody diarrhea, he knew it was much more serious.

"He tried to drive the both of them to a hospital..." she tears up. "But he was too weak, and he ended up driving into a ditch. A Deputy Sheriff found them about six hours later and called an ambulance. The bacteria had destroyed their kidneys, and by the time they got to the hospital, other organs were starting to fail.

"I'm glad he was with his dad, that they got to do something he loved. But damn it, it didn't need to happen.

"My husband and I had struggled for years to get pregnant. Todd was the product of three rounds of in vitro fertilization. Steve used to call him our science experiment. He used to joke about the lab mixing up the sperm because he couldn't figure out how a guy who barely made it out of high school math could be the dad of such a bright kid. But you could see it in their eyes, when they both laughed at the same goofy TV show, or cheered their favorite sports teams. They were the same. Best friends without losing that special father-son bond."

The smile, left over from her nostalgic reminiscence, fades.

"I drove to that roadside diner to confront that man... that killer." She turns to her left, looks past Barb at Brian. "Here comes the hate."

Some of the others nod.

"He had no remorse. He didn't even apologize. Told me there was nothing wrong with his food, people ate it all the time. I found out he was poker buddies with the Sheriff. The Deputy had told me there was nothing they could do. He's just sitting up there at that hole-in-the-wall diner waiting to kill someone else. And my boy, and my husband..."

She doesn't finish and doesn't need to. She just sits down and accepts a comforting hug from Barb.

ten

The next story comes from a young couple whose infant was the victim of obvious and blatant malpractice. Even substantial punitive damages in a lawsuit did not end his medical career, only caused their hate for his carelessness to fester.

Two more of the remaining survivor parents lost children to drunk drivers like us. Another to a fatal dog attack. Two others lost their little ones to cancer. They were the ones who seemed uncomfortable when anyone spoke of hate for the killers of their children, after all they had no one to blame—unless you count God, and there was no point in that.

Another single woman lost her two children to a psychotic ex-husband who burned them alive, but escaped with merely the loss of his hands and eyes. And the last couple of the evening lost their twelve-year-old daughter to gang violence. A stray bullet pierced their living room window and hit her in the neck while she was watching her favorite teen comedy on TV. The killer of their daughter was known, but no witnesses would come forward, and the district attorney (likely the same weak-kneed jellyfish that prosecuted Vitali) refused to indict let alone bring it to a trial.

After the stories are done, the gathering transforms into something more of a social event. Brian makes a point of engaging me in conversation, finds out I'm in I.T. and naturally has an ongoing computer problem to tell me about.

When we come to a pause in the small talk, I ask him about the old man, still sitting off to the side contemplating his liver spots. Doesn't he have a story?

Brian nods, "That's Old Harold. He does have one, but it's his to share and I suppose he'll tell it when he's ready."

And that's about all he's willing to say on the subject. "So, what do you guys do when there's not someone new to do the whole history thing with?" I ask.

"Mostly this. Barb gets us started, we recognize anniversaries, that kind of thing, then we just hang out. Some of the guys get together outside the group. If you're a poker player, there's always a seat available for another sucker—I mean player." He elbows me in the side with a deep chuckle.

"Maybe," is as far as I'm willing to go.

"Listen," he says, "I know we're supposed to let you share when you're ready, but the truth is I recognize you guys from the news. Your son was killed by that mob guy, Vitali." Then he adds, putting a hand on my shoulder, "I know how you feel."

"Thanks," I say, and leave it at that. The people in this room are the only ones who can say that and not leave me thinking they are total idiots.

I find Rebecca and we exchange pleasantries with some of the other parents. They are on to something in this group, it is good to be around people who know the specter you live under when you lose a child. It allows you to feel at ease, like you don't have to wait for someone to say something inadvertently insensitive, or unnecessarily compassionate.

It's about as close to *nice* as any of us can get.

eleven

Over the next few days, I spend most of my time thinking about how we're going to pull this off. I need to know everything we can about our target, find some way to spy on him without it interfering with our continuing alibi.

We're watching a TV show about people who bid on the contents of storage lockers, ones that have been abandoned for some reason or another, the bills unpaid and the hidden treasures within auctioned off.

In one unit, a couple discovers a spy kit, complete with a remote video recording unit that can store video discretely and be retrieved later.

"That would be perfect," Rebecca offers. "If we could plant cameras around his place, record what he does, then just pick up the video."

It is a good idea. "The trick would be how we can buy it without leaving a trail. If anyone digs deep enough, they'd wonder why we'd bought surveillance equipment," I say.

"Could you have it shipped to your office? There are a hundred people working there, if a package shows up with a name no one knows, what happens?"

"Probably sits in the mail room until someone decides to send it back."

"Could you get in and take it?"

"I don't see how. Plus there would be a record of it delivered to my office."

"We could maybe find a pawn shop that sells that kind of stuff?"

"They keep records, too. And probably have cameras of their own."

I stare at the TV screen as I ponder how we can acquire something anonymously.

"We can steal it," I announce. "From a detective agency."

"Brilliant. Let's go rip off a private eye, I'm sure they won't have any means or desire to track us down," Rebecca responds, sarcastically.

"No, we steal it from them before they know they have it."

"What are you talking about?" Rebecca asks.

I lay out my plan for her. We've been squirreling away cash for a few weeks now, there should be enough to get the equipment we'll need.

It's the first big risk we'll be taking in this endeavor, but by no means the last.

twelve

When I get to work, I lock myself in the server room, pull up my virtual machine and anonymously shop for the equipment we'll need.

The devices are remarkably affordable for what they are. Lipstick sized cameras with enough memory for up to twenty-four hours of compressed video and Wi-Fi radios to wirelessly transmit the data. I order six of them, request that they be shipped to the address of the private investigations firm that is on the ninth floor of my company's building and pay for it using a PayPal account that has been funded by auctions on eBay, the money going through several imaginary buyers and sellers I had set up.

I request the UPS shipping method and get a tracking number a few hours later. The order is timed to arrive on a day that Rebecca can be in the building.

I check the tracking information several times a day. There is an option to request a specific delivery window and I select an early one when I know there is very little activity at the investigation firm.

On the expected delivery day, Rebecca is in the ladies room between the elevators and the firm's office. From the break room in my office, I can see delivery trucks arriving and entering the loading bay. I send a coded text message to Rebecca. The rest is up to her.

We agree not to contact each other immediately after the pickup. It's not until I arrive home that evening that she shows me the box and the covert cameras inside.

She tells me about her part of the mission. "So, I stepped out of the ladies room and stood in front of the office door. When I heard the elevator ding, I put my hand on the door knob, then looked behind me at the UPS guy. I gave him a smile, he smiled back. I asked him, 'Is that the package from Covert Systems?' He checked the return address, then nodded. 'Great,' I tell him, 'I need to get that over to the surveillance site.'

"He handed me the electronic clipboard thing, I scribbled something illegible, he asked for my last name, typed in the made up one I gave him and he wished me a good day. I started opening the package as he disappeared into the elevator, then I took the stairs down and out to the parking lot. I got in my car and drove straight here. I don't know if I took a breath the whole time. It was kind of exciting."

I connect one of the cameras to a charger and we conduct a little experiment. She hides it on a shelf in the living room and I use my old laptop to create an ad hoc Wi-Fi network to pull the video from the device.

It works perfectly.

We spend a few hours making sure all the devices are fully charged.

That night we take a long walk in the overcast gloom foretelling a coming storm. We eventually wander onto the street where Vitali lives. It's a fairly modest home, a sprawling ranch-style house, but well appointed.

Rebecca takes in a deep breath and assumes an air of calm that I try to match. We don't see his car either on the street or in his driveway. There are no lights on inside his house. There are no neighbors out. Good fortune is on our side.

I reach up into a tree in front of his house and place a camera secured with a lump of putty aimed at his front door that will also capture activity in his garage.

Then Rebecca and I each walk around separate sides of his house and look for other spots to plant the remaining cameras to give us a glimpse around and inside his house. We meet in the rear. There is a gate that exits into the alley and we walk through it like people who belong there. The cameras have motion detectors and will only record when there is something happening. According to the instructions, the batteries should last a week in that mode.

We must have patience. Things are going so well.

thirteen

Sunday, we go to church. It is the Lutheran parish where we sent Nick for preschool. The congregation is small enough to notice a couple new faces, and the mother of one of Nick's preschool classmates recognizes Rebecca. She greets us, then offers her empty words of condolence and introduces us to some others. No one asks why we are there, but it is clear that they assume we are looking for spiritual solace.

After the sermon, the pastor introduces himself. He remembers Nick from the preschool Christmas pageant and as one would expect a minister to do, strikes the right tone by recalling a fond memory, but not pressing the issue. "I hope we'll see more of you," he adds.

I assure him he will.

There is a small reception we get pulled into in the basement. The room is divided into men on one side, and women on the other. The preschool mom takes Rebecca aside and one of the deacons takes it upon himself to introduced me to the "inner circle." They talk mostly of when it will be warm enough to return to the golf course and ask if I play.

The situation and conversation strikes me as a replay of the latter half of the support group, only these people are not burdened by the death of their children. These are the people Rebecca and I might have been if Vitali had never been born.

fourteen

Two days later I return to Vitali's house with a laptop I acquired from a thrift shop. I had wiped and reformatted the hard drive and installed a hardened version of Linux developed for security nuts. I risk parking on the opposite side of the street to scan for the signals from the cameras. Most of them are easy to lock in on and I quickly download the footage. The rest of them require me to make a slow drive down the alley. It seems none of them have been discovered.

At home, I use the laptop to sort the videos by time stamp and we go about the painstaking task of logging all the activity the cameras have captured. The work is wordless, I bring up each segment of footage, Rebecca writes it down on paper. When we are done, we transfer our written notes into an encrypted spreadsheet on the laptop and burn the paper, then flush the ashes down the toilet. Overkill, I know, but we are as careful as I can think to be.

So far, our picture of Vitali is getting more and more detailed. I have what information we knew about him from the trial and the events surrounding it, and I was able to hack into his Facebook account quite easily, his password was not very original—the letters on his license plate: "CHK MGNT"—chick magnet.

We learn quite a lot from the videos.

He has a job of sorts at one of his father's restaurants, the kind where he can come and go as he pleases and not screw things up too much. He drives a black Maserati which he keeps in his unusually sparse garage. He doesn't do his own yard work, so he doesn't have any of the typical lawn care equipment or really anything except some golf clubs to crowd the space allocated to his car.

His day starts around noon. He has a gym in his home with a variety of equipment where he works out after his morning cup of espresso. Around two or three in the afternoon he heads out to work. He gets home well after midnight, and on one of the nights we recorded, he brought a girl with him, but she left around two in the morning by cab.

There is an alarm company sign in the flower beds by his front door. That makes me second guess doing it in his house. But a little snooping reveals that the company named on the sign went out of business a year ago. Perhaps it was left over from the previous owners. Regardless, it is likely the extent of his security system. I'm sure he thinks that anyone who would contemplate ripping him off knows who his father is and wouldn't dare try. In the videos, whenever he returns home he doesn't unlock his door, he just opens it and walks in.

We agree that we should watch him for a couple more weeks, but no more. Watching him enjoying his life, not a care in the world makes us all the more anxious to end it.

fifteen

Flipping through the latest issue of "Popular Science" I come across an ad for a gadget that catches my eye. It is a GPS tracking device that can be hidden on a car and digitally record its comings and goings. I show it to Rebecca and we discuss whether it would be worth risking another third party delivery to acquire one. Probably not. But maybe we could check to see if something similar was available to buy for cash somewhere in the city.

At work the next day, I use my encrypted virtual machine, and a privacy focused search engine to look for the device and come up with a list of retail stores that might sell it. I memorize the names and addresses of a few prospects that are outside my normal sphere of activity, but not too far away.

On my way home, I drive by the first one and park a couple blocks down the street. I walk back to the small electronics store, browse the aisles for about ten minutes and come up empty. I don't want to make myself stand out by asking for it, so I casually walk out and head back to my car.

The second stop is a car stereo shop. I'm not as excited about my prospects there, but walk in anyway and am rewarded by a display of the devices front and center. I pick one up along with a pair of windshield wipers, pay cash and politely decline the clerk's offer to have someone replace my wiper blades for me.

When I get home, Rebecca and I discuss the best way to plant the device on Vitali's car. He has a private spot behind the restaurant where he spends his evenings pretending to work. Like his home it is within walking distance of Rebecca's apartment. We decide to wait till after it gets dark.

I plug the device—which consists of a featureless black box with a strong magnet on one side and a USB port on the other—into the laptop I used to download the surveillance camera video.

Rebecca comes out of the kitchen, wiping her hands on a towel. "I want to talk about how you're going to do it," she says.

I know what she means. She wants to discuss the exact method by which I'm going to end Vitali's life. She has developed a fascination in this part of the plan, perhaps unhealthily so, but I can't blame her. The whole point of this exercise is to bring justice to our son, and that justice is Vitali's death. So I satisfy her morbid need.

"I take an ice pick," I say plainly, "and stab him in the heart. Right here." I point a spot on my chest to the left of my sternum. "There is a mob killer who has that M.O. It's on that crime writer's website."

I walk up to Rebecca, take her hand and shape the fingers as if they're holding a weapon, then grab her wrist and guide it to my chest to demonstrate. She draws in a shocked breath when the imaginary weapon pierces my chest.

"Then he sort of swirls it around, to make sure the heart is sufficiently damaged to cause a quick death." I guide her hand in a circular motion around the point of penetration, then pull her hand away from me, and turn it sideways.

"He waits a moment to make sure the victim is dead, then—" I guide her hand quickly toward my temple and make the same circular motion there. "—just in case there's any life left in him, he pierces the temple and scrambles the brains as well. Each wound is usually fatal on its own, doing both makes sure the target is dead."

I let go of her wrist, but her hand stays pressed to the side of my head. I can see in her eyes that she's not seeing me, she's seeing Vitali, or rather his lifeless corpse.

"Can you do it?" she asks.

"Yes," I answer without hesitation.

"What if you can't?"

"I can and I will. I promise you. When the time comes, I will drive that ice pick into his chest without hesitation, and then I'll finish him off in the head. I promise."

"Swear on Nick's soul."

"I swear."

She seems convinced, and her hand uncurls from around the imaginary ice pick and falls to her side. She takes a deep, satisfied breath, then returns to the kitchen.

sixteen

We don't speak of it further during dinner, in fact we don't talk at all. As I clear the table and load the dishwasher, Rebecca changes into a dark running suit.

I check the GPS tracker to make sure it's charged, and that it's set to automatically track any movement, and that the internal clock is set to the correct time and time zone. Everything is ready.

"We have the group again tomorrow," Rebecca mentions.

"I know. I kind of like it."

"Me too."

I slip into a dark jacket and slide the tracker into my pocket. We walk outside. It's cooler than I expect. Rebecca takes my hand as we start our mile and a half walk to the restaurant.

On the way we bump into Nancy, the woman who was friendly to us at church, walking with her son.

"Hi, you two," she says with a smile. "Nice night for a walk."

"Yes," Rebecca answers, "my goodness, look at you Ian, you've grown!"

Ian wipes ice cream from the corners of his mouth with the sleeve of his jacket.

"Ian, what have I told you about that?" Nancy chastises, then hands him one of the paper napkins she has tucked away for such occasions.

"Sorry, Mom," he says as he takes the napkin and wipes at his now clean mouth.

"Boys," Rebecca says simply with a smile. "You know, I wanted to ask you," she continues, changing the subject, "I saw a sign on the bulletin board at the church about volunteers for the bake sale. Do you have anything to do with that? Are you still looking for people? And cookies?"

"I'm exactly the person to talk to. And yes, we're always looking for both. I can call you later and give you all the details."

"Tomorrow would be better. I'm off and will be home during the day."

"Terrific. Is the number still the same from the preschool list?" A fleeting panic crosses Nancy's face. She assumes that awkward, embarrassed look people get when they realize that their words are a reminder to Rebecca and me that we've lost our child.

We are fairly numb to such feelings at this point, and their attempts to compensate for a slight we do not perceive is more offensive than the one they imagine. It's a story we might tell at the group the following night. One our fellow grieving parents will understand.

"Yes, it's the same," Rebecca says, quickly defusing the situation. "I'll talk to you tomorrow then."

"Okay, goodnight."

"Goodnight," I add.

Ian waves, his mouth once again occupied with devouring the ice cream cone in his hand.

We each continue on our way. A few minutes later, Rebecca gives my hand a squeeze and I notice a tear falling down her cheek.

"I wish we could kill him tonight," she says.

"We can't."

"I know."

seventeen

We reach the restaurant and walk around the corner to the back. On our first pass, there are a couple of busboys hanging out by the dumpster near where Vitali's car is parked. We stroll down the alley. They take notice of us in passing, but then continue their conversation and smoking their cigarettes.

We walk around the block and enter the alley again, this time, I proceed alone, take off my jacket and drape it over my arm in the hope that if the busboys see me again, they won't recognize me as half of the couple that just walked past.

The busboys are gone.

I scan the back of the restaurant for security cameras and check Vitali's car to make sure there is no alarm engaged. Everything is clear. His hubris works to our advantage.

I whistle a signal to Rebecca and she continues to look out as I slide under the back of Vitali's Maserati and attach the tracker to an exposed piece of steel. It clings tightly and I slide back out, give Rebecca a nod and we continue our stroll down the alley.

My heart races. Rebecca seems calm and collected.

"Are you all right?" she asks.

I nod. "Just adrenaline."

She smiles at me as we make our way back onto the main street and head in the direction of her apartment. I slip my jacket back on and Rebecca slips her arm around mine, leans her head against my shoulder for a moment, and we finish our walk in silence.

It's not lost on me how perverse our relationship has become. We have formed a bond centered around revenge. We spend our time planning the murder of the man who murdered our son. At some point during this journey there is going to be blood on our hands. Vitali's blood.

Rebecca looks up at me as if reading my thoughts.

I smile at her.

She squeezes my arm, reassured.

eighteen

My boss calls me into his office.

The first thing that comes to my mind is that he's discovered my secret virtual machine and has somehow been tracking my carefully hidden online activities. This is, of course, ridiculous. I know what I'm doing and have covered my tracks completely. Everything I've done dead ends on a server somewhere in Finland that guarantees a completely anonymous proxy. Some Fins, at least, really value their online privacy.

Still, as illogical as my concerns may be, I can't help wondering if there isn't something I have missed.

"Have a seat," he offers.

I sit down in one of the pair of chairs in front of his desk. "Is anything wrong?" I ask, because that's what I would ask even if I wasn't planning a revenge killing in my company's server room.

"No, not at all. Quite the opposite. We're really very happy with the way things are working out. I want to offer you a full time position again. You can pick up right where you left off, seniority, vacation, pay grade, benefits... We'll call the gap a leave of absence. I've gotten approval from the CIO, he was glad to hear you're back on track."

"I feel back on track. It's good to be back at work. I mean some days it's still not easy to get out of bed, but I'm glad I have this place. There are good people here."

"There are," he agrees.

There is a pause.

"I understand if you need time to think about it—"

"Oh, goodness, no. I don't need any time. Absolutely, I'd love to come back." That's what a normal, non-homicidal guy would say, isn't it? "Yes, thank you!"

He rises and offers his hand.

I stand and shake it, smiling appreciatively.

"Great. H.R. will have some paperwork for you, and as of Monday, you'll be a regular employee again."

"That's great. Thank you so much."

"By the way, Sally and I are still waiting for you and Rebecca to accept that dinner invitation."

"Soon," I promise. "We're still in I guess a kind of second honeymoon phase."

He smiles knowingly. "Well, don't want to step on that. But don't put it off too long, or Sally will have my head."

"You got it, boss."

As he walks me to the door, he asks a few perfunctory questions about the projects I'm working on and I give him a few ideas for improvements in some of the automated processes. That makes him happy.

Just to reassure myself, I return to the server room and casually look around. My paranoia that security cameras have been added without my knowledge is laid to rest. It seems I have indeed genuinely earned their trust, and my job back. It's not some sort of trap to stop our plan.

Regardless, I stay off my virtual machine for the rest of the day.

nineteen

At group, there are a few members who we did not meet at the previous meeting, and we get their obligatory testimony.

First is a couple whose son was the victim of another drunk driver, an irresponsible middle-aged woman who actually drove her own kid to school with a point-one-four blood alcohol level. Then on her way home, she raced at fifty miles per hour through the school zone and hit their child while he was riding his bike to the same school. She got an expensive lawyer and probation.

The other is another single woman, Joan, who's in her late sixties. Joan's husband had passed away earlier that year, and she seemed happy that he was with their daughter—who had died of an alcohol and drug overdose incurred during a sorority initiation. The daughter had passed over thirty years ago, but Joan didn't find the group until twenty-some years later.

Barb asks if there is anyone who wants to talk about anything that had happened over the past week that they might want to share.

Rebecca considers for a moment telling the story of Nancy and her family, but then breathes a sigh of relief when Amy, the woman who lost her son and husband to acute food poisoning, speaks up.

"I drove up there last weekend," she begins, "to the roadside diner where it happened. Every time I tell the story here, I get the urge to go back and see if he's out of business yet, or better, dead.

"The restaurant is still there. There's a sign out front, one of those chalkboard things that fold out, and scribbled on it was 'Best Burgers in the State.' I parked on the shoulder across from the place and fantasized about going up to the gas station back a ways and getting a can of gas, dowsing that sign and the grease soaked shack he calls a restaurant and lighting the whole thing on fire. I even imagined him running out, wrapped in flames, screaming for someone to put him out. Screaming in pain.

"He did come out—sadly not on fire—and noticed my car parked there and me staring at him through the glass. I know he recognized me because a little while later a Deputy Sheriff drove up behind me and walked up to my car window. He urged me to move along. I told him I had every right to be parked there. He gave me some baloney about shoulder parking not allowed on county roads, but I pointed out the two beat up trucks parked on the shoulder by the restaurant. He suggested that I move along anyway seeing as how Buck—that's the guy's name, Buck, like in Fuck you very much, Buck Cooper, for killing my family—how Buck might take my presence there personal and do something like take a bat to my headlights or slash my tires. I got the distinct impression that Buck had done that before and that the deputy was sincerely concerned for my safety, not Cooper's complaint. So I promised him I'd move on.

"He got back into his car and waited until I started mine up and drove away. I thought about going back, but I don't think I could've stood another moment of knowing he was there, breathing, eating, living."

Barb pats Amy on the knee.

Amy looks directly at her. "I'm sorry Barb, it's another hate day for me. I wish he was dead, God forgive me, but I wish he was a charred skeleton by the side of the road."

"You can't think that way, dear," Barb tells her.

"How can I not? How can you not?"

"I try to forgive."

"Forgive? You forgive the creep who killed your daughter?"

"I said I *try* to forgive. God hasn't opened my heart that wide yet."

"I couldn't even try," Amy adds. She turns and scans the other faces in the room. "Can any of you?"

The Cancer Parents avoid her gaze, but the others meet her cold, determined stare head on, silently agreeing with her, sharing her frustration and passion.

When her eyes pass over Rebecca and me, she seems to pause for a moment, perhaps sensing kindred spirits in the desire for deadly revenge.

Barb steers the group to more mundane topics, and at the appointed hour we break up into little group-lets. Somehow Rebecca and I find ourselves bound to Barb and Brian and the new Drunk Driver Parents. I'm horrible with names and tend to label people by the characteristics that define them in my mind. Drunk Driver Parents they would be, even after I pull Brian aside to have him refresh my memory as to their names.

"Sorry about Amy," he says.

"No need," I answer, then add, "I know how she feels."

"Hmm, yes," he responds. "But imagine what would happen if we all went around killing everyone who did us wrong."

"Not everyone," I offer, "just the ones who kill our children."

Brian nods. I sense that like Amy, like all of us, his hate days are more than he's willing to admit to, especially to Barb.

During the evening, Rebecca breaks away from Barb and the Drunk Driver Parents mom, and shares a moment with Amy in a corner. Their brief conversation ends in a tearful embrace.

On the way home, I ask her what she talked to Amy about.

"Just mom stuff," she answers.

I don't press the matter further.

twenty

Over the next week, I download video from the cameras twice and retrieve the GPS tracker from Vitali's car. We now have a fairly complete picture of his daily activities. The batteries on the cameras seem to be holding up, so Rebecca and I decide to leave them in place until the night I kill him.

The GPS information turned out not to be as useful as we had hoped. In hindsight, it was an unnecessary risk, but it was a way to pass the time. The hardest part of all of this is the waiting. The adventure of purchasing, planting, retrieving and reviewing the information from the tracker was more for us to have something to do, rather than to do something to further the plan.

We lay a calendar from the neighborhood pizza place on the kitchen table and pick a day. Saturday night—actually, Sunday morning. Four a.m. is when he is reliably bedded down. And on Saturdays, he comes home very drunk and is likely to be more careless than he usually is.

Rebecca shows off the results of her recent shopping spree.

We found a medical surplus place that had disposable paper suits that emergency room doctors and nurses wear over their scrubs to keep bodily fluids from soaking their clothes. They also sell a lot of them to people who do home remodeling so our purchase wasn't remarkable. She also found a slick, polyester running suit for me, one that was jet black, and a black ski mask as well.

From a garage sale she purchased a box of assorted tools, one of which is an ice pick. Disposing of it is going to be a challenge, and I haven't quite worked that out yet, but I have a few good ideas involving a nearby river and a blow torch.

The remaining element of our plan is our alibi. If we do everything right, we won't need it, but we decide to establish one anyway. We have reservations at a romantic lovers' retreat and have worked out a way for me to get in and out without anyone noticing. It's actually only about five miles away from Vitali's place, so there shouldn't be a problem getting there and back undetected.

The only thing left to do, is wait.

twenty one

It's Friday. We've taken the day off from our respective jobs. My boss was happy to approve my request for a day off, especially when I told him Rebecca and I were having a little getaway weekend.

We drive to the cemetery and park near the entrance.

I haven't been here since the funeral, and I don't think Rebecca has either. I warn her that it might be dangerous doing something out of the ordinary. She counters that going on a romantic weekend with her ex-husband is out of the ordinary as well. People will see it as part of our road to reconciliation.

I reiterate my concerns, trying to convince her that if someone sees us, it could endanger all the work we've done so far.

She dismisses my paranoia. "They'll think it's a coincidence. Or divine intervention. Or they'll think it was part of an elaborate master plan we cooked up to exact revenge. I don't give a damn. I need to see him."

I have no argument for that. "All right. I'm sorry."

"You don't have to be. You're just looking out for me."

"I wish—" I start to say.

"Don't. Don't even think it. You looked out for our son in every way you could."

I start to cry. So does Rebecca.

"Do you remember what I told you at the hospital?" she asks.

I think back. Her words are seared in my mind. "You said, 'I forgive you.'"

"I did and I do. I needed you to know that, even though you didn't ask me for forgiveness. Because the only thing I could think of was what if it had been me driving him to school that day?"

My sobbing becomes uncontrollable. We sit on a nearby stone bench, and I bury my face in the nook between her neck and shoulder.

"He didn't run into the street. We always told him not to, and he was so good about that. Vitali drove onto the grass. He had to knock down a stop sign to hit Nick. If it had been me…"

She has trouble going on. I lift my face and look into hers. She has that same look she did at the hospital when she offered her unconditional forgiveness.

"There are a million things that could've happened that might have changed everything. But they didn't. And it wasn't your fault. Vitali killed him. Not you."

She holds me in her arms and we stay that way for a while.

My tears dry in the wind. Early spring smells are in the air along with the scent of flowers left by the graves.

Rebecca takes my hand, stands, and we walk the rest of the way to Nick's grave. There are some plastic flowers there, possibly left by his grandmother, or maybe someone from the school.

We didn't bring flowers. Instead, I pull out one of his favorite toys from my pocket. A small Lego minifigure. He loved rearranging their parts and adding various weapons, tools and other devices by which he imagined they could fly and do battle with his other toys.

I set what looked to me like an insane test pilot, cobbled together from a few other characters and outfitted with a helmet and goggles with a crazy, bared teeth expression on his tiny yellow face, on top of the stone marker. Rebecca adds some sort of futuristic looking ray gun to his tiny plastic hand. It's so big and heavy, we have to pose him sitting down. It makes us both laugh, thinking about how he would bring us little creations like that one, and show off every little detail.

"Yuck, what am I supposed to do with flowers," he would've said if we'd brought a more traditional offering.

Only of course he can't say anything now.

We hold hands in front of the marble marker. Etched deep into the stone are the words, "Nicholas Argent, beloved son of Rebecca and Richard," and the dates upon which he was born and died.

Rebecca is right, we need to be here today, no matter what.

After a while, Rebecca breaks the silence and tells me a story about the first time he dressed himself, his socks mismatched, shirt on backwards and wearing pajama pants.

I remember one about his irrational fear of vampires, how he was convinced that they were real and were going to get him, and how we drove to the grocery store to buy garlic to hang over the doors to my apartment.

We go on like that for a long time. In the parlance of Barb and Brian Brown, we're having a "love day."

And for the first time in a long time it feels good.

twenty two

We leave the apartment around noon on Saturday, me driving Rebecca's car.

I take us to the overnight lot next to the train station where my car is waiting. Rebecca slides behind the wheel and follows as I exit the parking lot and head back onto the street.

About two blocks from our final destination, I pull into the parking lot for a body shop that is closed over the weekend. No one will notice an extra vehicle parked there. I slide back behind the wheel of Rebecca's car and we drive on to the Sierra Winds Retreat and Spa.

Not much of a retreat, really, as it's surrounded by mini-malls and numerous building developments. Likely when they first opened the area was more remote, but there are strategically placed rows of trees and hedges that give it the illusion of seclusion.

We make a stop at the office, check in with the clerk and drive on to our personal cabana. The units are all separate, so there's no chance of hearing someone else's headboard banging against the wall. And much to our benefit, the doors all face away from the center of the compound, so when you look out of yours you see only the perimeter foliage, creating a rather respectable oasis amid a dense suburban community.

I park by the front door of our little cabin. Rebecca notices that there's an alley between a couple of the bushes, visible only from our unit. Another card stacked in our favor. Sneaking away in the middle of the night is going to be very easy.

I pull our bag out of the trunk as Rebecca unlocks the door. It's a very nice, cozy space, opening into a living room with a wide, deep couch facing a gas fireplace. A big screen TV hangs over the mantle, and there's a kitchenette with a bar off to the side.

A door leads to the bedroom, with a king size bed made up in silk sheets. On the other side of the room is a large, heart-shaped bath tub. Rebecca points out the mirrors on the ceiling.

"I'd hate to see this room with a black light," she jokes. "Do we have to stay here the whole time?"

I shrug. "Nope."

"Let's go to the movies. I haven't been in ages."

"Yeah, great idea. Any idea what's playing?"

"We passed a multiplex on the way. Are you feeling adventurous?"

"Maybe."

"Well, we walk up to the box office and the next show time at that moment is the one we see."

"Okay. I'm in. Could be a three-D horror movie," I warn.

"Could be a foreign chick flick," she counters.

"We can grab dinner after. Someplace with steak."

"Perfect."

I throw our bag on the bed, and we head on back to the car.

twenty three

It's dark when we get back. We make a point of waving at the clerk in the office as we drive by. He nods, recognizing us.

I park behind the cabana and we re-enter our weekend hideaway.

"I'm going to try to take a nap," I tell Rebecca.

"I don't think I'll sleep at all tonight," she tells me.

"I don't want to make any mistakes. This is it."

"Yeah, it is, isn't it?"

I nod, then cross into the bedroom and lie down on top of the sheets. Rebecca joins me, and we lie together like we did the night after the verdict. Only this time, I do fall asleep.

At two am, the alarm on my phone goes off and I wake up. I hear the TV in the other room. Rebecca is watching some reality TV show—I can't tell which one. She turns and sees me standing in the bedroom door.

"I was just about to wake you. I put out your stuff." Rebecca looks to the black running suit she bought neatly folded on the back of the couch with the ski mask draped on top. All laid out for my first day of being a killer.

"Thanks."

I pick up the clothes and go back into the bedroom. It doesn't take me long to change. Rebecca enters with a black knapsack. She opens it and shows me the contents: a paper gown, paper booties, a pair of rubber gloves, and a wooden handled ice pick.

"Second thoughts?" Rebecca asks.

"Not a one." I take the knapsack, cinch the top shut and throw it over my shoulder. I check my watch. "I'll be back as soon as I can."

"Don't forget the cameras."

"I won't."

We stand there, frozen. What else are you supposed to say to someone before you go off to kill their son's murderer?

"If anything goes wrong, just leave. Don't take any chances," she says.

"I won't. I promise." *You won't lose me, too,* I think but can't say out loud.

I take a deep breath, offer Rebecca a confident nod, then grab the ski mask and quietly make my way out of the cabana to the alley entrance.

I walk back to my car at the body shop.

I drive to Vitali's street, park a block away from his house and walk the rest of the way in the shadows.

No one sees me. No one drives by. The houses are all dark. Not even a dog barks.

I put on the ski mask as I sneak around Vitali's house.

I peek into the garage window. It's empty.

I check my watch. It's almost three. He should be home by now, passed out in his bed, but he's not. I walk around the house and recover the surveillance cameras we had planted and stuff them into the bottom of my pack. I debate waiting for him inside the house, but decide that's too risky and instead find a comfortable spot between a bush and a fence to the side of the garage and wait.

I play the plan over and over in my head, picture him lying on his bead and my hand driving the ice pick into his chest.

I know exactly what I have to do. Rebecca and I studied the video from the cameras for countless hours. Vitali was nothing if not predictable. Saturdays, the GPS showed him leaving the restaurant around midnight, stopping for an hour or so at what we assumed to be some random woman's apartment, then returning home alone. But he is late tonight. Was he even coming home?

Headlights sweep up the street.

The black Maserati pulls into the driveway.

The garage door opens. The car goes in to the garage and the engine shuts off.

A car door opens, then slams shut.

Suddenly, I second guess my plan of just assuming I'll find an unlocked door or window. I hear the door between the garage and the house open and close, then the overhead garage door starts to move along its track.

I spring from my hiding place and rush to step over the electric eye and duck under the door before it shuts.

I'm inside.

I sit against the car on the side opposite the door to the house.

The automatic light on the garage door opener clicks off.

I check my watch.

I hear the faint sound of glass clinking. Sometimes he has another drink or two before collapsing on his bed.

Random footsteps, I can't tell from where.

Then a laugh. A woman's laugh.

Rebecca's words come back to me. "If anything goes wrong, just leave."

The only way out now is through the house. But I can't chance it.

I wait.

The woman screams ecstatically while he fucks her.

It doesn't take long.

She's upset about something. There is more screaming, but not from passion.

More footsteps.

A door slams. I think it's the front door.

There are small, decorative windows in the garage door. I take a peek. A woman is walking quickly away from the house, a cell phone to her ear. She stops to put on her shoes, then continues on her way.

I wait.

Five minutes.

Ten.

There are no sounds.

I open the knapsack, take out the paper suit and put it on.

I squeeze my hands into the rubber gloves, slip on the booties and grip the ice pick in my right hand.

Slowly, quietly, I turn the knob on the door to the house and gently ease it open.

It's darker than I expected.

The paper suit makes a rustling sound, which barely covers the pounding of my heart.

I walk through the kitchen, into the living room and down a hallway where the bedrooms are.

I hear snoring and relax.

In a few moments it will be over.

The door to the bedroom is open.

I walk in. From the light that leaks in through the bedroom window, I see him sprawled out on the bed, naked.

Face down.

Shit.

In my mind, every time I played it out, he was lying face up. The hitman I'm mimicking always stabs his victims in the chest, not the back. I need to turn him over.

I've come this far. I need to take a chance. Just one.

I put the ice pick on his night table, then gingerly move his right arm against his side. He doesn't react, and just keeps on snoring.

I grab his left shoulder and his left hip and pull his slight frame toward me. Slowly. I get him on his side, then shift my hands to ease him gently onto his back.

"Who the fuck are you?" he says.

I jump, surprised.

He just lies there, staring at me with one eye, the other seemingly stuck shut. He's obviously drunk, but also obviously awake.

I remember why I'm there, but there's no ice pick in my hand. I look around furtively in the dark. Where the hell did I leave it.

The night stand.

I grab for the ice pick.

Vitali watches me, puzzled.

"What's going on? Am I in the hospital?" He looks around, trying to get his bearings.

While his gaze is averted, I raise my hand and then drive the ice pick directly into the spot I'm aiming for, just to the left of his sternum. It goes in easily, right between the ribs.

His eyes go wide. He looks at me and his mouth opens, wanting to scream but only able to make a weak gurgling sound. Then he grabs my wrist with his left hand.

There's something else I need to do. Something I'm forgetting.

Then I remember, the hitman makes sure to maximize damage to the heart by swirling the ice pick around in the chest cavity. It's a lot harder than you might expect.

A look of supreme agony crosses his face and he grunts in pain, but his grip is firm. I let go of the ice pick and use my left hand to try to pry his fingers off my wrist, but I can't work them free.

Then another hand, wearing a rubber glove and at the end of an arm clad in a paper suit identical to my own reaches over and pulls the ice pick out of Vitali's chest. Blood bubbles out of the wound.

I turn and see Rebecca. She doesn't look at me. She places her left hand on Vitali's face, turning it slightly away from us. Then she plunges the ice pick through his temple. His groaning stops and a trickle of blood leaks out of his mouth. She lets the weapon sit there for a moment, then moves her hands and grasps the wooden handle so she can better move the slender, steel spike around his brain, shredding whatever life remains in him.

His death grip on my wrist loosens and I take a step back.

Rebecca calmly pulls the ice pick out of his head and turns to me.

"The bag. Where is the bag?" she asks.

I look around, trying to remember. "The garage."

"Let's go," she orders.

I want to ask her what she's doing there, I want to yell at her for not sticking to the plan. I want to ask what the hell she was thinking.

Instead, I follow her to the garage. She strips off her paper suit, wrapping the ice pick in it and stuffs it and her gloves in the bag. I do the same without thinking about it.

"Did you touch anything?"

I look around. See the windows in the garage door. "Maybe the garage door, by those little windows."

She uses my ski mask to wipe it down, then adds the mask to the bulging knapsack and takes me by the hand and leads me back through the house and out the back door. We walk briskly around the house and down the street to my car. About fifty feet away I see her car.

"Go," she orders, "we'll talk back at the cabana."

She walks to her car, gets in and drives off. I get into my car, wait a couple minutes, then start it and drive back to the auto body shop near the resort. From there, I walk back to the alley and follow it to the cabana. Rebecca's car is parked right where it was when I left. The lights are out in the cabana. I walk up to the door, open it and then gently close it behind me as I step into the dark room.

She is standing there in the gloom, looking at me.

"I couldn't just sit here," she explains.

She waits for me to say something, but I don't.

"I needed to see him die. After you left, I got in the car, put it in neutral and was able to roll it most of the way into the alley before I needed to start it. I drove till I found your car, then waited for him to get home.

"When I saw the woman in the car, I thought you would call it off, and I almost left. But then I saw you sneak into the garage while the door was closing. When you didn't come out of the house, I figured you didn't see that he had brought someone home. So, I waited some more.

"Eventually, the girl came storming out the front door and walked past me on the opposite side of the street. She was so busy talking on her cell that she didn't notice me.

"I saw the lights go on in his bathroom, then off and after a few moments, I decided to go in.

"I had an extra suit and gloves stashed in the car. The front door was still open. No one saw me. Once I was inside, I put on the stuff, and then you came in. You headed straight for the hallway from the kitchen and didn't see me in the dark corner of the living room. I wanted to call out to you, but I couldn't. I didn't want to take a chance that if you saw me there you wouldn't go through with it.

"Then you went into his room. I followed. I watched from the doorway as you rolled him over. When he woke up, I almost ran to you, but then you grabbed the ice pick and drove it into his chest.

"Oh, God, that was so beautiful.

"When he was holding on to you, I thought... I thought, *he's never going to die!* I don't even remember walking across the room, or pulling the ice pick out of his chest. I saw his face, and even in the dark I could tell he recognized us.

"And then when I stabbed him in the head, I thought, *now it's over. Now it's done. And he knows who fucking did it.*"

I finally break my silence. "We had a plan. Everything we did to cover our tracks, to establish an alibi—"

"No one saw me leave. And when I came back, I turned off the engine and coasted in from the alley with my lights off."

"Someone might've seen your car. Or you sitting in it, walking in through the front door of the house of the man who killed our son. What if—"

"No one saw. It's okay."

She walks up to me, takes my face in her hands.

"It's okay. He's dead. You did it. *We* did it. It's over."

I grab her wrists. I'm about to say something, but she kisses me. She kisses me hard, and I kiss her back. Passion engulfs us. We start doing a clumsy dance toward the bedroom, unable to loosen our grip on each other until we fall onto the mattress.

It's the most incredible sex of my life.

twenty four

I wake up. The sun shines through a crack in the drapes.

Rebecca is asleep and I don't wake her.

I find our overnight bag and pull out my change of clothes.

Then I find the knapsack and take it over to the fireplace. It's gas, and lights easily. The paper suits burn quickly. The gloves melt into charred, gooey blobs. I take the ice pick and place it in a Ziploc bag along with the cameras, roll them up inside the knapsack and tuck it into the bottom of the overnight bag.

"We really did it, didn't we? It wasn't a dream?" she asks from the bedroom door.

I turn to her and nod.

"When do you think someone will find him?"

"I don't know. Could be today, may not be until later in the week. Depends on whether anyone really misses him."

"What time is it? I'm hungry."

I look to my wrist, but my watch isn't there. I experience a moment of panic like the one I had when my boss called me into his office. I imagine that I left it in the garage when I put on the paper suit and gloves. I imagine it coming off when Vitali was clamped onto my wrist and the police finding it in his hand when the body is discovered.

Rebecca turns back into the bedroom, ducks inside a moment, then returns. She tosses the watch to me with a laugh. "Don't worry," she tells me. "Breakfast? Lunch?"

I slip the watch on my wrist and check the time. "Lunch. Jeez, it's almost checkout time."

"Time for a shower?"

I nod.

Rebecca grabs her stuff out of the overnight bag and heads toward the bathroom.

I turn off the fireplace, gather up the ashes with a paper towel and wash them down the sink at the bar. I make a pass through the room, searching for anything that would betray us. There is nothing, of course. I've been very careful. And despite Rebecca's involvement, she's right. There's nothing to worry about.

At some point over the next few days, Vitali's body will be found. Someone will call us to ask if we've heard. We'll be surprised, disbelieving at first and we'll listen to everyone tell us how he deserved it, and how God works in mysterious ways.

I don't expect we'll hear from the police, or the district attorney who barely tried to prosecute him, but if we do, we're ready.

I turn on television while I wait for Rebecca to finish her shower. Flipping through the channels I come across a local midday news show. After a recap of the previous night's baseball games, there is a breaking story.

A reporter stands in front of Vitali's house. There is yellow police tape stretched across the front yard, and police cars parked in the driveway, their lights flashing.

"The body of Anthony Vitali, son of the notorious crime boss, Tony Vitali, was discovered early this morning by a female friend. Details of how he died are not forthcoming at this time, but it's obvious by the attention the scene is receiving that police are treating this as a homicide.

"Vitali drew attention some months ago for his involvement in a traffic accident that resulted in the death of a young boy. He was acquitted of charges in that case, but could not evade the fate that caught up to him last night."

I hear Rebecca's cell phone ringing in the bedroom.

Mine rings in my pocket. I answer. While I listen to my mother tell me the news, I hear Rebecca answer her phone. She plays it perfectly. Asking questions, "How? Do they know who did it? Thank God that bastard's dead," she adds.

I tell my mom that I saw the story on the news. She tells me she's been praying for something like this to happen. Praying for justice for Nick. She asks me if I'm with Rebecca. "Yes, she's here," I answer.

Rebecca ends her call and comes and sits down next to me. "Is that your mom?" she asks.

I nod and hand her my phone.

They talk for a while.

By the end of their conversation, Rebecca is in tears. She says goodbye to my mom, then we scan the local channels for more news.

It turns out the woman who stormed out came back a short while later. She had left her keys behind. I figured it out in my head and she must've come back just minutes after we drove away.

Another panic attack washes over me. How could we have been so reckless? I should've left the house when I saw the woman leave. That was not part of the plan.

Rebecca puts her hand on my leg. "Come on, we have five minutes to check out."

I collect our bags, put them in the trunk, then drive us to the office. The clerk is the same one who checked us in. When he asks, we tell him how great it was, and yes, we plan on coming back.

There is a restaurant across from the body shop. We stop to have lunch. Our cell phones continue to ring.

Rebecca posts a message to her Facebook page, thanking everyone for their thoughts and prayers.

I send out a Tweet to the same effect.

We answer a couple of the calls, then turn our phones off. It's the same conversation over and over.

Our food arrives and we dig in hungrily.

Rebecca looks at me with a combination of concern and uncertainty. "We should talk about what we did last night—I mean, this morning, the thing after the thing, when we..."

"That was... really nice," I say.

"Yes. And I think I'd like to do it again, but maybe not right away."

"Oh."

"I mean, it was in the heat of the moment, and we've been so wrapped up in everything else, that I think we should take some time to figure out where we are with each other."

"Okay."

"But you don't have to sleep on the futon any more."

"Good, my back hates that thing."

Rebecca reaches over and places her hand on mine. "Thanks for understanding," she says with a smile.

I finish off my sandwich. "You know, it's not completely over, yet. The first thing, I mean."

"I know."

"Still some stuff I need to do and there's always a chance someone will ask us questions."

"I'm ready."

"Good."

Rebecca pushes the rest of her half-eaten lunch away and gazes out the window. In some ways, I feel closer to her than I ever have, but in others, she's as far away as the moon.

twenty five

When I arrive at work on Monday, everyone looks at me expectantly. Before I settle down at my cubicle, a few coworkers gather around.

"Heard the news. Guess that guy had it coming, huh?"

"You're not going to get an argument from me on that," I reply.

"Do you know anything about how he died? Who did it?"

"Just what was on the news. Might have been something to do with the mob."

"I heard that too. His dad is some Mafia big shot. They gave him a Columbian neck tie. You know, where they slit the throat and pull the tongue out."

"That's a myth. You can't do that with a tongue."

"I heard he was shot in the head and had his balls cut off."

"I hope they did the second part first," I add.

"How's Rebecca taking it?"

"I think we're both kind of mixed about it. I mean, it doesn't bring Nick back, but damn, I wanted to do a jig when I saw it on the news."

"Well, the entire city can rest easier with him off the streets. I know I will."

"Yeah. They should've never let him walk."

"Not walking anywhere any more."

"Thanks, guys. With or without him, we still have work to do here," I remind them.

They sense my reluctance to continue the conversation, and return to their tasks. One of the junior admins approaches. "Hey, I was running some diagnostics on Friday when you were out. Found a weird partition on one of the drives in the storage pool on the SAN. Looks like it's encrypted. I couldn't find any reference to it in the configuration files."

I shrug. "Could be an old recovery partition. Some of those drives we reclaimed from old servers a while back. I'll take a look. Thanks."

He nods, seemingly satisfied with my explanation. I make a mental note to scrub the partition from the drive and run a shredder utility on the sectors where it lived. I won't be needing it anymore.

The mistakes I've made along the way start to pile up in my mind. It's a miracle everything turned out as well as it did.

twenty six

At the group, there is an upbeat vibe. Most everyone shares the relief we feel knowing that our son's killer is dead.

But no one says anything out loud.

Barb starts up the group. There are no new parents this week, so she opens the floor up for anyone who has anything share.

Eyes start turning in our direction.

Rebecca and I smile.

"We have a bit of news," Rebecca says.

"News?!" Brian interrupts. "Glory Hallelujah, that greasy asshole is dead!" He starts a slow clap.

Others join in.

Barb conspicuously sits with her hands folded on her lap.

Amy is the first to speak when the clapping dies down. "How does it feel?"

Rebecca turns to her, sighs. "I almost hate to admit it, but it feels great. I finally feel like Nick can rest. I feel like I can close my eyes at night, knowing that he's not out there still, having a life, maybe killing someone else. He'll never hurt anyone ever again."

"What about you?" Barb asks me, an almost scolding tone to her voice.

"Ding Dong the bastard's dead," I say casually, without a tinge of guilt or remorse.

"Well," Barb continues, "I suppose it's reasonable to experience some... joy in the realization of justice. But remember," she cautions the members of the group, "He was someone's child, too. His parents could show up here, with the same feelings all of us share, the same shadow over their lives. Is that something to celebrate?"

"Damn straight, it is," Brian says. "This was no innocent kid. He was a killer. His parents should be ashamed to have raised such a monster. And from what I've heard, it's probably his father's mob ties that got him killed. They can all rot in Hell."

"Brian!" Barb shouts.

"Sorry, hon, but I'm having a full on hate day. Wish whoever took him out would pay a visit to—"

"Stop. Don't you say another word, or I swear, I'll walk out right now and you can sleep in the garage."

Brian silences himself. I sense he is genuinely remorseful for voicing his feelings in that way.

Barb scans the room, daring anyone else to challenge her. "I think we should adjourn for the night. And I hope all of you take some time to reflect on your feelings, and think about who you are and who you want to be, and what your children would think of you if they saw you acting this way."

She gathers her coat and purse. Brian follows.

The Cancer Parents also depart.

The rest of us stay in silence for a while.

Old Harold, sitting unnoticed in a corner of the room, looks up and for the first time, speaks. "He was a really bad person and deserved to die." He turns his gaze to Rebecca and me. "If you don't rejoice and celebrate his death, then you're dead, too. Your son is doing freaking cartwheels around you, can't you see him?"

Rebecca looks to the empty space in front of us and smiles.

"I'm glad for you. I wish all of you live long enough to see the people who took your loved ones die an early and painful death. Even that is too good for them."

Harold stands. His coat and hat are on a chair next to him. He picks them up and puts them on while walking to the door.

Once he's gone, what remains of the group dissolves into a sea of babbling conversation. Old Harold gave us permission to embrace our most base human emotions, and we do so with abandon.

twenty seven

It's Sunday morning, and we sit in a pew at church. People cast inquisitive glances our way. Nancy and her family are directly across the aisle from us. She keeps on looking our way, too, but more expectantly than questioningly.

The pastor gets to the portion of his sermon where he offers blessings and prayers. The last one is for us. "And let us bless our angel, Nicholas, and his parents, and give them the strength to forgive the one who took him from us now that his soul is in God's hands for judgment."

Rebecca whispers in my ear. "I want to go."

"It's almost over," I whisper back.

The sermon ends and Nancy approaches. "How are you two? We've been praying for you since we heard the news last week. It was me that asked the pastor to include that last prayer."

"I'm not feeling well, we're going to go home," Rebecca replies curtly. She turns and walks out the far side of the pew. I follow, catch up and take her hand in mine. She shakes it off.

twenty eight

I'm watching TV. I see Rebecca pass through the hallway, wearing her coat.
"Where are you going?"
"Out," she says, "do I need your permission?"
"No, just asking."
"I'm meeting Amy, from the group."
"Oh. Okay. Have a nice time."
"I will." She gives me that smirk that means I'm an idiot and leaves. My phone rings. I answer.
"Hello?"
The voice on the other end says my name, and I reply, "Speaking."
"This is Eric Goldman. From the District Attorney's office. We met briefly during Anthony Vitali's trial."
"I remember," I reply snidely.
"I'm sure you've heard that he was killed last weekend."
"Yes."
"Well, I wanted to let you know that the police may be wanting to question you."
"About what?"
"Well, nothing, really. Just a formality. I mean, technically you have a motive—"
"My wife and I have been working hard to put all that behind us."
"Wife? I thought you two were divorced."
"We are. I mean, we're trying to reconcile."

"Oh, I understand. That's good to hear. I just wanted to give you a heads-up because the police asked me about the case and, well, I feel bad that we didn't have enough to put him away, I don't want you to feel like they seriously think you could've done it. It was clearly a mob hit—but you didn't hear that from me."

"Hear what?"

"Thank you. Just wanted you to know that it's just procedure. Nothing more."

"Okay. Thank you, Mr. Goldman."

"Sure, sorry to disturb you."

"Goodbye."

"Good—"

I disconnect the call before he can complete his farewell. I notice my hands are shaking.

The police.

I've been putting off getting rid of the cameras and ice pick. I didn't want to draw any attention to myself in the aftermath of Vitali's death. But now I feel I have to dispose of them. What if they have a warrant?

I grab my coat, leave my cell phone on the coffee table and calmly walk out to my car.

In the wheel well of the trunk where there normally is a spare tire, I have hidden the knapsack with the cameras and ice pick along with the wiped laptop, a gallon of bleach, a ball-peen hammer and a blow torch.

I drive to a forest preserve about thirty miles away. I've been there once or twice before. It's the kind of place that attracts a big crowd of kids on the weekend, looking for a place to drink beer and hook up.

It's as I remember it, overflowing with garbage. Mine is the only car there on a week night. It'll be dark soon, the park officially closes at sunset, but the gate to this picnic area is broken.

There are rusty charcoal grills bolted to posts anchored in the ground with cement. I lay the knapsack on the ground and pound the cameras inside to bits with the hammer. When I can no longer feel any pieces bigger than a pea, I drop the knapsack into one of the grills and light the blowtorch. The canvas of the knapsack must have some type of flame retardant since it takes a while to burn it to ash. The camera pieces melt into slag. I burn the handle of the ball-peen hammer, too.

I drop the ice pick into the grill and char its wooden handle. I hold the torch on the metal spike until it's red hot. Then I douse everything with the bleach. A noxious gas fills the air and I step away quickly, feeling light-headed.

I wait till a breeze clears the air, then gather the ash and slag and the remnants of the hammer and ice pick into a heap and slide it onto a piece of cardboard I fished out of the trash. I follow the road past the pavilions to a boat launch next to a murky, smelly river and heave the stinky slush as far out into it as I can. The laptop—which I've carefully purged of any traces of what it was used for and drilled holes into until any information was unrecoverable—follows, making a loud splash and bobbing in the current for a moment before sinking out of view. I rinse my hands in the foul water, then again under a pump near one of the covered pavilions.

Dusk descends as I pull out of the parking lot. I'm still alone. No one sees me come, carry out my evidence destruction, or leave.

Finally, something goes exactly to plan.

twenty nine

The detective sits on a chair. Rebecca and I are opposite on the sofa. He sets the glass of water Rebecca got for him on a coaster, then pulls out a notebook.

Just like they do on TV.

"Okay, like I said, this is just a formality. I hate to ask, but where were you on the morning of May eleventh of this year between the hours of three a.m. and four a.m.?"

"We were at the Sierra Winds Resort down route thirty-four," Rebecca replies.

"You were together?"

"Yes," I answer.

"Anyone see you there?"

I think for a moment. "There was the clerk in the office. He checked us in, then he was still there when we got back from dinner. We left right at checkout time the next day."

"You got a receipt or anything."

Rebecca and I look at each other, she answers. "I don't know if we kept it, but it'll be on my credit card bill. We can look for it if it's important."

"No, that's fine. Like I said, just a formality. I've got what I need." He gets up. We rise also, and all of us move toward the door. "Do you mind if I ask where you were when you heard?"

"At the resort, still," I tell him. "Seems like everyone we knew was watching the news and started calling us."

"Yeah, I guess they would. Just so you know, I was at the station when the news came in. There was a bit of a cheer, actually. Real scumbag, that guy. This is one of those cases I really don't give a shit if we solve. Let those thugs kill each other, right?"

I nod.

"Sorry for your loss—your boy I mean. I hope you get some peace out of this."

"Thank you," Rebecca says.

He lets himself out and disappears down the hallway.

Once he's gone, I wait almost a whole minute before taking a breath.

"I think that's it. We're in the clear."

Rebecca sighs with relief and smiles. She gives me a quick kiss and a tight hug. "I knew we would be. Thank you. If I had planned this whole thing I'd be sitting in jail right now."

"Orange is the new black," I add jokingly.

She pushes away and gives me a playful rebuke. "Okay, Mr. Master Assassin. If you're so good, tell me, how would you off that guy who poisoned Amy's family?"

"The 'Best Killer Burgers in the State' guy?"

"Mm-hm. Tell me, if that guy had killed Nick…"

I find myself pulling together various thoughts in my mind. "Well, I think Amy had the right idea, but instead of a gas can, maybe start a grease fire. The way she describes that place, it would probably only take a match or two to set it on fire."

"But how do you make sure he gets incinerated along with the place?"

I think about that for a moment. "Tie him up with rags, or a greasy apron, something that wouldn't leave any marks, but would burn away once he caught on fire. Douse him with grease, light him up. Let him run around till he falls down, just a charred skeleton. Guy probably drinks all day long, he'd burn like a gas lamp wick."

"And how do you get him to sit still long enough to tie him up?"

"Surprise him. Get there when the place is empty, maybe after the lunch crowd. Sit at a table, when he takes your order, jump him from behind, knock his head on the floor, or smack him with a chair. With any luck, he'll be in shock long enough to get something around his wrists and ankles, the coroner would think the injuries happened in the fire..."

Then it hits me.

She's been spending a lot of time with Amy.

"Did you tell her?" I ask.

"Who?"

I don't answer her question. She knows full well who and what I'm talking about.

"I had to tell somebody," she confesses, "she won't say anything."

I'm furious. "To our graves. We agreed we would take this to our graves. What does she know?"

A pause. "Pretty much everything."

"What?"

"She was so amazed that we actually did it. She pressed me for every detail."

"Rebecca. I... I can't believe this. We swore."

I collapse on the sofa. My mind racing with the notion that the truth would spread on whispers through the group, and someone—probably Barb—would get wind of it and wouldn't be able to keep quiet and would tell the police.

Rebecca sits next to me, rubs my arms reassuringly. "She's not going to tell anyone. She just wants some help."

Oh, Jesus! "Help?" I ask.

"She wants to kill Cooper. We've been putting together a profile just like you and me did with Vitali. Nothing on paper, all in our heads. She's been there enough times to know what the place looks like. She's even been inside."

"No. Stop."

"She's going to do it whether we help her or not."

"No, stop her. We barely got away with it."

"She needs to do it. She needs to kill him. We need to help her."

"No."

"*I* need to help her."

She's pleading now. I look in her eyes and see that same desperate drive that she had when we visited Nick's grave. "Why?"

"It's what we're supposed to do. It's why we found the group. It's a reason to go on."

"It's too risky. He's in a whole different state. There's no chance to establish an alibi—"

"But we don't need to. Who would suspect us?"

"We can't. We're not killers."

She looks at me, puzzled. "Yes, we are," she states. "We are killers, cold-blooded murderers. We killed Vitali. You know we can do it. We have to do it. For Amy. So she can have the peace we have."

Peace? "How is going on a killing spree peace?"

"If you don't want to help I'm going to do it on my own."

"No."

Rebecca crosses her arms. Her mind is made up. She would do it on her own. Or worse, take Amy with her.

I have no choice. I sternly make a hasty ultimatum. "We take no chances. We have to do it exactly as I say. If we get there and everything is not perfect, if one thing is not according to the plan, we walk away."

"I promise. You're in charge. If you say we walk, we walk."

I consider. I run the plan I sketched out for Rebecca over in my head, smooth out the rough edges, figure in a couple contingencies... it could work. We could be in and out in minutes, and she's right. Why would anyone suspect us?

We could do this.

My God, I *am* a killer.

TODD

The Dead Kids Club

one

Rebecca, Amy and I sit around Amy's kitchen table.

I question her relentlessly about every detail she has on Buck Cooper and his little roadside diner. She uses knives and forks and salt and pepper shakers to illustrate the layout of the place. I get her to describe the roads leading to and from, where the nearest intersections are, farm houses, gas stations, everything she can think of.

Both she and Rebecca are getting impatient. It's been two weeks since Rebecca got me to agree to this, and they want to get on with it. I insist that there be some time between our killing and hers. The people in the group know we're friendly with each other and may start jumping to conclusions—however correct they may be—regarding the synchronicity of the deaths of the monsters who killed our children.

They don't care, and assume that everyone in the group, if they had such suspicions, would keep them to themselves. Everyone will assume it's a happy coincidence. When it rains, it pours.

I see it differently. Each lapse in judgment, each mistake in planning led to potentially fatal errors when we killed Vitali. It was mere luck that kept us from getting caught, and I don't want to leave anything to chance this time.

Amy wants us to take pictures or better yet, a video. I absolutely forbid it. We don't make any type of recording or leave any traces. There must not be anything that could potentially tie us to the scene. If all goes well, this is going to look like an accident.

Just in case, Amy is going to establish an alibi, spending the weekend with her sister.

No credit cards is my other absolute rule. Rebecca and I purchased stuff online for the Vitali killing, albeit through several proxies, but I always thought that was a weak link in that plan.

"We can do it this weekend," Rebecca tells Amy.

I look at her, she looks back, challengingly. I've known her long enough to know when not to even start an argument.

"All right. But if we do it now, you can't tell the group until next month."

"What?" Amy asks. "Why?"

"Think about it. This is an accidental fire and death in another state in a rural area. How would you find out about it? In a month or so, you do one of your drive-bys and come back to the group with a smile on your face. The fucker burned himself to death. Fry cook gets fried."

"Poetic justice."

"Agreed?" I ask, or rather demand.

"Agreed," Rebecca answers, then looks at Amy, who hesitates.

"Or else we wait," I insist.

Amy thinks about it for a minute, then nods. "Agreed."

two

My boss presses me again to bring Rebecca to his house for a weekend barbecue. I tell him we're planning another getaway and ask for a rain check. He demands that I commit to the following week, or else his wife will have his head.

I relent.

At work I have a new virtual machine that I keep on an encrypted USB key. When I plug it in, I can use it to cover my tracks like I did with the previous version on the server—now digital history—but there will be no footprint left behind anywhere for nosy junior admins to stumble across.

I pull up satellite maps of the area around Cooper's diner and memorize every road, every path, every fence line.

I scour the internet for information on Cooper himself, but he does a good job of living off the grid. From the overhead views, it's obvious there's a residential building in the back of the diner where Cooper likely lives. There's nothing in Amy's intelligence that indicates there is anyone else living there. If we get there and discover that there is, we walk away.

This is a very different scenario from the Vitali killing. That one we made to look like a murder—which wasn't a stretch since that's what it was.

This one has to be an accident.

Part of me hopes he dies when I smash his head against the floor in our initial attack. But Amy is adamant about him burning alive. I tell her we'll do our best, but no promises. Our first priority is getting away with it. There are no style points if we're in jail.

I pull the USB key out of the port on the server and clip it back onto my key chain. Not an unusual accessory for a computer guy.

It's time to call it a day. Time to head back home. It's Wednesday, and there are a couple shows on TV that Rebecca and I like to watch together. Like we used to.

There has not been any more sex since we killed Vitali. She hasn't offered and I haven't asked. Part of me is afraid to. I don't want to push the issue.

That awkwardness that existed between us after Nick's death is gone, but there are other barriers still up. The last couple weeks have been good, though. Rebecca is genuinely excited about killing Cooper, and her enthusiasm is a bit contagious.

I step out of the office into the late spring evening. The air is fresh, like after a rainstorm. The sun is at that point where it casts a golden glow over everything, like a sepia tone Instagram filter.

Then it hits me.

What the hell am I doing?

Killing Vitali made sense—in a way. But it also had a purpose personal to me.

This plan to kill Cooper... this is Amy's shadow. How did it become ours?

What if we refused? Would she feel spurned enough to make an anonymous call to the police about the Vitali murder?

I've spent so much time and effort making sure my plan has a way out at every conceivable point, that I've neglected to make sure I had a way out of the plan itself.

Is this what my life has come to? Computer-guy-slash-contract-killer? Hell, not even a contract killer. Strictly speaking, I'm an unpaid amateur.

A year ago I would've adamantly derided the notion that I'd kill another human being, let alone two. I find my lack of revulsion at the notion now a bit disconcerting. True, they deserve it, they are not innocent victims of circumstance, but callous killers with no remorse for their actions.

But isn't that what I am now?

I sense that Rebecca and Amy might be planning to "help out" another member of the group. I swear to myself that this is the last time. After Vitali's death, I finally felt like I could go on living, maybe even enjoy life a bit. But Cooper I'm doing out of what? Sympathy for Amy? Concern for Rebecca? Because I want to? Because I want that feeling of handing out justice to someone who so undeservedly avoided it?

Is that how I'm justifying it to myself? Is it a way to cover the possibility that I get a thrill from killing? From planning the perfect crime? Am I willing to do anything to feel closer to Rebecca, the way we did after killing Vitali?

I reach my car and vomit onto the pavement. I catch my reflection in the side-view mirror and see the face of a specter who's been haunting me since Nick's death. How long has he been hiding in the shadows, waiting for an excuse to come out and kill?

three

It's early morning. As I drive, I go over the plan with Rebecca. She is weary of hearing me repeat the same situational contingencies over and over again. So am I. But I am determined that nothing will surprise me this time, and that there won't be any needless errors.

We have four hours of driving ahead of us and I intend to use every minute of it making sure we are prepared.

Five minutes later Rebecca shuts down. She stops responding to my questions, reaches into her bag and pulls out her phone and ear buds and literally tunes me out, reclines her seat and closes her eyes.

We approach an exit and I think about making a U-turn and returning to our apartment. But I know the cost of that action is too high. I imagine Rebecca getting into her car with Amy and carrying out the plan without me, getting caught, and all of us going to prison.

I drive on.

An hour and a half later I stop for gas. Rebecca is sleeping—or at least is pretending to—and the cessation of motion is enough to rouse her.

"Where are we?" she asks, rubbing her eyes.

"Gas," I answer. "I'm going to grab a Coke or something, you want anything?"

She undoes her seatbelt and opens the passenger door. "I want to stretch my legs."

We head into the minimart. I give the clerk some cash for the gas while Rebecca browses among the rows of chips and candy.

When I'm done pumping, I walk into the shop and grab a small bag of mixed nuts on my way to the drink cooler. I pick out an energy drink in a big can and look around for Rebecca.

I don't see her right away, she's not in the food aisles. Instead, I find her in the automotive supply and tools section. She hefts a heavy wrench in her hands, then sets it down and tries out a few different sized sledgehammers.

"What are you doing?" I ask.

She turns to me, smiling, holds up a hammer. "What do you think? This should make a good dent in his skull."

I take the hammer from her hands, put it and the food I was going to buy down on the nearest shelf, then guide her out and back to the car. I open the passenger side door for her and she gets in, shooting me a quizzical look.

I get in the driver's side, start the car and head back to the highway.

"What were you thinking?" I ask.

"What?"

"The plan is to use something at the diner. If we bring anything that doesn't belong, it could be noticed, traced, we can't take that chance."

"Okay, Mr. Stick-To-The-Plan. Sorry."

"I'm not being this way to annoy you. We have to be careful."

"I know. I just hate it when you dismiss any ideas I have."

"What do you mean?" I ask, confused by her comment.

"I mean, this whole plan, every step of it, is yours. You didn't like any of my ideas, or Amy's. Why does everything have to be your way?"

"It's not about my way or your way, it's about not getting caught."

"And you're the only one smart enough to come up with any ideas that don't get us caught?"

"No."

"Sure seems that way."

"Come on. We can't do this if you're going to be mad at me."

"Of course not. That's not in the plan."

My grip on the steering wheel tightens as I struggle to keep from shouting. "That's not what I meant. I'm sorry. It's just, you know me, I'm a bit of a control freak." These are the words I say when I want to change the trajectory of an argument with Rebecca. I confess the flaws she sees in me. Next, I blame myself and insist it's out of concern for her. "After Vitali, and the whole thing with the woman, I'm just on edge. It has nothing to do with you, I'm just afraid there's going to be something I didn't think about. And I don't want anything to happen to you. I couldn't live with myself." Sometimes this works. I wait to see how she reacts.

"It's okay," she finally says. "I want us to be in this together, though. Partners. I don't want to be your... assistant, or whatever. I want to be your equal."

"You're right, I haven't been treating you like I should. I'm sorry. I'm just... I guess I'm afraid."

"I've been asking so much of you," she says. "First Vitali, now Cooper. And you've been great. You really have. I really appreciate what you've done. Not just anyone could have pulled it off. You've been really smart and careful about it, and I've wanted to rush in and just do it."

"I can understand that. I certainly have felt that way, too."

"I need to clear my head. I think the constant talking about it is what's really got me annoyed. Can we talk about something else?"

"Of course," I tell her.

I launch into a long retelling of the progress I've been making at work, how my boss constantly insists that we come over for a barbecue, how there might be a management position opening up in the near future.

She tells me how I totally would be great for that. I have a natural skill for managing projects and working with people.

"And killing them," I add.

"Best to leave that off your resume," she jokes.

We settle back into a ridiculous conversation about an imaginary job interview where I explain our unusual hobby and the interviewer finally ends up offering me *his* job.

It raises both our spirits.

I take the exit that leads to Cooper's diner. It's another forty-five minutes on rural highways. I am scrupulous about obeying the speed limit and coming to a complete stop at every red light and stop sign.

Rebecca teases me about only being a good driver when I'm about to commit murder.

I assure her I'd be just as careful for a mere bank robbery. Or even if I was driving to my accountant's office to cheat on my taxes.

four

I almost miss Cooper's diner as we drive by it the first time. The place really is a tiny little shit hole. There are several cars and trucks in the weedy gravel patch that serves as a parking lot, including Coopers F150. It's a mystery why he spends money on a new truck, while his restaurant is run down to the point of being condemned.

I have several routes that will take me in wide circles around Cooper's place. It's just after one in the afternoon, and the "lunch crowd" should be winding down about now.

"Didn't see the 'Best Burgers in the State' sign," Rebecca remarks.

"Someone probably ran it over."

She laughs. We mustn't get relaxed to the point of being careless, but I'm glad we aren't at each other's throats.

It takes two drive-bys before Cooper's customers are gone. We pull into a far corner of the parking lot that is mostly obscured from the road. There is an empty cardboard box that I position next to the car to hide the license plate.

I take Rebecca by the hand and we walk toward the diner.

"Remember, if anyone comes, we have to walk away," I remind her.

"I know" she reassures me.

five

Inside, the place is exactly as one would imagine it. There are a lot of neon beer signs, mismatched chairs and tables, and a counter that doubles as a bar.

Cooper sits at the counter, paging through a car magazine. He glances up when he hears the screen door slam shut behind us. He sizes us up. I nod and lead Rebecca to one of the cleaner tables. There are four chairs at it, perfect for our purpose.

"Still serving lunch?" I ask.

"Hmm." he answers unresponsively.

We sit. The menus are worn eight-and-a-half by eleven sheets of paper folded in half. I pluck two out of the clip on the napkin holder and hand one to Rebecca.

Cooper walks up, a pad in one greasy hand as he pulls the stub of a pencil from behind his ear with the other. "What can I getcha?"

I already know what I'm going to order before I looked at the menu. "Burger. Rare."

He looks to Rebecca. She makes a show of scanning the entire menu before responding.

"I'll have the chili," she says. "With a Diet Coke."

"Two diets," I add.

He doesn't bother to jot the order on his pad. He simply sticks the pencil back behind his ear and turns to the counter.

This is it. This is my chance.

Time slows down. I turn my head to look at the parking lot

through the grimy windows. Ours is still the only car there, and there is no traffic on the road.

I rise, taking a step toward Cooper while grabbing one of the empty chairs between him and me.

The chair is fairly heavy, but I manage to raise it above my head as I continue closing the distance between the clueless fry cook and myself.

Using my forward momentum, the weight of the chair and all the strength I can muster, I bring the chair heavily down on the back of his hair-slicked skull.

The blow knocks both him and me off our feet. I crash to the floor, landing awkwardly on my left arm. I hear a loud snap and pain explodes from my elbow, through my shoulder all the way up to my neck.

I look over at Cooper. Blood trickles from the wound in his head, but he's still conscious and moaning.

Rebecca sees that I'm not getting up and rushes to my side.

"Are you all right?"

"I think I broke my arm," I tell her.

"What do I need to do?" she asks.

Get out, is my first reaction. But I know that is not an option. If we leave him alive, he'll be able to describe us to the police. We have to go forward.

"Tie up his hands, use his apron strings."

Rebecca nods, and crosses over to Cooper, kicking the chair now laying across his back aside. It didn't splinter into pieces like it would in the movies. It's solid wood, but she manages to move it easily. She kneels on his back, keeping him from moving as she quickly wraps his hands securely with the frayed strips of fabric at the back of his stained apron.

While she does this, I manage to get to my feet. Any movement in my arm is excruciating. I tuck my left hand between the buttons on the front of my shirt, creating a makeshift sling to keep my arm still. That helps.

Rebecca looks to me, expectantly. "What do we do next?" she asks.

I try to call the plan up in my mind, but my thoughts are interrupted by flashes of pain.

"His feet," I manage to say. "Need to tie up his feet, too."

Rebecca looks around for something to tie him up with.

I see a dish rag on the counter. "The dish rag, tear it into strips."

While Rebecca sets to making bindings for his feet, I take another look at the parking lot. Still clear. No one is coming. I cross to behind the counter. The fryer is full of hot oil. I check the grease collection bin under the griddle. It is nearly full. I slide it out with my good arm and manage to drag it across the floor around the counter. It splashes a bit, but that's okay.

Rebecca has Cooper's feet bound and comes to help me.

"Pour about half if on him. Spread it out, then we'll need to turn him over."

Rebecca picks up the bin, heavy with gallons of grease and hauls it over to where Cooper lies. She dowses his back, then I use my good arm to help her roll him over and she pours more grease over his face, chest and groin. He is still groggy, but his eyes open and look up at me.

He looks exactly like Vitali did that night not so many weeks ago, when I turned him over in his bed to stab him in the heart with an ice pick.

He moans but doesn't question what happened or why he's tied up. Likely he doesn't realize it yet. After all, he has a visible dent in his head.

I stand up and Rebecca splashes the remaining grease on the floor and furniture as we walk back to the kitchen area. I grab another rag and start wiping every surface I can remember touching, and any others that I might have touched. I see what constitutes the bar area. There are some bottles of high proof whiskey. I pick one up with the dish rag and break it over the stove. I smash another on the counter.

"Hand me one of those," Rebecca requests.

I hand her a third bottle wrapped in a rag. She carries it to Cooper, smashes the top off of the bottle and empties it over him. Then she tosses the bottle aside and uses the rag to wipe off the chair I smashed him with and sets it back at the table where we were sitting and cleans everything at the table as well.

I look around the kitchen for matches and find some on a shelf. I bump my injured arm reaching for them and they spill over the stove. I feel light-headed. The combination of the pain and the fumes from the liquor set me back on my heels.

I spy the doorway in the back of the diner that leads to what I assume are his living quarters. I take a step and nearly stumble.

Rebecca arrives at my side. She puts my good arm over her shoulder.

"We have to check the back. No surprises."

Rebecca nods and leads me to the doorway. I push it open with a foot. Inside is a medium sized room with a bed against one wall, an enormous flat screen TV on another and a stained easy chair facing it. The floor is littered with empty beer cans, cups, snack food wrappers and dirty clothes. There is no sign of any other inhabitants. No indication of a female presence.

I sigh, relieved and satisfied that our due diligence has paid off.

"Ready?" Rebecca asks.

I nod. There are a few matches clutched in my hand. I offer them to Rebecca. "Has to start in the kitchen."

Rebecca takes the matches and leads me back to the counter. She strikes one on the underside of a stool and tosses it onto the stove. The alcohol laden grease catches fire easily, then spreads down to the floor. Blue and orange flames dance and spread quickly. More quickly than I had imagined they would. Smoke quickly fills the space. It stings my eyes and burns my lungs.

"We need to get out of here."

"Come on," Rebecca says, pulling me after her.

I catch a lungful of noxious fumes and immediately lose my balance. My arm smashes against the edge of the counter. The pain is blinding, and I suck in another deep breath of the smoke that is quickly filling the restaurant.

The room goes black.

The last thing I remember is falling.

six

"Careful with his arm, I think it's broken," Rebecca says.

Rebecca somehow drags me across the floor as flames chase my feet.

I look to the side and see Cooper, his body convulsing from coughing, the fire creeping closer to his grease and alcohol-soaked overalls.

"Hurry, this place is going up fast," says another familiar voice.

My arm slips out of my shirt, banging my elbow against the floor.

The pain is intense, but momentary, as I slip back into darkness.

seven

A splash of water on my face returns me to consciousness.

I open my eyes, and Rebecca comes into focus. Behind her, Cooper's diner is almost entirely engulfed in flames.

"We have to get out of here," I tell her.

"Can you get in the car?"

I sit up, lean on my right arm and push myself to my feet. Rebecca opens the back door for the car, and I manage to slide in. She gets in behind the wheel and starts the car.

"We need to get you to a hospital," she says.

"Not here. We need to get back home," I tell her.

"Can you make it?"

"Yes. And don't speed!"

"I know, I know," she says, annoyed at my continuing caution.

She starts the car and backs over the cardboard box I had left blocking our license plate. The only thing I can think of at that moment is what if the tires leave a tread mark that can uniquely identify this car?

As we drive back onto the road, a shape crawls out of the diner, a body wrapped in red-orange fire.

Cooper.

Out of the corner of my eye I think I see a car parked across the road, tucked into an overgrown driveway. I can vaguely see there is someone sitting in the front seat, watching the diner burn.

Watching Cooper die.

The other voice when I was being dragged out.

Amy. She and Rebecca must've arranged for her to be there to watch our handiwork.

I also know that if she hadn't been there, I might still be inside burning to death myself. I'm both mad as hell and grateful.

I sit quietly in the back seat, keeping an eye out for any other cars. There are none.

I spy Rebecca watching me in the rearview mirror.

"I think we're okay," I tell her. "Do you have any aspirin or anything?"

"Yes, in my purse." Rebecca fishes around in her bag, and hands back a bottle of ibuprofen.

I take the bottle, squeeze it between my knees as I try to open the child-proof cap one-handed.

"Do you need help with that?" she asks.

"I think I got it." After a few tries, I manage to get it open and pour four or five of the reddish-brown pills into my mouth and swallow them dry. I put the cap back on the bottle. "Do you know how to get back to the Interstate?"

"Yeah." She knows I have forbidden the use of our phones or a GPS device. "Why don't you lie down?"

"I think I will." My arm is throbbing. I slowly lower myself across the back seat, waiting for the pain killers to kick in. I close my eyes. Every little pebble in the road sends a twinge of pain from my elbow to the back of my neck.

Rebecca turns on the radio. The music helps distract me from my injury and pass the time. After a while, the rhythm of the road slows as Rebecca pulls onto the on-ramp and then quickens to a soothing pace as she accelerates down the Interstate.

Somehow, I fall asleep.

eight

Rebecca shakes me awake.

"We're at the hospital. What are we going to tell them?"

I push myself upright, look out the window. We are in the parking lot for the emergency room of the hospital a little over a mile from our place.

"I fell in the garage, bumped my head." Which is true. I can feel a lump on the back of my head. "You found me and brought me here. Do I smell like smoke?"

She nods. "We both do."

I try to think of something, some explanation. "We need to go home, change."

But Rebecca has a better idea. "We were working in the yard, burning some tree trimmings."

"We don't have a yard."

"At your mom's house."

My mom is out of town this weekend, visiting her cousin. Makes sense we would help out with some yard work while she's gone. That's something we'd do. "That's good," I say, satisfied we have a plausible story to cover our tracks.

"Okay. Can you walk?"

"Yeah." The pain is now a dull throb. I let my arm dangle as Rebecca opens the back door as I push myself out.

We walk toward the emergency room.

"I guess I should be grateful that Amy broke our rule about not being there," I say. The subtext is obvious to Rebecca.

"We were careful."

"You shouldn't have let her come. It was too risky."

"You can thank her for helping to save your life once we get your arm set," Rebecca says, purposefully bumping my elbow gently enough to appear as an accident, but hard enough to induce another piercing bolt of pain.

Even as we enter the hospital, no one the wiser that we've just come from the scene of a murder, I think about all the things that went wrong. How incredibly lucky we are to have gotten away with it.

How lucky I am to be alive.

When will the luck run out?

nine

With my arm in a cast up past the elbow, and a fresh dose of the prescription pain killer they gave me at the hospital dulling the pain, I follow Rebecca into the apartment. "Hungry?" she asks. "I just remembered, we never did get our lunch." She smiles, somewhat amused by her joke.

I find it a bit disturbing. Not the joke, but the fact that she is in such a good mood. More than good, almost euphoric.

Her phone rings. "Hello... Yes, come on over." She hangs up.

"Amy?" I ask.

Rebecca nods. "She's on her way, I asked her to pick up some take-out."

"When did you do that?"

"At the hospital. She offered to help. I knew you'd be starving. I am."

Rebecca puts out some plates and silverware. I shuffle over to the table and sit. Rebecca pours me a glass of wine. I hesitate a moment, wondering if it's a good idea to mix alcohol with the meds I took earlier, but at this point I just don't care. I take a drink.

"Amy was supposed to be at her sister's place. That was supposed to be her alibi." I say.

"She was," Rebecca answers, matter-of-factly. "She told her sister she was going to do a spa day. Made an appointment and everything. She had to see it. You understand, right? Like I had to watch Vitali die."

I nod, then reach for the wine bottle Rebecca left on the table and refill my glass.

"You're going to need to take some time off from work. Want me to call your boss?"

"No. I'll email him later."

She turns on the TV. The weekend news is on. I half expect to see a story about a murder by arson connected to a local widow. Or perhaps the fire we started spread into the neighboring woods and is now a raging wildfire burning across three states.

Instead it's just stories about a lost dog, crooked politicians and big-hearted musicians. The usual local fluff.

There's a knock at the door. Rebecca answers and Amy walks in, carrying a couple bags of Chinese takeout. Rebecca gives her a hug, and the two of them, happy as clams, take the food into the kitchen and prepare our dinner.

I help myself to a bed of rice covered with beef and pea pods.

Amy and Rebecca serve themselves lighter dishes as Rebecca gives Amy all the details about our time in the emergency room. How the doctors were rude, and the x-ray took forever, and how she's probably going to get TB from the old woman who sat across from us in the waiting room.

Amy turns to me and gives me a look of appreciation mixed with pity. "You poor thing. I'm so sorry you got hurt."

"Well, lucky thing you were there," I say with a hint of admonition.

Amy glances to Rebecca, who gives her a reassuring pat on the arm.

"I had to go," Amy explains. "I needed to see him suffer."

"We agreed it was too risky."

Rebecca cuts in, "You agreed. We took every precaution. Rebecca has an alibi. She arrived before us and left after us, and no one saw her parked in that overgrown driveway."

"Don't blame Rebecca," Amy says, "I would've been there even if she hadn't helped me.

"I was there probably about a half an hour before your first drive-by. Once the parking lot emptied, I got out of my car and hid in the woods behind the diner and I waited for you to arrive.

"After you went in, I went up to the window that faces away from the road. I saw him take your order and then watched you pick up that chair and slam it into him.

"I think he saw me at the window just before you struck. He looked surprised, then confused when he felt the chair smash into his head. And at that moment I felt so... relieved."

"I know what you mean," Rebecca tells her. Amy has that same look that Rebecca did when she told me about watching me stab Vitali in the heart.

"Then I saw that you were hurt. I caught Rebecca's eye, but she waved me off. So I waited and watched. I could smell the grease and whiskey, even from outside. The fire burned so fast. I wanted to watch him burn, but then I saw you fall the second time, and Rebecca struggling to drag you.

"I ran around to the parking lot just as Rebecca came rushing out, calling for me. We went back inside and got you out. By then the building was burning so hot. I thought he had to be dead.

"Rebecca told me I should get back to my car, so I hurried back. I had a perfect view of the front door when he came crawling out. He was trying to shout, but I don't think his lungs were working anymore.

"You left about then, and he rolled over onto his back, reaching up toward the sky. Maybe he was praying for an angel to pull him up to heaven before the demons came to claim him. But I didn't see any angels.

"I could see his skull as the hair and skin burned away from it. He stopped moving, but his arm stayed reaching upwards. He kept on burning, his arm was like a torch. I couldn't believe how long he burned. He was like a marshmallow in a campfire.

"Then the diner collapsed. Fell in on itself.

"He looked like he was lying in front of the gates to hell. Want to see?"

Amy reaches into the purse at her side and pulls out a camera.

She turns it on and shows Rebecca the image on the display on the camera's back. They flip through a couple shots, laughing at something funny on one of the pictures.

I stare at the pair of them, incredulous.

"Are you kidding me?" I finally ask.

Rebecca, takes the camera from Amy, offers it to me. "You've got to see this. It looks like—"

"Pictures. Of a man who killed your family and was killed two hundred miles away while you were supposed to be in a different state on your camera. How were you planning on explaining that? Who else have you showed them to?"

"No one," she protests. "I just put them on my Facebook page."

My jaw drops open.

A second later, Amy and Rebecca burst out in laughter.

"Relax, I just wanted to show you guys. I'm not going to keep them."

"You need to lighten up," Rebecca adds.

"I've done nothing for the last few weeks but make sure I did everything to keep us from getting caught, and you bring the evidence of the crime into our home. We can't take any chances. None. Destroy them right now. Burn it."

"I'll just erase them," Amy offers.

"No!" I almost scream. Then pull myself back as close to calm as I can get. "That won't do. A forensic investigator could still pull them off the card. You need to destroy it. There can be no connection between Cooper's death and us, or you. None at all."

Amy turns to Rebecca, who nods in agreement with me, her lightheartedness replaced with a more somber expression.

"Okay. Sorry. I'll do it when I get home."

I drop my fork on my plate, no longer hungry. I hold out my hand. "Give it to me."

Amy seems offended by my obvious distrust, but removes the memory card from the camera and drops it in my hand. I stand, cross to the kitchen, and paw through a drawer looking for a pair of tongs. I find them, then remove the grate from one of the burners and turn on the gas. I hold the memory card in the flame with the tongs. It melts, giving off a noxious smell and a cloud of gray smoke.

When I'm convinced it is beyond the ability of anyone to read, I drop it into the sink and run it through the garbage disposal.

"I'm going to go lie down," I tell them. "Anything else I should know? Did you cut off his charred balls for a souvenir?"

"No," Amy answers, then adds, "sorry."

I nod my acceptance of her apology and cross into the bedroom.

I'm still hungry, but even more tired, and I manage to fall into a shallow slumber.

ten

I rouse when I hear the front door close as Amy leaves, and a second time when Rebecca turns on the shower.

The gentle caress of her hand on my cheek wakes me the third time.

She sits on the side of the bed, wearing a white silk robe. One I had given to her one Christmas when we were still married.

"You need a bath," she says.

"In the morning," I tell her.

"It's okay, I'll do it. Can you roll over a bit?" She gives me a gentle push, and I roll onto my right side. She tucks a beach towel under me, sets a basin of water on the middle of the bed, then puts her hands around my neck and pulls me toward her.

My face rises toward her breasts, she smells of the lavender scented soap she likes.

Slowly, with great care not to disturb my broken arm, she unbuttons my shirt and gently guides it off my body. She helps me lay back slowly, then takes a washcloth from the basin, wrings it out and wipes it across my chest, my shoulders, up and down the length of my arm. It smells of the same soap that she does. Once she's finished with my chest, arms and face, she puts the washcloth back in the basin.

With the same gentle deliberateness, she undoes my belt, unbuttons my pants, and wriggles them down my legs, taking my socks off with them. I'm naked now, except for the cast. Rebecca reaches for the washcloth and continues bathing me, slowly, carefully. Her touch arouses me quickly and completely. She smiles at me, drops the washcloth back in the basin and then sets it on the floor.

She loosens her robe and lets it slip off her shoulders.

Then she climbs on top of me.

Her passion is less violent than it was at the resort, but no less intense.

I don't know where this woman was when we were married but I am blissfully grateful she is here now.

She knows my body well enough to guide me—along with herself—to the edge of pleasure, and then back again, several times before we finally climax.

She falls on top of me, a human blanket radiating lavender-scented heat, tinged with sweat and the smell of sex.

Our breathing falls into a synchronous rhythm, slowing until we fall asleep.

I realize that all my vows, oaths and promises that we would never kill anyone again were in vain. I'll do anything for this woman. If I have to kill for her to make love to me like that, I'll do it.

I'll do it gladly.

eleven

I wake before Rebecca. She must've gotten up at some point in the night because she's wrapped in the robe and sleeping under the covers beside me. I check the time on the bedside clock, then get up and go into the living room. I find the satchel where I keep my laptop, turn it on and fire off a one-handed email to my boss explaining my "accident" and requesting at least a couple sick days.

I return to the bedroom and silently crawl under the covers with Rebecca. I keep my plaster encased arm resting on my hip so I don't wake her. She still smells of lavender.

The next time I wake up, there is sunlight pouring into the bedroom. Rebecca is gone, but there's a note: "Call me if you need anything! Love, Rebecca."

I take a moment to reflect on just how screwed up my life is. But, considering I thought it was essentially over less than a year ago, I shrug it off.

There's a knock at the front door.

I sit up and realize I'm still naked. I try to slip hurriedly into my pants, but it's not easy with one arm bent in a permanent ninety-degree angle, offering painful complaints each time I move it.

More knocking.

"Coming!"

I don't even try to put on a shirt, instead I slip my right arm into Rebecca's robe which is laying at the foot of the bed and wrap the rest of it around me.

I hurry into the living room and approach the front door. We have one of those peepholes that gives you a fish eye view of whomever is in the hall.

It's a man. His back is turned to me, but I can tell he has an unruly head of shocking red hair, a description that fits no one I know.

"Who is it?"

He turns to face the door, looking directly into the peephole as if he can see my eye on the other side. Under the hair are green eyes and a thin face framed by long sideburns. He wears a skinny black tie and a shirt that used to be whiter than it is now, and a dusty brown leather jacket.

"Hello?"

"Who are you?"

"My name's Horne, Eddie Horne."

I know that name. It's familiar. How do I know that name?

"I'm a freelance crime writer. I was wondering if I could talk to you about Anthony Vitali."

Shit. The guy with the website. The one where I got the M.O. for the ice pick killing. Why does he want to talk to me?

He answers my unspoken question from the other side of the door. "I understand he killed your son. I'm very sorry for your loss. I'm putting together a book on the Vitali family, and I came across your story. If it's all right, I'd like to talk to you about it."

I think for a moment. Nothing he said leads me to believe he has any interest in me beyond being one of the sad victims the bastard left behind. I unlock the door and open it a crack.

"You've caught me at a bad time," I tell him, showing off the cast.

"Oh, I didn't mean to bother you. I wasn't sure anyone would be home, I was actually going to leave a note."

"People don't do that much anymore. It's all texts and emails."

"Yeah, well, I'm a writer. A bit old fashioned about words. They should be written down. On paper, don't you think?" He reaches inside his jacket for something, a leather-bound pad and pencil, like one you'd see a reporter carrying in an old black and white movie.

"Can you maybe come back later?" I ask.

He tucks the pad and pencil back in his pocket. "Yes, of course. Listen, how about we meet for lunch? There's a place I sometimes hang out at down the street, the Ale House."

"Sure, I know it."

"Around noon? I don't want to bother you, but I'd really like to get your story. Normally I like to be in the courtroom during a case. Reading the transcripts just isn't the same, but I was out of town during his trial. It won't take long."

"Sure," I tell him. After all, what reason would I have to say no? Wouldn't I love to get Nick's story out?

"Great, thanks. I'll see you then." He nods appreciatively, then strides down the hall, pulling out his notebook once again to jot down some thoughts.

I close the door and return to the bedroom and search for some clothes I might be able to get on fairly easily. I find a loose-fitting T-shirt and a zip-up sweatshirt that I manage to squirm into without too much pain.

I take a large pill from my prescription bottle and follow it with a swig of orange juice from the carton. After that, I check my email to make sure there's nothing on fire at work.

It's ten past ten. Still almost a couple hours before I promised to meet him. I open his website, and follow the link to his book on Amazon, a collection of true crime stories. It's only a couple bucks for the electronic version, so I buy it and start reading.

The writing isn't bad, but the subject matter is boring. I can tell he's struggling to find something interesting, compelling or shocking about his topics, but they all fall just short. Embezzlement, road rage and domestic violence can only go so far.

By the time noon has rolled around, I've made it into the fourth case, and don't have the desire to continue. Though I think if he does pull together a book on the Vitali family, he might really be able to do something with it.

I find some slip-on shoes—laces are not a strong suit of mine at the moment—check my email one last time and head on out.

It's strange to think that my story is probably the closest thing he'll ever come to a best seller, but he'll never know it.

twelve

Horne sits at a window booth in the restaurant with various scraps of paper scattered around, and a yellow legal pad on which he's scribbling what looks like shorthand. I walk up to him, and he waves me to the seat opposite him and finishes jotting down a thought. Then he gathers his notes, tucks them into a messenger bag by his side as I sit, leaving the legal pad out.

"Thank you for coming," he says.

I nod. "I'm glad someone wants to shine a light on Vitali's crimes."

"Well, there's a lot more to him than just the incident with your son. He ran a money laundering operation at a restaurant his father owns, and there is more than one disappearance of a former girlfriend that is linked to him."

"I had no idea," I say honestly.

"They've got financial connections all over the county." He glances around the restaurant. "He's even got a stake in this place."

"Well, then I'll be sure to walk out on the check."

Eddie smiles. "Yeah, poor choice, I guess."

"It's all right," I tell him, "To be honest, I'd never even heard the name until…"

"Right. Well, the old man was grooming him to take his place. He was made on his eighteenth birthday."

"I thought I heard that his death was some kind of hit."

"Yes, had all the earmarks, except…"

I cock my head curiously.

"I'm going to tell you this in confidence. I'm asking a lot for you to share your son's story with me, so I don't mind sharing this, but it's for the book, and I don't want it getting out."

"You have my word. What is it?" I ask, my curiosity piqued.

"Well, the killing was made to look like it was done by a hitman who has killed quite a few people over the years, someone who's knocked off a lot of Vitali's enemies. So it was kind of weird that someone who worked for the Vitalis would kill Anthony."

"I see your point."

"The thing is, the killer was definitely not the hitman, just someone trying to make it look that way."

"How can you be sure?" I ask.

"The police always hold back a detail of major crimes from the press. That way they can weed out the crazies. You wouldn't believe how many people try to take credit for murders they didn't commit."

"Doesn't sound like a sane thing to do."

"Definitely not. Anyway, all the of the previous victims of this hitman—who I'm pretty sure is Mikey Manzonetti, but you didn't hear that from me—had a certain part of their anatomy removed."

I cringe. "You don't mean…"

"Oh, goodness no, it was their left pinkie toe. The guy must take it as a trophy or something. But Vitali had all ten of his little piggies, and there was no indication that the killer was in any particular hurry, doesn't take long to snip off a toe, you know. That and there were other details that didn't jibe with the other murders, little things like how the killer got in the house, and the fact that he usually helps himself to a glass of wine—but the big thing is the toe. I'm the only one outside the police who knows about it—well, you, too, now."

"So what does that mean? Why would someone want it to look like a mob hitman did it? Are you sure he didn't just forget, or run out of time?"

Horne shrugs. "Well, I guess the only one who knows the answer to that is the killer. What I wouldn't give to sit down to lunch with him."

I nod, suppressing a smile.

"It would be just the hook my book needs to sell. But these mob guys are so tight, it's likely we won't find out until one of them gets caught with his hand in the cookie jar and the feds can make him sing.

"I do have my own theories, though. Could be a feud in the family. Could be a rival wanting to plant the seeds of discord among Vitali and his people. Could be a scorned woman—Lord knows there were enough of them in his life."

"Well, whoever it is, Nick's mom and I are eternally grateful. If you ever do get to meet who did it, please pass along our thanks."

Eddie smiles at that. "I will. I hope I get that chance. But, I really think a chapter about how he managed to so recklessly kill your son and get away with it will be a compelling part of the book—especially now that it ends with his death." He picks up a pen and starts scribbling on the pad. "I don't want to make you uncomfortable, I have most of the facts of the case, but I want to know more about Nick, and how you and your wife have made it through this."

"Thank you. I appreciate that. Nick's mom and I aren't married anymore. We've been back together for a while now, I guess the grief brought us closer, but we divorced about three years ago when he was in preschool."

"I'm sorry," he offers. "I'm hoping to talk to her as well, do you think she might be willing to give me some time?"

"Possibly. I'll ask her."

"Thanks."

I take a deep breath, and then tell him all I can remember about Nick, from the day we brought him home to that morning dropping him off at school ending with the day the verdict was read in the courtroom. He scribbles it all down on his pad. Somewhere in the middle, a waitress comes and we order coffee.

Horne lets me ramble on from start to finish without interrupting, allowing me to tell the story my way, not trying to shape it to fit some specific narrative for his book. I appreciate that. Makes me glad I took the time to talk to him.

"Where were you when Anthony Vitali was killed?" he asks when

I'm done.

"Excuse me?" I sound a bit more defensive than I mean to. Is he asking for an alibi? Is this some sort of setup?

"Where were you when you found out that your son's killer was dead?"

I collect myself. "We were actually at a little romantic getaway place just out of town. We were packing up when it came on the TV news. Then of course our phones rang almost non-stop the rest of the day."

"It wouldn't happen to be the Sierra Winds Resort and Spa?"

"Yes, how did—"

"I've been meaning to take my wife there for ages. Any good?"

"Well, we're still making a go of it together afterward, if that means anything. The cabanas are relatively private, and if you can get past the kitschy decor, it's not too bad."

"I'll have to check it out. I put in some long hours—which doesn't go over too well with Melissa. We could use a romantic getaway." He puts the legal pad into his bag. "Do you mind me asking how you broke the arm? Sorry, curiosity is an occupational hazard in my line of work."

I look down at the stark white plaster. "Fell doing some yard work at my mother's house. I feel like one of those people you hear about who trip and break a hip. Not fun getting old."

"I hear you," he adds. "Well, again, I really appreciate your time. And if your ex-maybe-not-so-ex-wife would like to chat," he says with a smile, "I'd love to get her point of view, too." He hands me a card. The font looks like what would come out of an old typewriter. "I don't have a cell phone, but you can leave me a message at that number."

"No cell phone?" I ask. "I would think someone like you would want to be connected and available all the time."

"Well, it wasn't so long ago that people didn't have electronic leashes in their pockets. I don't even have a computer. The email address on the card gets converted to a fax that is printed out at my home office."

"A real-life Luddite," I say. "Did I mention that I'm in I.T.?"

Eddie laughs. "I won't hold that against you. Thanks again for your time. If it ever goes to press, you might get a call from the publisher's fact checkers, but I'm putting the cart before the horse. If I can put a name to that killer, I'll have something I can sell, and your son's story will get heard by more than just the people who look past the coupons in the local paper."

"Well, if you do come up with anything, I'd love to hear about it. Like I said, I owe the guy a thank you."

"Right." Horne checks his watch, and rises from the table, leaving a few bills to cover the coffee. "I hope things work out for you guys."

We shake hands and walk out of the restaurant together. He gets into a wood paneled station wagon, and waves goodbye as I walk back to the apartment.

Pinkie toe. Who knew?

thirteen

I check my email when I get back. My boss sent a friendly note reminding me that I'd better be well enough for Rebecca and me to join him and his wife for dinner this coming weekend like I promised. I assure him we will, and that I will probably be back at work by Wednesday. Might as well use the sick days, they go away if I don't.

I end up reading the rest of Eddie Horne's book. As a courtesy, I post a positive review on Amazon. He really is not a bad writer, and I feel sorry that he'll never find Vitali's killer—especially if he's chasing down mob leads.

I take a chance and start a private browsing session, then use an anonymous proxy to check for news on Cooper's death. There is a story on a newspaper website about the fire, attributed to an unsafe kitchen and the alleged drinking problems of the owner who was the only victim of his apparent recklessness. By the time fire crews arrived, the establishment was reduced almost completely to ash, and Cooper had to be identified by x-rays, since he wasn't one for going to the dentist. Turns out he had some screws in his leg from a motorcycle accident when he was younger. There is no indication in the article that there is any suspicion of foul play.

I continue searching, find a photo tweeted by one of the county firefighters who responded to the call. The only thing recognizable is the steel grill where he made his "famous" burgers that killed Amy's family. It is littered with charred wood and covered with soot and ash.

Rebecca comes home from work. I show her the article and photo.

"Wow, there's nothing left," she remarks.

"Well, that's what happens when there's not a fire department within ten miles, and no fire hydrants. Just keeps on burning till it runs out of fuel."

"Good for us."

"Yes."

She crosses into the bedroom and starts changing out of her work clothes. "I'm going out tonight, with Amy. We're going to see a movie."

"Oh."

"Girl's night," she offers as an explanation for not inviting me along.

"Great. Say, do you remember that Mob website I told you about, the one with all the details about hit men and stuff?"

"Sure."

"The guy who writes it came by today."

She steps out of the bedroom, looking puzzled. "Here? Why?"

"Nick. He's doing a book on the Vitali family and thought Nick's story would make a good chapter."

"What did you say?"

"Well, it didn't make sense for me to refuse, so I had lunch with him, told him about Nick, and all the bullshit with the trial and that stupid A.D.A. He'd like to talk to you, too, if you want." I hand her the card.

"Sure, why not? If you think it's a good idea."

"I do. Just don't confess to killing Vitali or anything." I smile, teasing.

"I think I can manage that."

"He has a theory that it was someone in the family, or a rival trying to put the old man off his game. Turns out that the hitman we were trying to imitate also had a habit of cutting off the pinkie toe of his victims as a souvenir."

"Gross. What does he do, make a necklace out of them?"

"Probably keeps them in a box somewhere. Or maybe he uses them as proof of death to get paid. Anyway, only the police and this Horne guy knew about it, so the theory is that there's someone who tried to make it look like it was the Vitali hitman. Either way, the trail doesn't come anywhere close to us."

"That's because you are such a great criminal mastermind." She bends over and gives me a kiss. It's quick and perfunctory, void of the passionate hunger her kisses had the night before. I crave those kisses and wonder if I really only will get them if we kill someone else. "Gotta go. I'll call him tomorrow."

"Okay. Have fun."

"Thanks."

And she's out the door.

I consider going out myself, but then settle on a cable channel showing a marathon of "Twilight Zone" episodes.

I fall asleep on the couch not knowing what happens to the little old man who emerged from a bank vault to find he was the last man on earth.

The Dead Kids Club

JEREMY

The Dead Kids Club

one

The week passes slowly. I spend Tuesday at home but do some work remotely. It's slow going with only one hand.

The next day, back at the office, I get the requisite teasing from my coworkers about breaking my arm and settle back into a regular routine. It feels a bit strange not to be stealing moments in the server room to plan another killing.

Thursday night we go group.

No new members this week. Just the regulars with Old Harold sitting in his corner. Amy is under strict orders to pretend not to know about Cooper's death. But when Barb gets to the point when it's time to share, she can't keep it to herself.

"I got a call from a deputy sheriff up where Steve and Todd died. He had some news he wanted to share with me."

I look to Rebecca. She avoids my stare and instead squeezes my hand, reminding me not to betray anything by my reaction.

"He told me that the man who killed Todd and Steve died in an accident at his diner. He's not going to be killing anyone else's families. He's not going to keep on living while the souls of his victims lie restless, waiting for justice."

"How did he die?" Brian asks.

Amy shrugs. "I didn't ask. I was just… glad to know he's dead."

"I hope it brings you peace," Barb adds.

"It does, actually," she responds.

There's a shared moment, a silent communication between all of us that we understand completely how she feels, Rebecca and I more than the rest of them.

Then the silence is broken.

"I wish the bitch who killed Jeremy was dead," says Tina, the mother of the boy who was killed bicycling to school by a drunk driver.

Her husband, Larry, nods. "They say things happen in threes. Maybe God will take that woman and send her to Hell."

I'm surprised. I didn't take Tina and Larry for the vengeful type. It had occurred to me that Vitali's death would foster such feelings in some of the other parents, but the intensity in their eyes is unexpected.

I can tell they look upon Rebecca and me—and now Amy—as the lucky ones. They still have to live with the knowledge that their children are dead, and their children's killers are alive. They have to worry that they'll see them at the store, or driving down the street, or laughing and having fun with their own families.

"Let's pray," Barb suggests. She reaches out for Brian's hand, and the hand of the woman sitting next to her and bows her head. The rest of us follow her lead, except for Tina.

"Pray for what, Barb?" Tina asks.

"Pray that God will give us the strength to endure our sorrow," Barb answers.

"I don't want to endure," Tina responds.

The moment of prayer dissolves, and everyone turns their attention to Tina.

"I think we should pray that He drops a piano on Sharon Dempsey, or gives her a particularly painful case of cancer, or a lion escapes from the zoo and eats her."

I admire her imagination.

"That's not what prayer is for," Barb insists.

"Why not? Whatever happened to an eye for an eye?"

"Please, Tina—"

"I'm supposed to ask God to what, give me the strength to forgive that bitch? Her kid is still alive. She gets to see him every day. I have to drive to the cemetery to see Jeremy. I have to stare at a cold stone instead of my son's face."

Barb responds, "I know it's hard, I miss Betsy as much as you miss Jeremy, Tina. But it does no good to keep hate in our hearts."

"What good does it do to hide it?" Tina asks. "We've been coming to this group for six years. And don't get me wrong, Barb..." she starts to cry, bites her lip as she calms herself to continue. "I think I would've killed myself if it wasn't for you and Brian. You helped us deal with Jeremy's passing at a time when no one else could give us any comfort. But love and forgiveness can only get us so far. I feel like I'm at the end of my rope."

She turns to Rebecca, Amy and me. "And forgive me for saying so, but God, I envy you. Ever since I saw the story on the news that Nick's killer had been murdered, I've been wishing that I'd see a report that Sharon Dempsey had met an untimely and horribly painful end. You're so lucky to have that closure."

We made our own luck, I think to myself.

"I don't know how much peace it actually brings you to know that the people who killed your children are dead, but it has to be a hell of a lot more than I get from praying."

Barb doesn't respond. She actually looks a bit scornful. And who can blame her? Her group—the one she founded and fostered on the premise of keeping love in our hearts—was being hijacked by open calls for vengeance. Rebecca and I had really stirred the pot, but as I look at the people in the room, it is clear to me that it was on the verge of boiling over before we ever got there.

"Maybe we should stop coming," Rebecca offers.

At once, the group erupts into a cacophony of pleas to stay, and voices insisting she put that idea out of her head.

Barb is conspicuously missing from that chorus. I think she does wish we would stop coming, that we could cease being the wind that fans the flames of hate she has labored so hard to quench in the hearts of everyone in her group.

Brian speaks up. "No one is leaving this group," he says with authority. He pauses to make sure he has everyone's attention. "Believe me, I struggle with the same feelings you have, Tina. And if it wasn't for this woman by my side, I might've done something long ago that I know I'd be regretting right now."

No regret over here, I think to myself.

"I think it's healthy for us to voice these feelings." He looks at Barb. "I know it makes you uncomfortable, but we're not all like you. And the thing I love about you is that you have a heart big enough to accept everyone in your life as they are."

Barb softens at the compliment.

"We would never ask anyone to stop coming," Brian continues. "There is a bond between us, an understanding that we desperately need. Whenever we take a vacation, we leave on a Friday and come back on Wednesday so we don't miss a meeting. Five hundred and twenty-two of these we've had. People have come and gone, but those of you who have been here for the long haul, you've been more than just people we see once a week for a couple hours.

"You're our friends.

"You're family." He chokes up a bit. Emotions are running high among all of us.

I glance over at Old Harold, and even he seems moved. He's bent over with his face in his hands. I think he's weeping, but I can't really tell.

"So, like all families we're going to have our disagreements, but it's important that all of you know that this is the place—this is the only place in the world—where we don't have to live under glass, where we don't feel like exhibits in the Pity Museum, where people don't point and whisper when they see us, feeling sorry for us.

"And as hard as it is for us to accept sometimes, it is the love we have for our children that binds us, not the hate. The hate is hard to put aside, I know. But let's try. Because we've been doing this a long time and as hard as it is to do sometimes, it does work. And it does bring us all comfort.

"You know, something we used to do a lot when we first started, but haven't for a while now is to just share with each other something we love about our children. Say something that you remember about them, something that makes you smile or even laugh when you think about it. I know you all have a lot of things like that you can share. So let's do that.

"We don't have to let go of our hate, but let's put it aside for tonight, and share our love."

Barb looks at Brian, lovingly. I get the feeling he's had to make a speech like this before. And he's good at it. Most of the cheeks in the room have trails of tears running down them.

Brian continues, "Betsy, when she was five, wanted a puppy so bad. She begged, and pleaded, but I kept on telling her she was too young, how she needed to be older to take care of a dog, I would try to set the bar high enough to discourage her. I told her she needed to keep her room clean and make her bed. I told her that she needed to make sure all her toys were always put away, because a puppy would chew up anything she left lying around. I told her she had to be able to get up early in the morning to take him for a walk, and she'd have to pick up his poop—that grossed her out at first, but she decided she could pick up poop for her puppy." He laughs to himself, you can see the memories lighting up his eyes, filling his heart with love.

"For a month, she was diligent in doing everything I said. She even got up early every morning, came into our room and announced to me that it was time to walk the puppy. She even had a name for her—it had to be a girl, puppy. Princess. Princess the Puppy.

"Well, between Betsy and Barb I finally wore down and got her miniature poodle. A thousand bucks that damn dog cost me. But you never saw a kid and a dog so much in love with each other.

"The breeder had suggested that we crate the dog at night, but that didn't last long. Princess was snuggled up with Betsy every night. And every morning, she took that dog for a walk. Of course, I had to get up and go with them, but I didn't mind."

"When Betsy died, Princess still slept in her bed every night, but you could tell her heart was broken, too. It was just a few months later that Princess passed away. Not even death could keep those two apart."

Brian smiles, chuckles to himself at something else he remembers, but keeps to himself.

Barb is next, and tells us about the first birthday party Betsy had where she got to invite her friends, and how she agonized over the list and it grew and grew because if she invited one friend, then she'd have to invite another so she wouldn't hurt anyone's feelings. They ended up with over thirty kids at that party.

One by one, everyone in the group shares a story. Brian was right. It was exactly what we all needed.

Tina is even able to take a break from her hate-driven frustration to tell us about the time Jeremy put on a puppet show with his stuffed animals for her and Larry.

The only one who doesn't participate is Old Harold.

By the end, we've gone well past the time we usually break up, and it takes quite a while before any of us actually leave because of all the hugs that are shared. I understand Barb's faith in love a bit more, now.

Love is all you need, as the song goes.

But I can't help feeling that revenge is still nice to have, too.

two

I flip the computer on, and it blinks to life.

"Don't know how to thank you," Brian says, "Thought for sure that thing was a goner."

"Yeah, well, it is on its last legs," I warn him, "wouldn't be a bad idea to pick up something from this decade. But the online backup I added should keep you from losing anything until then."

"Thanks. Wouldn't want to lose those vacation photos—although if the ones of me in those pink Bermuda shorts happened to evaporate into the ether..."

"I think the ether would spit them right back," I joke.

Brian is in the midst of a sip from his beer and nearly spits it all over the computer I have managed to resurrect with my one good arm. "Ain't that the truth," he adds, wiping his mouth with the back of his hand.

I take a big swallow from my own beer. It's cold, which is about as much as I can say for it.

"That's something about that guy who killed Amy's family, ain't it?" Brian says casually.

"Hmm?"

"That guy, what was his name... Corker... Kramer..."

"Cooper," I correct, without thinking.

"Yeah, that guy." Brian looks at me, inquisitively, then takes a deep breath and another sip from his beer. "Reminds me of the Crawfords. A nice couple we had with us for a few years."

"They don't come any more?" I ask.

"Nah, stopped when the bastard doctor who operated on their daughter while he was high on oxy and put her into a coma, drove himself into a quarry not too far from here."

"I'm sure that made them feel like Karma was making its rounds."

"Sure did. They announced a couple weeks later that they didn't need the group anymore, haven't heard from them since."

"Oh."

"I'm telling you this—in case you hadn't guessed—because I want to make sure that you and Rebecca aren't thinking that you don't need us anymore. I mean, not that I wouldn't be glad if that was the case. But we've met far too many parents doing this, and you get a feel for the ones who need it and the ones who don't."

"I see," I tell him. "Rebecca and I don't have any plans to stop coming to meetings. Your speech the other night about us being a family was right on. We really do appreciate what you and Barb do for us. For everyone."

Brian nods, empties his beer and sets down the empty bottle.

"You know, for a while, there was a stretch of time when it seemed like almost every year we would have someone get a visit from the Karma fairy." He grins, "At one point I thought there was some sort of avenging angel out there, looking out for people like us."

"Really?"

"Ah, just wishful thinking. Everybody dies sometime, but if you're waiting for it to happen, you just notice it."

"Right," I agree. "Like shooting stars. There are probably hundreds of them every night, but if you're not looking…"

"Trees falling in the forest when no one's around," Brian finishes. "Another beer?"

"Sure." I finish off the one in my hand.

How many trees, I wonder, can I knock over before somebody hears one fall?

three

It is the second time I've noticed the man in the last week.

The first time I saw him was when I stopped at the drugstore a couple nights before. I was checking out, and he was standing at the front of the store by the ATM. He wasn't using it to get cash or anything, just reading the instructions and ads on the screen.

Now he stands next to a black SUV three pumps down from me at the gas station. I fill up the tank on my car, but he doesn't seem to be doing anything except watching me—though I can't be completely certain of that since dark sunglasses sit between me and his eyes.

The reason he jogs my memory is that he's wearing the exact same clothes. Black slacks, black shirt unbuttoned to reveal what can only be described as a shaggy coat of chest hair, and a black leather jacket. He wasn't wearing the shades in the drugstore, but his attire is identical.

I finish pumping my gas and drive by him as I leave the station. He watches me go but doesn't follow. I pass it off as a weird coincidence.

four

We arrive at Roger and Sally's house right on time. Rebecca has made a lemon meringue pie and I hold a bottle of wine.

"Rebecca, so nice to see you again," my boss says.

"Nice to see you again, too, Roger. Where's Sally?"

"Out back. She doesn't trust me around the grill. I'm only allowed near the bar."

"I don't rate a hello?" I ask.

Roger puts his arm around Rebecca and guides her inside. "We really only wanted to see Rebecca. You're here out of pity," he jokes.

"Fine, I'll be out in the car with the wine then."

"Good luck opening it with that arm," he says, calling my bluff.

I follow them inside. My boss takes the wine and brings it into the kitchen, pulling four glasses from a cabinet.

Sally enters from the back porch, a smile on her face. "Rebecca!" They embrace. "It's been too long! And I'm so glad to see you two together again."

Rebecca reaches out for my hand and I hold it. "Well, thank you for the invitation," she says. "Feels like we're finally getting back out into the world."

"You've been in our prayers," Sally adds. "I hope you know if there's ever anything we can do…"

People with the best intentions will never understand how painful it is to hear them say that. How ridiculous it is to think that they have some special power they can call upon to make us feel better. But putting aside the ill feelings that accompany that misguided sympathy has been getting easier, almost second nature.

"Thanks."

Roger hands out the wine.

"Come give me a hand outside. I need information. Roger is horrible at getting anything out of that tight-lipped guy of yours."

"Do I smell your cedar plank salmon?" Rebecca asks as Sally opens the back door.

The aroma that sweeps in with a breeze answers the question.

They walk outside and start talking like they were picking up a conversation they were having earlier that day.

"She's looking good, considering," Roger says.

"Yeah. It's been going well. We're going to this group for surviving parents. And we started going to church, too. That helps."

"Well, the good thing about having a wife who insists on doing all the cooking, is I get to watch all the games. The Blackhawks are just getting started," he suggests.

"So weird that they're still playing hockey this time of year," I say.

"It's either that or golf."

"Hockey."

He leads me to his famous "man cave," something he likes to give regular updates about at work. It's equipped with the latest video and audio technology and we settle into his plush theater seats, drink the wine and watch hockey on his hundred-and-eleven-inch projection screen.

There is no talk of work, no questions about what's in the cards for me and Rebecca. Just a couple of guys watching a bunch of other guys smash each other as they try to smack a thick disk of black rubber into a net. It's like a micro vacation from the insanity that has been my life, and I sit back and enjoy it.

five

After dinner, Sally entertains us with stories about some of the crazier clients from her interior decorating business.

Rebecca coaxes me to tell everyone about the writer who interviewed me for the book about the Vitalis.

"I think I saw something about that family on Lifetime or T.L.C. or something like that. One of those shows Bill Curtis narrates."

"Yeah," Rebecca says, "seems everyone knew what a shit he was except for the jury. This writer guy thinks he was killed by someone in his own family."

"Or a rival, wanting to make it look that way. Or a particularly clever disgruntled ex-girlfriend," I add.

"Who cares, the bastard is dead," Roger offers.

"Let's talk about something else," Sally suggests. "I was telling Rebecca about the lake house." She looks to Roger. "We should invite them to come up with us."

"Of course," my boss agrees. "You'd love it. Nice and quiet. They don't allow any gas motors on any of the boats on the water. Great fishing. What do you say?"

I look to Rebecca, she has a look of eager excitement. "Sure. That'd be great."

Sally puts her hand on Rebecca's knee. "I'll call you this week, we'll pick a date."

"Can't wait."

The conversation shifts to Roger's fishing stories up at the lake. Sally is teasingly skeptical about all his claims and we laugh away the rest of the day.

I drive us home and Rebecca is flirty. I get my hopes up that when we get home, we might have a repeat of the night we got back from Cooper's—without the messy homicide.

"You know who else has a place up on the lake where Roger and Sally go?"

The question surprises me. My mind is in a different place.

"No."

"The Dempseys."

I try to remember where I heard that name before. "Who?"

"You know, Sharon Dempsey. The woman who killed Tina's son, Jeremy. Weird, huh?"

"How do you know this?"

"Amy found out. I thought it was such a strange coincidence when Sally brought up inviting us there. It's like fate, isn't it? Apparently, Sharon Dempsey is there pretty much every weekend."

Part of me was wondering how and when Rebecca would bring this up. I didn't expect it so soon. I only heard the name Sharon Dempsey a few weeks ago. Rebecca and Amy must've been looking into her for at least that long. Maybe even before we killed Cooper.

"No." I say. "It's not fate."

"It's the perfect opportunity to help Tina and Larry."

"They haven't asked for our help."

"What do you mean? Of course they did. At the meeting."

I think back on the events of that evening. "You didn't tell her about Vitali and Cooper, did you?"

"No. We don't have to. I think everyone there has put two and two together. We show up, a grieving young couple whose lives are destroyed by Vitali and shortly thereafter, he's dead. Then Amy goes on about how she wants to see Cooper die, and a couple weeks later, he's dead. Now Tina is asking for help. She may not know who's involved, or how, but she's asking for help. Our help."

"That's ridiculous."

Rebecca assumes a pouting pose and averts her gaze from me. "Fine, if you want to just leave them suffering..."

And there we are. She knows which button to push, which string to pull to get me to do her bidding.

Even as my anger grows, and I think of new ways to curse this Pandora's box I've opened, I start thinking about the seeds of a plan. How Rebecca may be on to something. We'd be in proximity to Sharon Dempsey completely at the whim of someone else. And like Cooper, there would be no reason to connect her death to us, and keeping Tina and Larry in the dark would assure that we wouldn't have a repeat of Amy with them showing up at the scene of the crime snapping photos.

Rebecca takes my silence for what it is. Tacit acceptance of my fate.

Here we go again.

six

At work, I fire up my secret computer and try to find out what I can about Dempsey. There is a lot of news coverage about the accident that took Jeremy which dredges up memories of Nick that are far too recent. It's hard to read about the tragedy they endured. I remember the incident being discussed on local talk radio stations, there was quite a public outrage about a mom who not only drove her own children to school intoxicated, but took the life of another child. The cries for her to go to prison were only surpassed by the voices clamoring for her children to be taken away from her.

In the end, neither happened.

The case dragged on in the courts for years. The trial ended in a hung jury, and the district attorney felt it wasn't worth the expense to the "public treasury" to retry her. Without a conviction, her lawyer was able to sweep away the threat of putting her children in foster care. She and her family moved out of the neighborhood where they had lived, but not too far away.

Not far enough away for Tina and Larry.

Searching public tax records confirmed what Rebecca and Amy had already uncovered. In addition to their home in a posh suburb, they had a lakeside property in the same border town as my boss and his wife.

There is a real estate agency that caters to the area and has a lot of information and links to many of the community organizations surrounding the lake. Only sailboats, canoes, kayaks or pontoon boats with electric motors are permitted there. A weekend ritual of paddle powered craft gathering at the center of the lake where the stars reflect off the still surface of the water is supposed to be spectacular.

It's almost second nature the way my mind starts to fill in the details of a plan—and more than a bit frightening.

I'm stuck on how she should die. Tina's suggestion of her being eaten by an escaped lion seems impractical. There are no zoos in the area. This is something that will require a bit more thought and research.

The door to the server room opens and closes.

Footsteps.

I yank the USB memory key from the server and switch over to a diagnostic screen just as my boss peeks around the corner.

"Hey, don't you ever take a break?"

"Thought we were getting some latency on the SAN. We might need to replace some of the solid-state drives."

"Well, whatever you need, we have plenty of room in the capital budget, so I leave it in your hands.

"Listen, Sally is so excited about you guys coming up to the lake. How is the fifteenth for you guys?"

Two and half weeks. That should be enough time to figure out a suitable fate for Sharon Dempsey. "Sounds good. I'll tell Rebecca, she's excited, too." Although for completely different reasons.

"Great. One other thing, Bob is coming in from Dallas for the big management retreat next week. We should set up a lunch, he needs to meet you."

"Okay." Hanging out with the boss sure had its perks. Fast track to management was something I hadn't even thought about since before Nick's death. But it seems Roger still had it on his mind. "I can make time whenever."

"All right. I'll set it up. And I'll email you directions for the lake. GPS always gets it wrong."

"I'm sure it's on purpose to keep the riffraff away."

"You may be onto something there, the local chamber of commerce is very protective and resistant to change. The local movie theater only has one screen—by city ordinance."

"A regular Mayberry, huh?"

"Yeah, except Floyd's barber shop charges a hundred bucks for a haircut."

I laugh. My boss takes his cue to leave and disappears back out the way he came.

I finish the diagnostics I'm running, jot down the specs of the drives I need to replace and head back to my desk, thinking of ways to kill a middle-aged mother of three.

Just your average homicidal computer guy.

seven

The next time I see him I know it is not a coincidence.
And he knows I know it.
The man in black is looking at me over the stacks of citrus in the produce section of the grocery store.
"You're that guy," he says.
"I'm sorry?"
"I saw you on the news, that guy killed your kid, right?"
I nod, offer a weak smile, then toss a grapefruit into my basket and move on. Obviously, he's not a cop, the first irrational conclusion my mind leaped to when I saw him tossing an orange up into the air and catching it in his left hand.
He follows me as I head toward the dairy case.
"That was something how he died, huh?"
I know now that I'm not going to be able to just ignore him, so I go along with the conversation.
"Yeah, yeah. That was something."
"Some people think it was a mob hit."
"I heard that."
"You know what? I got a theory. You wanna hear it?"
"Sure."
I grab some cheese and move on to the yogurt.
"I think it wasn't a mob hit at all. I happen to know a thing or two about mob hits. This wasn't done by a pro."
I swallow hard. Who the hell is this guy? What does he know?
"A pro wouldn't have killed a guy right after he fucked some chick.

Chicks come back. It's what they do. A pro would've walked away, come back another time."

"That's interesting," I say, selecting a few tubs of yogurt and turning down the freezer aisle.

"I get the sense you're patronizing me."

"No, not at all."

"I hate when people patronize me. I find it very annoying."

"I don't mean to offend you, it's just I'm sensitive talking about anything surrounding the death of my son, and I don't know you—"

"Forgive me, where are my manners." He extends a hand with thick, strong fingers. "Mikey Manzonetti."

I put my hand in his to shake before realizing where I had heard that name before. He squeezes tight. Too tight. My hand is awash in pain. He lets me wince for a moment, then lets go.

"Well, Mr. Manzonetti, it's been... interesting to meet you. But I need to get home."

"Right, you got that pretty ex-wife of yours waiting for you. Rebecca, ain't it?"

I freeze. What's his game?

"So, don't you wanna know who I think really killed my friend Anthony?"

No, I don't.

"Could've been that bitch who found the body," he says.

Liar. If you thought that you'd be stalking her, not me.

"That would be awfully bold of her," I suggest.

Mikey nods. "Yeah, but bitches do crazy things. How 'bout that wife of yours? She ever do crazy shit?"

"No, not really."

"Of course you say that. I mean, you ain't gonna talk shit about your lady to a complete stranger."

"Good point."

"Hey, you're not doing that patronizing thing, are you? I think I mentioned I find that very annoying."

"No. I just want to get home."

We reach the checkout lanes and I pick the one with the shortest line. Normally, I'd go through the self-checkout, but I want to limit Mikey's opportunity to continue his disturbing conversation. I still don't know what he wants from me, and I keep on playing back Eddie Horne's theory that this is the guy who is the real ice pick hitman.

"Well, I don't want to keep you. Just wanted to say I'm really sorry about what happened to your boy."

"Thanks, I appreciate that," I say, hoping Mikey won't find it patronizing.

"Yeah, you must've been as torn up as Anthony's father is. You know, he put out a contract on the boy's killer."

"Really."

"Half a million bucks."

Curiosity gets the better of me. "How will he know if he has to pay out? I mean it seems someone could just knock off some poor guy and say he was the killer and cash in."

"Good point. You're a smart man. He needs a confession first, of course."

"Of course."

"So, that makes it a bit harder. Omelets," Mikey adds cryptically.

"Excuse me?" I ask.

"Gotta break a few eggs, sometimes. You know, to see if it's a good egg or a bad egg."

I sensed he didn't quite grasp the expression he was mangling, but I wasn't going to bring that up for fear of sounding patronizing.

"You seem like a good egg," he says.

"Thanks."

The checkout line finally moves to where I can start unloading my cart.

"Course you never really know if an egg is good or bad unless you crack it open."

I force myself to empty my cart onto the conveyor before I look back toward Mikey.

He's gone.

But his threat still hangs in the air.

eight

I tell Rebecca about Mikey.

She listens attentively, but seemingly unconcerned. "He's just trying to shake the trees. He doesn't know anything. You handled it well."

"What if he decides to grab me and torture me, just for the hell of it? Half a million dollars is a big incentive to 'break a few eggs.'"

"He's bluffing."

"Maybe I should go to the police. I mean, that's what I would do if…"

"If you weren't guilty of what Mikey thinks you are?"

"Well, yeah."

"Okay. You might want to talk to that writer, too."

"Horne?"

"He seems to know a lot about these mob guys, maybe he can reassure you that Manzonetti is all bluster," she adds.

Not a bad idea. "What if he comes after you?" I ask.

"If he tries to threaten me, I'll scratch his eyes out."

She crosses into the kitchen and starts fixing herself a snack. It's hard to tell if she's serious, or just masking her fear with her own bluster.

I fish Horne's card out of my wallet and flip it over and over between my fingers. I decide I'll talk to him before I go to the police.

I just hope the cops don't agree with Mikey that I could be the killer. Don't need a mob hitman and a detective on my ass while I'm trying to kill a suburban mom at her weekend lake house.

nine

Friday night arrives and I still have not gotten a reply back from Horne. His outgoing message said that he was out of town, and judging from his Luddite tendencies, I suspect it was an answering machine I spoke to and not a cell phone voice mail service.

I haven't seen Mikey either, so I convince myself that Rebecca was right, and the guy was just trying to scare me.

Rebecca and I drive up to the Lake. I would prefer to go by myself, but I know how far I'm going to get suggesting that to Rebecca.

When we get there, we pass by the Dempsey's house. There are lights on, and a car in the driveway. I wish I hadn't destroyed the spy cams we used on Vitali, they would come in handy now.

We drive through town and find the canoe rental place I had looked up online and join the throng of tourists waiting to make the Saturday evening excursion to see the stars in the lake.

Once everyone is seated in an aluminum canoe and equipped with wooden paddles, the guide gets our attention by gently rapping the gunwale of his canoe with his paddle until everyone is silent.

"Three rules," he begins, "number one, stay with the group. There is a red light that flashes every five seconds on the back of my canoe. If you get separated, paddle toward shore and head toward the dock, there's a flashing red light there, too."

Everyone turns around to look at the dock, and a few seconds later we are rewarded with the brief flash of a red light attached to a piling.

"Rule two," he announces, then waits for everyone to focus back on him. "Keep the noise to a minimum. Your paddles should not bang against the sides of your canoes, keep the splashing down and no talking.

"Rule three, once we're out in the lake, pull your paddles in and keep as still as you can. We'll hold on to each other's canoes like I showed you earlier. When the water is still, the effect is amazing, but if you're making waves, it ruins it for everyone.

"Okay, let's go."

He leads the way, expertly spinning his canoe silently so that his red flashing stern is facing the group. Initially, there is a cacophony of banging and scraping as all of us canoeing neophytes noisily get underway. After the first couple hundred yards, everyone falls into a steady, smooth and mostly silent rhythm.

Rebecca and I stay at the back of the pack—she does most of the work, I only can manage to use my paddle as a rudder with one arm in a cast—and allow the distance between us and the group to grow until we are left alone in the dark. We head back toward the shore, away from the flashing red light on the dock, and toward a group of piers jutting out into the lake.

One of them belongs to the Dempseys.

I had studied the satellite maps from my virtual machine at work. The Dempsey's property was very distinctive, with a large white boathouse at the base of a long white pier and a floating raft belonging to a neighbor nearby. Of course, it is impossible to tell how old the photos were, but with any luck, we should be able to pick out their house from the water.

Turns out, luck is on our side. The configuration of the piers is exactly what I expected it to be. We paddle up to the boathouse and it's empty. We slip in, tie off and sneak into the yard, keeping to the shadows.

Our cover story is simple, we lost track of our canoe group, and they had told us to go ashore if we got lost and ask for help. Plausible, but we aren't expecting to get caught.

We get close enough to peer into the large picture window that faces the lake. There are no blinds or curtains. Sharon, and a man who I assume is her husband, are snuggling on the sofa watching a hockey game on a big screen TV. Everything in the house appears to be top of the line. Mr. Dempsey must do very well for himself, though I'm sure he spent a good portion of his fortune on defense lawyers.

"That's not her husband," Rebecca says.

"How can you tell from the back of his head?" I ask.

"They're snuggling."

"So?"

"He hates her. Hates that he had to stand by her while she was paraded around as the most vile woman in the state. There's no way they're having sex, let alone snuggling."

"So, who is it?"

"A lover?," she suggests.

We sneak around the house to the driveway. The make, model and license plate match Sharon Dempsey's Mercedes. Rebecca taps me on the shoulder and points to a bicycle leaning against the railing leading to the back door.

"Local guy?" I ask.

"Makes sense."

"Where are the kids?"

"Probably back home with the nanny."

"Wow, she's a real winner."

"Maybe she should run for congress."

We snicker quietly, then make our way back down to the boathouse. I stop to give the handle of the back door a turn. It is unlocked and opens easily. People in these communities sometimes are lax about security, hopefully this is typical and not an exception. From the lake-side yard, we stop to get another view of what's going on in the house.

Sharon sits on her lover's lap, blocking his view of the hockey game on the screen. She tries playfully to draw his attention away from the game and is not having much luck. She leans in to kiss him, and when she pulls back, he pushes her aside to see the replay of the goal that she made him miss.

Offended, she storms off and up the stairs. He yells after her, pleading, but a fight breaks out on the hockey game, and he is seduced more easily by the action on the enormous flat screen than his pouting paramour.

I'm not surprised. There's nothing really attractive about her except a pair of exceptionally large breasts, which at the moment for this guy is not enough.

"Let's go," I say.

I lead Rebecca down to the boathouse, and we climb back aboard the canoe and silently make our way back out onto the lake, Rebecca again handling pretty much all the paddling. While we wait for our group to make its way back to the dock, the water is still enough to show us the incredible reflection of the night sky that this little lake is famous for.

The night tour group is a bit noisier coming in than they were going out. We blend back in seamlessly and thank our guide for a spectacular evening.

By the time we get back to the apartment, we are both exhausted and I fall asleep nearly the second my head hits the pillow.

ten

The phone rings.

The call is very confusing.

It's someone from the hospital. They tell us a boy has woken up from a coma, and he's not who they thought he was. Somehow, Nick was confused with another kid who was brought to the hospital at the same time. Our Nick has been in a coma in the Pediatric Intensive Care Unit, and we buried someone else's child.

I demand answers. How can this be? Who is responsible?

The voice on the other end of the phone ignores my questions and tells me Nick is asking for his mom and dad.

Rebecca is ecstatic. She wants to see him right away.

Before I know it, we're at the hospital being guided to a room by a smiling nurse.

Nick looks up at us from the hospital bed, his eyes light up when he sees us, but his limbs are so atrophied that he cannot even raise his arms to hug us.

Rebecca is completely accepting of the staff's apologies.

I am furious. Do they know what they put us through? What we've done because we thought our son was dead?

Vitali arrives, he heard that the little "bugger," as he calls Nick, is awake and brings him a giant stuffed animal. No one else seems at all surprised that he's there.

Next, Cooper enters with a plate of cheeseburgers. Sharon Dempsey is hanging on his arm, cooing, bragging to anyone that'll listen that, "This one prefers my tits over a hockey game."

Nick calls out to me. I cross to the bed. "I missed you, Daddy," he says. "Don't go away."

"I'm not going anywhere," I tell him, but the policeman who came to our house after we killed Vitali—we did kill him, didn't we?—puts handcuffs on me and reads me my rights.

"Don't go away, Daddy!"

"It's okay, Nick," Rebecca tells him, "Daddy did some bad things, and has to go to jail, but he'll be back when you're older."

"Did what? They're alive. Both of them."

I turn to the cop. It's not the cop anymore, it's Mikey Manzonetti.

Eddie Horne takes notes in his leather notebook. "This is great," he says, "just the twist I needed to sell my book."

"But I didn't do anything," I protest.

"It's okay," Rebecca reassures me, "Nick's alive."

I look back to the bed. Nick is older now, twelve or thirteen. Amy is on the other side of the bed. She and Rebecca each hold one of his hands.

"Come on," Mikey tells me, "time to break some eggs." He pulls out a black gun, as black as the leather jacket he's wearing, and brings it down as hard as he can across my face.

I sit upright in my own bed, gasping for breath. There is no hospital room, no Vitali or Cooper, or Dempsey... no Nick.

Rebecca lies next to me, undisturbed.

The clock glows, telling me it's just before four a.m.

I wait for my pulse to slow before lying back down.

I try to close my eyes, but sleep doesn't come right away.

And when it does, I don't dream.

eleven

The phone rings.

It's Eddie Horne. "Sorry to take so long to get back to you," he tells me, "I was out of town, chasing down a story. You said in your message that you had some questions?"

"Yes, thank you for calling back. Can we meet? I'd rather not talk over the phone."

"Oh, okay. Same place? Eleven?"

"I'll be there. Thanks."

"No problem."

I hang up. Rebecca is gone, likely meeting up with Amy to share the results of our reconnaissance.

I check the clock. It's just after nine.

I take a quick shower, throw our clothes from the previous night into the laundry, then go out to the car to make sure we haven't left any traces except a few extra miles on the odometer.

There is an email from work, alerts coming from one of the servers, so I set up a remote connection and check it out. By the time I'm finished, it's time to head off to meet Horne.

I get there before him this time, sit at the same table and order a coffee. He walks in a few minutes later. I stand, we shake hands, make some small talk about my cast. He waves his coffee cup at the nearest waitress.

"So," he says as he slides into the booth, "what can I do for you?" He sits with his elbows on the table, hands clasped, a friendly grin on his face.

"I met a man who said his name was Mikey Manzonetti," I say.

Horne's hands unclasp and reach inside his jacket for his leather notepad and pen. "Mikey Manzonetti? Are you sure?"

"Big beefy guy, wears a lot of black, doesn't like it when people are 'patronizing.'"

My abbreviated description is enough to convince him—and me—that it was indeed Ice Pick Mike that had been following me.

"What did he say?"

"He told me that Vitali's father has a bounty out on his son's killer, and he implied that I was on his list of possible suspects."

"How much is the bounty?"

"Half a mill."

"Shit."

"Is that a lot for something like this?"

"Yeah. Most hits are in the ten to fifty thousand range."

"He said that there needs to be a confession along with it."

"That explains the amount. It's a lot easier to just whack someone than to extract a confession. And the old man is smart enough to tell if someone confesses because they've been tortured. Sounds like he's trying to scare you."

"It worked."

The waitress comes and fills his coffee cup.

I tell him the whole story.

"He's hoping if you're the killer you'll make some sort of move that will expose you" he says at the end.

"I'm not the killer."

"Of course not, but Manzonetti is very methodical when he needs to be. And patient. You're a name on his list, and he won't strike you off until he's found the guy who murdered Vitali's son. Have you gone to the police?"

"Not yet."

"Did he say not to?"

I replay the conversation in my head. There were no admonitions of that type. "No."

"Then you should." He scribbles something on a page from the back of his notebook. "Talk to Detective Kort. He's the one in this town most plugged into Vitali's activities. He'll take you seriously."

"Do you think I need to worry about him coming after me or Rebecca?"

He shakes off my suggestion. "These guys are smart. They wouldn't have been around for so long if they weren't careful. If he really thought that you killed Vitali's son, he wouldn't have tried to scare you, you would be dead right now, pushed into a barrel with a few cinder blocks and dumped into the river."

"That's comforting."

"Listen, you just had the misfortune to cross paths with the Vitalis. They don't think the same way you and I do. If someone kills one of their own, they want blood."

They think exactly the way I do.

"But Vitali has a code he follows, makes an effort to minimize collateral damage. You're a civilian. Unless Mikey has solid proof that you killed Vitali's son, they're not going to touch you. And once Manzonetti catches another scent, he'll leave you alone.

"Go see Detective Kort. That's probably the best way to convince Mikey you have nothing to do with the murder. A guilty person would maybe run or hide, or try to destroy any evidence that could link him to the crime."

"I'll stop by the police station today," I assure him.

"Good. If I hear anything, I'll let you know."

"Thanks."

He tucks his notebook back into his jacket and pulls out his wallet and fishes out some bills.

"I've got it. Thank you for seeing me," I tell him.

"Anytime," he says. "Have a slice of pie, they've got apple today." He gets up and leaves, checking his watch as he goes. Obviously, I was an unexpected detour in his day, but the conversation was reassuring and helpful.

The waitress passes by, and I ask her for a slice of apple pie. She jots down my order and moves on.

I look at the name on the scrap of paper Horne gave me.

How good of a detective is Kort? Will he take Mikey's interest in me as a lead he should be pursuing as well? Or will he dismiss the notion as quickly and completely as Horne did?

I eat the pie slowly, wishing to put off the answer to that question as long as possible.

twelve

I stop at home first, hoping to see Rebecca and fill her in. She's not there.

I call her cell phone. There's no answer, so I leave a message telling her that Horne suggested I go to the police about Mikey and I'm going to go do that.

I wait almost an hour at the station before Detective Kort will see me.

He walks me back to an area not unlike the bullpens you see on every TV cop show. I sit in a solid wooden chair to the side of his desk, while he sits back in his modern office chair.

"I'm very sorry about your son," he begins, "we were all frustrated as hell that the D.A. couldn't make the case against Vitali. I know it's a small consolation that Tony is rotting in his grave, but I hope it gives you some comfort, nonetheless."

"Thank you. It actually does."

"What can I do for you today?"

"Eddie Horne suggested I talk to you."

"Really? How do you know him?"

"He interviewed me for a book on the Vitalis. Wanted to include the story about Nick's death and Anthony's murder in a chapter or something."

"Eddie's quite a character. What does he think I can do for you?"

"A man who called himself Mikey Manzonetti has been following me around lately. He came up to me at the grocery store and told me he's looking for the guy who killed Anthony Vitali. And he led me to believe that he thought it might have been me."

"Was it?" he asks.

"No," I answer with a note of offense at the suggestion.

He pauses, evaluating my response. After a few seconds, he puffs out his lower lip and nods like a human bobble-head. "Then you have nothing to worry about."

I breathe a sigh of relief.

He asks a few more questions about dates, times and locations.

"We know about the bounty, but if Vitali or Manzonetti really thought you killed Tony, you'd be dead already."

"That's what Eddie said," I tell him.

"Chances are, he's making a show of going after you to lull someone else into a false sense of security. My money's on someone inside the family. There'll probably be a body dumped in an alley somewhere in the next month or two."

"Not the bottom of the river?"

Detective Kort smiles. I'm not sure if he thinks it's funny, or he's amused by my naivete about mob hits. "They'll want to make this one public."

"So, nothing to worry about?" I ask hopefully.

"Keep an eye out, if he accosts you again, give me a call." Kort hands me his card.

"I will, thanks."

"Not at all. Can you find your way out?"

"Yes, I think so."

"Take care."

I get up and wind my way out through the maze of desks. Before I go, I turn around and see that Kort is now speaking with the detective who paid Rebecca and me a visit not too long ago.

My heart races and I get out of there as fast as I can without drawing any attention.

When I get home, I collapse on the sofa in front of the TV. I'm in the mood for some sort of distraction. It feels like everything is closing in around me lately. But after talking to Horne and Kort, I'm reassured that Mikey is not going to slip an ice pick into my heart and temple while I sleep, and then snip off my pinkie toe.

thirteen

Rebecca finds me sleeping in front of the television when she returns home and wakes me.

She asks me about my day and I replay the conversations with Horne and Kort as she takes off her coat and goes through the mail.

She sits next to me, an air of excitement in her eyes. "So," she begins, "Amy and I had lunch with her sister-in-law. They live in the same town as the Dempseys."

I don't like where this is going.

"Turns out we were right about the other man. Their marriage is 'strained'—to put it mildly—and she practically lives at the lake house on the weekends when her husband isn't working. She never takes the kids. Sounds perfect, right?"

I nod.

Rebecca detects my concern.

"What's wrong?"

"Amy's sister-in-law?" I ask.

"Don't worry about that. We didn't just grill her about the Dempseys, in fact, she's the one who brought it up. She's a terrible gossip."

"The fewer people who connect us to the target the better. Once she's dead, there are going to be a lot of questions, and if a nosy investigator detects a connection to the group, or us, or—"

"They won't."

"And why not?"

"Because we're going to make it look like the husband did it. Or the lover. There's already a motive hanging out there, all we need to do is make it look like a crime of passion."

Rebecca whispers the word "passion" and moves closer to me.

"Oh, that's all?" I ask, trying to detect her mood.

"Yes," she replies simply, now an arm's length away from me.

I realize that she's right. It is a perfectly simple and brilliant plan, and puts minimal suspicion on a third party, let alone us. She arches her back slightly and bites her lower lip that way she sometimes does when she's about to kiss me. "Okay," I agree.

Now she's next to me, I slip my good arm around her waist.

"Knife?" she whispers in my ear, giving it a little nip.

"Sounds good," I answer, "we can find something in the kitchen."

She pulls back slightly, reaches around and takes my hand into hers.

"During the midnight 'Lake of Stars' thing?"

"No one will notice us coming or going."

An inspiration strikes her. "Sally mentioned that they have a pontoon boat. I'll suggest to her that it'd be a nice romantic thing for us to do and she'll keep Roger from insisting on joining us."

"There's a playoff game that night, he'll be eager to have an excuse not to go."

She squeezes my hand, I can see the excitement growing in her eyes, and part of me grows eager with the hope that all this talk of taking a human life will engender the same type of animal lust that the actual act had before.

"So, now all we have to do is wait," she adds, seductively.

"Hardest part of any plan."

I move in to kiss her, but she deftly dodges my attempt with a playful smile and instead changes the subject.

"Wanna go to the movies?" she suggests.

"Sure," I answer. I guess the notion that tonight will be an exhausting round of unbridled sex is off the table.

fourteen

The two weeks before the trip to the lake pass uneventfully.

I finish a major project at work, everything goes smoothly. My boss brings up Sally's excitement at us joining them at their lake house, but I suspect he is looking forward to it just as much. We are actually becoming rather good friends. More than just coworkers. We share more and more lunches and even a dinner.

Rebecca and Sally become fast friends as well. They go out to dinner and shopping a few times. There is a natural synergy between their careers, Rebecca as a real estate agent and Sally as an interior decorator.

There are no more visits from Manzonetti, or the police, or anyone else threatening to kill or arrest me.

At group, the sessions return to a normal rhythm. Barb reasserts herself as the leader, and we share our trials and feelings, and even welcome a new couple into the group. They're cancer parents, so they don't stir the revenge pot at all. Rebecca tells Nick's story when it's our turn. Will hearing it ever not make me cry?

The dreams are getting stranger and more frequent. Ever since that nightmare after we returned from our reconnaissance of the Dempsey house, they've been coming every few nights, this evening is no exception.

I'm at work and a teenage boy shows up, telling me he's Nick, asking why I left him at the hospital. I don't question his assertion, just apologize to him and promise that I'll make it up to him. The senior

Vitali appears, and tells me he knows what I did, and before he kills me, he's going to kill Nick and Rebecca. My son and his mother plead with me to kill Tony Vitali before he kills them. I have a gun, but the bullets seem to move in slow motion. Vitali easily evades them. When I finally get close enough to have one of the bullets hit him, it does no damage, just bounces off of him. We fight, but my arms and legs feel like they're covered in molasses and he pushes me to the ground, holding me down with my arms pinned to my sides while I struggle to get free. Rebecca stabs him with a knife. Nick kicks him in the ribs, but he won't let go.

I wake to find myself twisted in the sheets, Rebecca has rolled over next to me, tightening the bedding's grip. I'm swaddled like a baby.

I don't wake her, or even stir. Instead, I lie awake, unmoving, waiting for the first light of dawn, or the alarm clock to stir Rebecca and free me.

fifteen

We have three bags for our trip to Roger and Sally's. One for my clothing, one for Rebecca's, and one we call the Kill Bag.

In it, we have more of the disposable surgical scrubs and gowns including caps and booties like those that we used at Vitali's, along with a supply of rubber gloves and a couple of the rubber sleeves I use over my cast when taking a shower. There are also two black rain suits to wear over the scrubs, since we could only get the former in a dull yellow color—not much good for sneaking around in the dark of night. Layered on top of our supplies is a first aid kit, bottled water, and a mylar blanket, so if anyone were to get curious, they'd just assume it was an emergency road kit.

There are no weapons included, the plan is to use something from the house.

Neither is there any sort of electronic equipment, or other tools.

Amy has strict orders not to be anywhere close to the lake.

I am firm on the condition that if we don't find a door unlocked, or if there is anything that is not how we expect it, we walk away. Rebecca seems on board with that, but I know she'll agree to anything to get closer to another kill.

The plan is to wait for Sharon Dempsey to be alone. According to the amazingly detailed information from Amy's sister-in-law, we have an idea that the man Sharon is having an affair with is married himself, and doesn't spend the night. He pedals his bicycle over when his wife falls asleep, or during the days when she's out doing

The Dead Kids Club

something. It seems everyone in town knows the details of their affair except their spouses.

We'll make our first attempt tonight, and if she's not there, or he is, we'll reassess and determine if it's worthwhile to try again the following night.

On the drive up, I don't drill her on the plan like we did with Cooper. Instead, we take the time to catch up on each other's lives, speculate about the new couple at the group, joke about Roger and Sally's sex life. Rebecca goes off on a riff about what we might hear at night, Roger directing Sally's efforts to arouse him in the same manner I describe him running a project meeting. I laugh so hard I nearly lose control at one point, forgetting that my left arm is bound in a cast.

Then she casually adds, "Oh, did I tell you? Amy's pregnant."

"What? Who's the father?"

"Her husband. She had some eggs left over from the in vitro."

"When did she do this?"

"A couple months ago. Right before..."

"Well, good for her," I say.

"Yeah," she adds wistfully. "It's nice to think she'll have someone to love."

On the way, we stop at a farm stand and pick up some fresh produce.

We arrive a bit earlier than we had intended, but Roger and Sally are there, eager and glad. Sally and Rebecca embrace and immediately disappear into the house, making plans.

"We won't see them for a while," Roger warns me.

"Of course not, there's stuff to unload."

"Looks like you could use a hand," he jokes, knocking on my cast. "When do you get that thing off?"

"About three weeks." I pop open the trunk from my key fob and start handing Roger bags. He takes the luggage, I grab the produce.

"Think you can manage some fishing with that arm?"

"Sure. Only need one good arm to drink a beer."

Roger laughs. We joke some more as we carry the luggage and

groceries into the house. Roger gives me a tour of the place, starting with the room where Rebecca and I are staying. It is on the complete opposite side of the house as Roger and Sally's room and even has its own kitchenette. French doors open out onto a porch with a panoramic view of the lake.

The center of the house is the great room, a large open space with a fireplace on one end, and an enormous, big screen TV on the other and a variety of eclectic seating in between. There is a picture window that again affords a spectacular view out onto the lake.

Roger and Sally's room is ridiculously large and connected to a master bath that looks like something from one of those TV design shows. Obviously, Roger is doing rather well for himself. Management has its perks. And judging from the quality of the decor, Sally's success as a decorator is well deserved.

We meet the women in the kitchen. Rebecca and Sally are stuffing some Tupperware containers into a picnic basket.

"Are you boys ready?" Sally asks.

"Indeed we are," Roger answers, giving his wife a peck on the cheek.

"Then let's go."

Rebecca walks over to my side and takes my hand. "Sally and Roger are taking us for a cruise on their pontoon boat."

Sally directs Roger to pick up a large cooler by the door. She reaches for the picnic basket.

"Let me," I offer.

"When you have two working arms, you can be a gentleman. For now, you're our guest. All you are required to do is relax, have fun and laugh at Roger's jokes—those last two may be mutually exclusive, but I'll do my best to keep him in line."

Sally hefts the picnic basket off the counter and directs us to the back door. Rebecca and I exit out into the yard.

There is a lush, green lawn stretching down to a strip of sand at the water—much nicer than the weedy waterfront Sharon Dempsey has—and a dock stretching out into the lake with a nicely appointed pontoon boat moored at the end.

Roger loads the cooler on board, then grabs a captain's hat from atop the pilot's chair and dons it.

"Permission to come aboard?" I ask.

"Permission granted," he replies with a limp salute. "It's a three-hour tour, but I can promise you if we get stranded on a desert island, I do know how to make a radio out of a coconut and a piece of string."

"Thank you, Professor," Sally chides.

Rebecca and I board followed by Sally, who hands the basket to Roger. He carries it to a dining area at the rear of the boat and urges us to take a seat.

"We'll be reaching a top cruising speed of seven knots, so please keep your hands and arms inside the boat. If you need to piss or heave, check the wind."

Sally smacks him on the arm, and Roger unties the boat, and takes his position in the pilot's chair.

We do spend roughly three hours out on the water on the nearly silent electric powered boat. Roger points out some interesting features of the lake and its shoreline, while Sally fills us in on who's got the most expensive houses, and how gauche their decorating decisions are.

We move out to the middle of the calm water where Roger cuts the engine as Sally sets up our lunch.

I ask Roger about the pontoon boat. He brags that it's the fastest craft on the lake. The rule is it can't generate a wake greater than three inches and must have an electric motor that operates under a certain noise level.

"It is nice to be out on the water without the roar of a gas motor and all those fumes getting in the way," Rebecca remarks.

"That was one of the selling points of this place for us," Sally says.

"You guys are free to take it out later, do the whole star thing," Roger suggests. "There's a bunch of blankets in that compartment. This boat has been known to generate a wake greater than three inches with the engine off—if you know what I mean."

Sally swats him on the arm.

"What was that for? You were there, too!"

Another swat. We all laugh.

"We may take you up on that. I read that it really is a spectacular site."

"It is," Sally confirms, sharing a confidential look with Rebecca.

We finish the meal, and Roger takes us on a meandering, wake-less course back to the dock.

sixteen

Later, Rebecca and Sally sunbathe on the lawn while Roger and I spend some quality time watching spring training baseball.

Dinner is a modest, yet delicious meal. After, we drink wine in front of the picture window, watch the sunset and turn on the gas fireplace—wood burning ones are not allowed around the lake.

It's nearly eleven thirty when Sally reminds Roger about our midnight star cruise. He walks me down to the end of the dock, shows me the controls, retracts the automatic awning and warns me about only using the low intensity red safety lights. He also cautions me to shut them down completely when we get out to the middle of the lake or else we'll get some not so friendly words from some of the regulars.

Rebecca and Sally catch up to us. Rebecca is carrying the Kill Bag. I cast her a questioning glance.

"You forgot to unpack our jackets, Sally says it can get chilly out there at night," she explains.

I marvel at her ability to spin a quick cover story.

Roger and Sally see us off as Rebecca unpacks some blankets from the storage compartment and makes a show of spreading them out on the deck.

Sally takes Roger's hand with a mischievous glint in her eye, and they almost skip back up to the house like a couple of young parents who've just dropped the kids off for a sleepover.

Once we are a sufficient distance from the dock, I bring us to a heading toward the Dempsey's place. We see a couple of other boats in the darkness, some red lights bobbing here and there that grow fewer as we get closer to the shore.

Rebecca undresses and puts on the disposable scrubs, then the black rain suit over them. Then she takes the wheel as I do the same. It takes me considerably longer with my cast, but I manage it well before we reach the Dempsey's dock.

We glide silently into the empty boathouse, check to make sure we have our shoes covered and gloves on and then disembark and make our way up to the house.

There is a light on in one of the upper bedrooms. We watch for a while, but don't see or hear anything going on.

We make our way around to the other side of the house. I can see the lover's bicycle in the front drive, leaning against the light post. I try the side door and it opens freely. Rebecca and I enter, close the door, then look around. It's dark, but we can make out the layout easily enough, and we decide to wait in a den off the living room. From its shadowy darkness we have a view of the staircase that leads to the second floor. We take off the rain suits, arrange them so we can slip them back on easily, then find a spot to sit and wait.

Once we're settled, we hear a yelp followed by laughter, first a woman's alone, then joined by a man's. The noises shift to moans, then rhythmic cries of passion accompanied by the creaking of a bed. A few minutes later, it's over.

"That was quick," Rebecca remarks in a muted whisper. "How lousy of a lay is her husband if she cheats on him with a minuteman."

"Shh," I caution.

Footsteps upstairs.

"Stay," a woman's voice pleads.

"You know I can't," a man replies.

"When are you going to leave that bitch?"

"As soon as you leave your husband."

"You know we don't have anything of a marriage left. I'm as good as divorced."

They appear on the landing above us, she flicks on a light. We are safely in the shadows where we sit, waiting. He finishes pulling on a shirt. She has a thin robe over her shoulder that does a poor job of covering her ample breasts.

"Good as isn't the same thing. Besides, I thought you liked things the way they are. You get to enjoy your husband's money during the week, and me on the weekend."

"I'd rather see you every day," she coos, kissing him, guiding his hands to her chest.

He gently pushes her away, taking a moment to fondle her as he does so. "You know I want to, but she'll be back from her bridge club soon. I'll see you tomorrow."

"You better," she warns.

He gives her a final goodbye kiss, and she disappears back into her bedroom as he bounds down the stairs and out the back door.

We wait a minute before emerging and making our way toward the kitchen. I select a knife from a butcher block holder, one that looks sufficiently lethal.

It hits me that this killing will be completely different. I don't have that revenge driven determination I had with Vitali, and unlike Cooper, who ultimately died from the fire, it will be my hand taking the life of another human being who hasn't personally done me any harm.

I reassure myself that this woman deserves to die, and Rebecca has made the argument to me on many occasions that we don't have the right to deny others the peace we received from Vitali's death.

This isn't murder, I tell myself, *it's justice.*

And as I look at Rebecca, and the determination in her eyes, I know I'm right. Sharon Dempsey drove her car over a little boy who was riding his bike.

Vitali drove his car over a little boy who was standing on the sidewalk.

She did it while she was legally drunk and dropping her own children off at school.

He did it while under the influence of alcohol and narcotics on his way home from a party.

She showed no remorse.

He showed no remorse.
A judge let her go.
A jury set him free.
This is right. And it needs to be done. Sharon Dempsey deserves to die, and we are the means of her execution.

One of the things I spent time looking up on the internet during my sessions on my secret virtual machine connection was where the best places for a mortal wound were. Slitting the throat was a popular option, but a blade into the heart would be more in line with a death blow from a jealous husband or lover.

We start up the stairs when there's a loud crash from outside, some softer thumps and then nothing.

"Raccoons?" I mouth to Rebecca.

She nods. We wait a few seconds more before climbing the stairs the rest of the way to the landing.

There are several doors, only one is open. We tread softly toward it.

Our plan is a sneak attack. She lies on the bed, naked, resting on her side facing away from us with a sheet half draped over her body,

I exchange looks with Rebecca. We're ready.

We continue creeping silently across the room. When we get to the edge of the bed, Rebecca motions that she'll pull Dempsey onto her back while I stab her.

A shot rings out, piercing the night.

Sharon Dempsey stirs. "Derrick? Is that you? What was that noise?" She stretches her arms over her head, yawning as she rolls onto her back.

Rebecca grabs her wrists and pins them behind her head. Dempsey's hair is draped back over her pillow, and Rebecca hops onto the bed and kneels across Dempsey's arms and hair, rendering her immobile.

Without even thinking, I raise the knife and bring it down between Dempsey's enormous breasts, just to the right of her sternum.

My first blow hits a rib.

I jerk the knife back.

Dempsey starts to scream.

Rebecca grabs a pillow and presses it over her face.

I bring the knife down again, this time slipping it through the ribcage and deep into her chest, which heaves as she tries to take in a breath.

I pull the knife out once more, this time blood pumps out of the wound in time with her pulse.

Once, twice, three times and it's over.

Her body goes limp.

The flow dwindles to a trickle.

Rebecca removes the pillow and climbs off the bed.

Dempsey's eyes are closed, and her mouth agape.

We look at her for a moment, half expecting her to gasp and come back to life.

But it's clear from the wound that my blow was sufficient.

"Did you hear that gunshot?" I ask.

"Probably just a firecracker, or a car backfiring," Rebecca answers.

"We have to get out of here."

Rebecca nods and we turn to exit the room.

A man stands in the doorway holding a gun in his gloved right hand.

seventeen

We stare at him for a moment.

He looks us over. Sees the bloody knife in my hand, the spatter across my scrubs and the lifeless body of Sharon Dempsey behind us.

"Is she dead?" he asks.

Rebecca and I exchange a look before she nods in answer.

"Good," he says. "I didn't know if I could kill her. She is the mother of my children after all."

He notices me staring at the gun.

"He's dead, too," he tells me. "Murder-suicide, is what the police will think. Let me have that." He motions to the knife and I obediently hand it over.

"Get out, I'll take care of the rest."

We hesitate, processing the situation we've found ourselves in.

"Go on," he urges. "I know you're not burglars in those getups, and you're also not the parents of that poor boy." He starts to sob. "If you know them, tell them I'm sorry. I'm so very sorry. I hope this brings them some comfort to know she's dead."

Ding, dong, the bitch is dead.

He steps aside from the doorway.

Rebecca and I walk past, rushing down the steps. We pause long enough to slip the black rain suits on over our scrubs, then without looking back, head for the side door and down to the dock.

Rebecca pauses, turns to me with a big grin on her face. "That was incredible!"

"No it wasn't," I tell her. "He saw our faces. He can describe us."

"To whom?" she asks. "Like he said, the police will think it's murder-suicide. And he's the only other suspect with a motive. And if he comes out with some story about how he was going to kill his wife, but two strangers beat him to it, they'll think he's desperate. We were careful. There's no evidence we were in that house."

"He saw us."

"Hey, it's done. Bitch is dead, boyfriend's dead—thank you jealous husband—and we were never here. It's our original plan, only better."

"An innocent man died."

"We had nothing to do with that. And you heard what he said, he probably couldn't have killed her himself. Win-win."

I shake my head. Logically, she's right. But I still find the whole thing unsettling.

"Come on, we have to go," she urges, and grabs my hand and starts pulling me toward the dock.

I let her drag me along. My gloved hand is slippery, though, and she loses her grip.

She staggers down the dock, trying to regain her balance.

Her foot catches in the space between planks on the pier.

She falls heavily onto the dock.

Her head bangs against a piling and her momentum carries her into the water.

She disappears into the inky blackness.

I jump into the lake. It's only about waist deep, but in the darkness, I can't find her. I reach out wildly with my feet and good arm.

Nothing.

I spin around, searching for any sign of her.

A fish jumps behind me.

I stop moving, but breathe heavily, panicked almost to the point of losing control.

Then I hear a faint gurgle coming from under the pier.

I duck under the water, open my eyes and scan the murky darkness.

There is a faint bright spot.

I swim toward it.

I reach out and touch Rebecca's face.

She doesn't react.

I grab the collar of her rain suit and drag her to the water-side entrance of the boathouse and place her arms on the platform at the back of the pontoon boat where swimmers can board. I climb aboard myself, my water-soaked cast making it a nearly impossible task.

Once I'm on deck, I kneel over Rebecca, grab the waist of her pants and pull her aboard. Her water-soaked clothes slide across the aluminum of the deck.

I turn her onto her back, position my broken arm so I can use it to pinch her nose shut, then force my breath into her lungs.

Then again.

I do one-armed chest compressions, a count of ten is what I seem to remember from a CPR class years ago, then two more breaths.

Ten more compressions.

Two more breaths.

Five compressions.

I fill my lungs as full as I can, then squeeze all the air I have into Rebecca's airway.

I take another full, deep breath and lean over to give it to her.

She expels a spout of water into my mouth and nose.

I cough.

She coughs, too. Violently, turning her head to the side as water comes up out of her lungs and she gasps for air.

"Rebecca, are you okay? Can you hear me?"

She nods. "What happened?" she asks in a weak voice.

"You fell off the dock into the water."

"Where are we?"

"We're still in the Dempsey's boathouse."

"Are you all right?" she asks, seeing that I'm soaking wet and scared out of my mind.

"I'm okay," I tell her. "We need to go."

She nods.

I take a moment to assure myself that she is indeed okay, then untie the pontoon boat and engage the quiet electric motor.

I back out, then turn the boat back toward the middle of the lake.

I look back to the shore.

The lights in the Dempsey's neighbors' houses are all off. Either there's no one home, or they didn't hear the gunshot or whatever commotion we made in our poorly executed getaway.

I look back at Rebecca. She is still coughing up lake water as she peels off the rain suit and the soggy scrubs underneath.

She's okay.

I take us out away from the Dempsey's, then turn back toward Roger and Sally's place, going at as slow a pace as I dare, keeping the safety lights off.

Rebecca comes up behind me. Coughs.

"You sure you're okay?" I ask.

"Yes, feels like I inhaled half of the lake, but I think I've got most of it out, now."

I turn to look at her, she's smiling.

And completely naked.

"Turn that thing off," she commands.

I hit the kill switch.

"You saved my life. You're my hero," she says, playfully.

"You scared the shit out of me."

"Shut up."

She wraps her hands around my neck, kisses me with wet, cool lips. She starts to strip my wet clothes off. Peeling them carefully, paying special attention to my broken arm. The cast weighs twice as much as it usually does, and my elbow is starting to throb with pain.

After a few minutes, she has me naked, too, then pulls me toward the back of the boat. She jumps into the lake. The water is only about chest deep. I jump in after her.

She moves toward me again, her kisses interrupted by an occasional cough. It doesn't take long for me to get aroused, and once I am, she wraps her legs around me and guides herself onto me. It's difficult in the water, but she's determined.

Once we're fully engaged, she takes a deep breath, pulls me back onto her and we fall. I grab a deep breath myself as she rides me under the surface of the water. She kisses me, breathing into my mouth, then inhaling my breath into her lungs. We're able to exchange a couple breaths that way and stay under longer than I would have thought we could.

I bring us back to the surface, and we both inhale deeply, then go back under, this time I take control. My heart is racing from the oxygen deprivation, which at the same time heightens the ecstasy that comes to both of us rather quickly.

We surface again, this time keeping our heads above the water. She grabs me tightly, her legs and arms wrapped around my body, clinging firmly and passionately.

We breathe in unison, frantically filling our lungs with the sweet, cool night air.

She kisses me again, then stares deeply into my eyes.

"I saw Nick," she says. "When I was dead, I guess, I saw him. He was there, and there was a light, and he told me he loved me and to go back to Dad."

Her face is wet from the lake water, but I can still make out the tears rolling down her cheeks.

"I'm glad you came back."

"Me too."

We kiss again, long and deep. Then the chill of the night air gets to us and we climb back on board the boat, huddling under a blanket.

After a brief respite, we make love again. Like we used to when we were first married. It's nice, but the passion has faded.

We dress and drive the pontoon boat slowly over the glass surface of the lake back to Roger and Sally's under the moonless night.

Rebecca wrings out our wet scrubs as best as she can and stuffs them back in the Kill Bag. We discuss weighing it down and dropping it in the lake, but the risks are too great. I'll burn them later.

It's a little after two in the morning when we get back.

We go straight to bed.

I dream about Nick, but this time, for a change, it's not some twisted nightmare.

eighteen

I wake up and look at the clock. It's half-past eight.

Rebecca is not in bed.

I pull on some clothes and wander out to the great room. No one is there, but I hear voices in the kitchen.

Rebecca and Roger are drinking coffee at the table while Sally talks excitedly on the phone. Rebecca pours me a cup of coffee and I join her and Roger.

"What's going on?" I ask.

"Bit of excitement this morning," Roger reports.

"Someone was killed last night," Rebecca adds.

"Really?"

Sally hangs up the phone and joins us at the table. "Well, turns out she was stabbed."

"Who was stabbed?" I ask.

"Sharon Dempsey," Sally says with a note of contempt.

"Good riddance," Roger says.

"Sharon Dempsey?" Rebecca asks.

"Oh, she was big news up here a few years back. She killed a kid in a drunk driving accident and totally got away with it."

Once Sally says the words out loud, they hang in the air for a moment. She gasps with embarrassment, seeing the echo of our own story play across my and Rebecca's faces. She looks to Roger for support. He starts to say something, but I cut him off.

"It's okay," I assure them.

"Don't give it another thought," Rebecca adds, then turns to Sally. "I remember hearing about that. She lives around here?"

"They're weekend-ers, like us," Roger explains.

Rebecca gives Sally a reassuring pat on the hand. She smiles, then continues. "She didn't bother showing her face around here for a long while, then about six months ago started spending weekends alone at their house. The neighbors on either side stay away when she's there."

That's why we didn't see any lights, I think, *and why the gunshot didn't alarm anyone.*

"Apparently she was sleeping with Derrick Long."

"Total hippy," Roger chides. "Guy makes Ed Begley, Jr. look like the Sultan of Brunei."

"Nobody knows who those people are," Sally tells him.

"Of course they do."

"Rebecca, do you know who Ed Beagle, Jr. is?" Sally asks.

"Never heard of him."

"Begley," Roger corrects, he looks to me, questioningly.

"St. Elsewhere?" I answer, thinking I remember him from an old TV show.

"There you go," Roger states, vindicated, "St. Elsewhere. Also launched the careers of Howie Mandel and Denzel Washington."

"I have heard of Denzel Washington," Rebecca offers.

"Shut up, Roger. Anyway, she's been a total blight on the community. I feel sorry for Dorothy, though.

"Who's Dorothy?" I ask.

"Derrick's wife. After he killed Sharon, he found her husband's gun and shot himself."

Rebecca gasps. "We heard that!" She turns to me. "Didn't I tell you that was a gunshot we heard?" Back to Sally. "We totally heard that. He said it was a firecracker, or a backfire."

"Well, as exciting as this is," Roger says as he gets up, putting a hand on my shoulder, "this guy promised to go fishing with me."

"I thought the fish don't bite once the sun is up," Rebecca remarks.

"I said fishing, not catching," Roger answers.

nineteen

During the rest of the weekend, we get more details from the lake community's grapevine via Sally. Neighbors stop by and offer their theories. The Sunday paper has a photograph of the house from the street with police tape across the driveway. The lover's bicycle is visible in one corner.

Rebecca and I listen intently, eating up every detail. There is no talk of anything but a lovers' quarrel. Some people wonder if the husband could be involved, but the rumors and Sharon Dempsey's reputation as a child killer cement the spurned paramour story.

One of the neighbors is a doctor, who notices the smell of stagnant lake water coming from my plastered arm and offers to re-cast it for me. Roger drives me down the road to the doctor's clinic, where he has the latest lightweight fiberglass and resin materials and even does a quick x-ray to make sure it is setting properly. The new cast feels lighter and is certainly cleaner. He refuses payment and instead asks me to look at his office computer, which I'm happy to do.

By dinner time on Sunday, the excitement dies down, and after another one of Sally's remarkable meals, we pack up our things and say our goodbyes. Roger plans on going directly to the office in the morning from the lake, but neither Rebecca nor myself have packed suitable work clothes, so that's not an option for us.

On the drive back, Rebecca goes on about all the cooking tips she picked up from Sally.

"This was the last one," I tell her.

Rebecca says nothing.

"I almost lost you. I can't take a chance like that again."

"It was an accident," she says. "A *freak* accident. Nothing like that would happen—"

"The last time," I insist, softly.

She falls silent. She doesn't nod or agree with me or even argue any more. I'm glad. We've been lucky. I play back the killings of Vitali, Cooper and Dempsey in my mind, and in each case there are at least a dozen different points where if things has gone just slightly differently, one or both of us would've been caught or killed.

I won't do it again.

"No more," I add, then turn on the radio and let a deejay and a parade of the top forty hits fill up the rest of the drive.

I remember from some TV series I used to watch frequently that once a murderer has three victims, they are officially classified as a serial killer.

There's a club I never thought I would join.

The Dead Kids Club

ERICA

The Dead Kids Club

one

I stop to pick up some groceries Tuesday night after work.

At the butcher counter I find myself standing next to Mikey Manzonetti.

"How you doing?" he asks.

"Please, leave me alone."

"I'd be happy to do that, but I got a couple questions for you."

"I don't know anything about Mr. Vitali's murder," I insist.

"Okay. What about Sharon Dempsey?"

I nearly fall over. "Who?" I manage to inquire after a brief, hopefully imperceptible pause.

"The lady who done killed a kid with her car 'cause she was drinking," Mikey replies. "You were up at that lake where she was murdered by the guy she was having an affair with—at least that's what everyone is saying."

"Yeah, I heard about that."

"I find it interesting," he says, letting the statement hang in the air while I give the butcher my order. "Interesting that the night Anthony Vitali died, you and your lovely ex-wife were away on a romantic getaway. And now another person who, like Mr. Vitali—and I don't excuse what he did, it was reprehensible—killed a kid, goes ahead and dies while you and that lovely lady of yours were away on a romantic getaway."

My god, had he been following us the whole weekend?

"Most people wouldn't put too much stock in such a coincidence, but me, I don't believe in coincidence. I believe in patterns. And I'm starting to see one here."

"Mr. Manzonetti, I really don't know what you're talking about. I've already told the police—"

"—that I was bothering you. Yeah, I know that, too. You think I don't got ears in every police station in the county? What are you going to do, tell them I think you and your ex go around murdering child killers? Personally, I would, under other circumstances, congratulate you. But unfortunately, one of your little projects was a friend of mine."

"Listen, I didn't kill your friend, I didn't kill anyone. And if you don't stop bothering me, I will go to the police again. I have nothing to hide from them."

He considers. "I'm sure you don't. You're a smart guy. But even smart guys do dumb things. And I'm a patient man."

"You're wasting your time," I assure him.

Mikey sizes me up. I stare him down, hoping that will either convince him that I really have nothing to hide, or maybe at the least confuse him.

"Maybe. But it's my time to waste." He turns and starts to walk away, but then spins back and leans in to whisper in my ear, "You should wait till you get that cast off before you go skinny dipping with that fine lady of yours again."

He quickly slinks off, not looking back.

Shit.

two

I shake uncontrollably as I pace between the kitchen and the living room.

Rebecca finally arrives.

"Where have you been?"

"I had dinner with Amy. What's wrong?"

"Manzonetti. He knows."

"Knows what?"

"Everything."

She grabs me by the shoulders, holds me still until I stop shaking. "Sit down and tell me what's going on."

Rebecca guides me to the sofa and has to almost push me down to get me to sit. I look into her eyes, calm pools of reassurance. I tell her about my encounter with Mikey.

She takes my hand into hers. "So he or one of his guys followed us to the lake. They saw us take a midnight cruise along with a hundred other people. We came back soaking wet. He's just trying to rattle you."

"It worked."

"Don't let it."

She's right.

"Didn't that detective tell you to call him if Manzonetti showed up again?"

"Yes."

"So call him. Tell him what happened. You're the one who told me we need to do everything that we would do if we were totally innocent. If he really knew we did anything, do you think you would be here right now instead of in some dark basement, or in some run-down warehouse on a pier being fitted with cement shoes?"

I laugh at the picture she paints, right out of some old gangster movie.

"Okay, you're right. He got to me. And that's probably what he wanted to do."

"Have you had anything to eat?"

"No."

"Let me fix you something. Give that detective a call. If you wait too long, it might seem strange."

"I will."

Rebecca retreats into the kitchen. I fish Detective Kort's card out of my wallet and dial the number on it. It goes to voicemail. I leave my message. By the time I finish, Rebecca has a sandwich ready for me. She turns on the TV and snuggles up next to me while I eat and we watch whatever sitcom is on.

Rebecca laughs.

I pretend to laugh.

three

At group, Tina and Larry are not there.

Barb makes an announcement.

"The Portmans won't be joining us anymore. They sent me an email letting me know that they're moving and wish everyone the best."

It's obvious that everyone has heard about Sharon Dempsey's demise. It's made the local news, but Barb is determined to keep it from being a topic of discussion. I wonder if she even asked that Tina and Larry not return, even to say goodbye.

There are no new members of the group. That's always a mixed blessing. Although new members mean additional support, it also means there is one less child in the world.

Frank and Lexi tell us about the anniversary of their son's death to leukemia.

"Throughout it all," Lexi says through sobs, "he was the one who comforted us. He wanted us to have some brothers and sisters for him that he could be a guardian angel for. To the very end, he always had a smile on his face when we walked into his room.

"The doctors and nurses told us that the kids are the strong ones. They couldn't do what they do if it wasn't for their spirit, even when things are bleak. Ronnie was everyone's favorite. We still hear from some of the nurses at the children's hospital."

Then Yule and Wendy talk about going to a family reunion. There were photos at the event of the participants of previous reunions.

The Dead Kids Club

Erica is in one of the old ones, smiling gleefully delighted to have discovered a whole new batch of cousins to play with.

Wendy puts her hand on Yule's.

"She loved playing baseball. We have this big family softball game at the reunion, and she always wanted to be the catcher because she got to throw the ball almost as much as the pitcher.

"We passed a ballpark the other day. Kids were playing. I saw a little girl that looked just like Erica. Same hair, in a ponytail, poking through that space in the back of her baseball cap."

She sobs for a moment.

We all allow a tear or two. How could one not?

"I wanted to go over there. To watch them. But…"

Yule squeezes her hand, comfortingly.

"It's silly. One of the families had a dog."

I remember Yule and Wendy telling their story some months back. How Erica had died in an accident at a block party. But they didn't go into much detail.

"It was a small dog, and there were kids playing with it. But it didn't matter. I saw what those beasts did to Erica.

"I know that those dogs were put down. I knew that this dog wasn't one of those. I grew up with dogs. We talked about getting a rescue for Erica when she was older, she loved them so much.

"But that man. What he did to those dogs."

"And what they did to Erica."

Wendy falls silent. She closes her eyes and leans against Yule, unable to go on.

I can tell by the looks on some of the other group member's faces that this is the first time they've heard any of this as well.

Barb is the only one not looking at Wendy and Yule.

She is staring directly at me.

"Sorry, I'm the one who thought we should share that with all of you," Yule says. "You have all been very forthcoming about the tragedies in your lives, it's always felt like we were lying to all of you by holding it back. Some of you know our story, but I think we needed to say it out loud."

Wendy nods to him.

Yule steels himself for the words that come next.

"Our daughter had her throat ripped out by a pit bull. Two other dogs ate parts of her as well before the police could rip them away."

Wendy buries her face in Yule's chest, her sobs muffled by the fabric of his shirt.

"We had a closed casket. Most of her face was..."

"Yule, you don't need to do this," Barb interrupted.

"Yes, we do, Barb. Isn't this what we're all here for? To support each other? To be a safe place to share our feelings and bare our souls?"

Barb opens her mouth to say something but thinks better of it.

"The man who owned the dogs raised them for fighting. The children all knew to stay away from them, and there had been several occasions when they had escaped from their kennel and roamed the neighborhood. We complained to the police, and animal control and even tried to get the TV news to check it out. Everyone knew he had dog fights, but he knew people with the county, and every time there was a chance someone might do something, it just went away.

"He wasn't invited to the block party, but he showed up anyway, ignoring everyone's stares. He stuffed himself at the potluck buffet after adding a half-eaten bag of stale potato chips to the table. It was like he was throwing all of our efforts to shun him back in our faces.

"What we didn't think about at the time was while he was at the party, there was no one at his house."

Wendy continues the story.

"You know how kids are, when a bunch of them get together there's going to be someone who dares someone else to do something stupid. It wasn't Erica who did the daring or the doing, but she was there when another little girl climbed to the top of the fence surrounding the dog kennel.

"The dogs were chained up out of reach. The other kids kept on daring her to go further. To sit on top of the fence, to hang over the other side. They dared her to drop down in front of the dogs, but she was too afraid. There were three of them, snarling and pulling at their chains.

"She started swinging her legs back over, but she slipped, lost her grip and fell to the ground inside the kennel. The dogs were straining on their chains. The girl was screaming and crying for help, and Erica..." The words get stuck in her throat. She takes a deep breath, then continues. "Erica climbed over the fence to help her. She got the girl up onto the fence, pushed her up to the top, and started climbing back over herself when the steel stake that was holding the dogs at bay finally pulled free.

"They grabbed her by the ankles and pulled her back. The other kids screamed, and some ran to get help, but the dogs were fast. They got their teeth around her throat. The medical examiner said it was quick, but I can't help but think of the terror she must have been feeling, and I wonder what her last thoughts were.

"By the time anyone got there, it was too late." She prepares herself for the next sentence, determined to get it out despite the obvious pain it caused her. I don't think I could've done it. "They had eaten her face. Her tongue. Chewed on her fingers. One dog had ripped open her stomach and pulled her intestines out across the dirty yard."

The room is silent. Even Barb offers Wendy a compassionate look.

Yule has his arms around Wendy. She buries her face in her hands and finally lets it all out. He wraps her up in his large, muscled arms, engulfing her, protecting her.

"He got a fine," Yule says. "A five hundred dollar fine. And even that he's never paid," he says to us, explaining their frustration and pain.

Heads shake in disbelief. Rebecca grabs my hand and squeezes.

Wendy straightens herself up, Yule loosens his embrace, and she wipes the river of tears from her face with the back of her hand.

"I'm sorry, I know that was hard for everyone to hear."

How hard was it to say?

"It was hard the first time I was told how she died. It was like a dream. A nightmare. I couldn't believe that something like that could happen to a child let alone my child. I still have dreams where I find

Erica, sleeping in her bed, or dancing down the stairs for breakfast."

I have those dreams too, about Nick.

"We can't afford to move. The funeral wiped out our savings, and with the economy, we're so upside down on our mortgage. I just pray, I pray that—"

Barb cuts her off. "We all pray, that God will grant you the strength to be there for your other children." She breaks into a warm smile that is comforting, while sending a clear message that what Wendy wants to say, how she prays to God not for strength, but for vengeance, will not be tolerated.

Barb is our leader. Our queen. And without saying another word, she makes sure we all know it. She dedicates the rest of the time to affirmations, coaxing fond memories, and happy thoughts out of the group. She's good at it. More and more she is taking the group back.

Back to the way it was before we joined.

I scan the faces, happy to see that Barb's efforts have lifted the veil that falls over all of us whenever the conversation turns to unfulfilled justice and revenge.

The meeting ends. Old Harold is the first one out—I hadn't even noticed he was there. He moves with a purpose, to avoid talking with anyone. I think about following him, trying to start a conversation, when I hear my name and turn around.

"Can you help me take some stuff out to my car?" Brian asks.

"Sure."

He loads me up with the box that holds the coffee cups, sugar, creamer, spoons while he packs up the coffee pots. He casts a glance back toward Barb, who is engaged in a conversation with some of the newer members, before urging me out the door.

"You heard about Sharon Dempsey?" he asks once we're outside.

"We were there," I tell him, "at my boss's lake house. It was all anyone in the town was talking about."

"Barb thinks the Portmans had something to do with it."

"What? That's crazy."

"I know. She even suspects that Amy had something to do with Coopers death."

"How can she think that?"

"She's bipolar. Keeps it in check with medication, but now and then, she gets these fits of paranoia."

"I'm sorry."

"For the most part, she's okay. She won't admit it, but I think she's starting to think that closure is something that maybe she wants, too. All this happy talk shit, sometimes it just feels like a show. You know what I mean?"

"I do. Knowing that Vitali is dead is a whole lot better than knowing he's alive."

"You only had to deal with it for a few months. We've been marking the milestones in what would've been our daughter's life for over a decade. It wears on you."

I expect him to start crying. I can hear it in his voice, but years of damming up emotions has made him impenetrable.

Barb sneaks up behind me, puts a hand on my arm.

I jump imperceptibly.

"Thanks for helping out," she says.

"No problem," I tell her. "See you next week."

"See you then," she finishes, then guides Brian to the passenger door where he opens and closes it for her. He continues on around the front of the car, conscious of her eyes following him. He doesn't look back as he gets in the driver's side, starts the car then drives away.

I see Rebecca say goodnight to Amy.

She notices me standing alone in the parking lot, gives Amy a parting hug and crosses to join me. "What did Brian want?"

"Just help with the boxes."

"Is it just me or was Barb really weird tonight. And the whole thing with the Portmans."

"I think she feels like the group is slipping out of her control."

"Well, she has been running it for a long time. Maybe she needs a break."

"I don't know. She kind of is the group. I don't think it would last without her."

We cross to the car and get in. I start it up and drive home, playing with the radio to fill the silence.

"That was some story Wendy told," Rebecca casually mentions.

"I can't imagine knowing that your child endured all that," I reply.

"And all he gets is a five hundred dollar fine," she adds.

I realize where this conversation is going.

"Someone ought to do something about it," she says in a way that almost dares me to challenge her.

"Rebecca, we talked about this. We've already tempted fate twice too many times than we should have."

"I know, I know. I didn't mean us. I'm just saying. There's got to be something. They destroyed the dogs that killed Erica, but he has more. Wendy told me. He's still doing the dog fights. Everyone knows it. Maybe that writer guy you know could stir up some interest. Shame someone into doing something."

"Eddie Horne? I don't know if this is in his wheelhouse, he's more of a mob guy."

"Doesn't hurt to ask."

"Okay, I'll give him a call."

"Thanks."

She sits back in her seat, a sense of satisfaction settles across her face.

That went better than I had expected.

four

Saturday morning Detective Kort finally calls me back. He is polite but perfunctory as I tell him about my encounter with Mikey.

Kort thanks me for the information and promises to let me know if anything comes of it. I hang up knowing full well I won't hear a word. I notice Rebecca getting ready to go out.

"Going somewhere?" I ask.

"Amy has an ultrasound appointment. She asked me to be her birthing partner."

"Oh," I say, a bit surprised, "tell her I said hi."

"Okay," she says, offhandedly, "Bye." She leaves.

I shuffle through a shower, get dressed and step outside into the warm, summer day.

I'm on autopilot as I walk toward the diner where I'm meeting Eddie Horne, thinking about how I'm going to persuade him to take up the child murdering dog fighting story, and I don't see the black Cadillac limousine pull up next to me.

The heavily tinted driver side window slides down. "Get in," Mikey Manzonetti grumbles.

I'm surprised to see him. My heart starts to race. There's no way I'm going to get into a car with him. "No," I say.

He points a gun at me.

I'm so terrified, I almost laugh. He reminds me of one of those old character actors that's in every mob movie.

"Seriously?" I ask. "You're going to shoot me in the middle of a busy street with a red light camera recording everything you're doing?" I nod over at the device mounted on the pole that holds the traffic lights.

A look of genuine surprise crosses Mikey's face. I don't think anyone has ever reacted that way before to his pointing a gun in their face. He looks up at the camera and tucks the gun back away inside his jacket.

Somebody says something from the back seat. I can't make it out, but Mikey nods in response.

"I'm sorry," he says somewhat reluctantly.

I'm caught off guard by his contrition.

"Would you please get in the car? My employer would like to talk to you."

"No," I repeat. "No offense," I add, louder for the passenger's benefit, "but I'm not getting in this car no matter how politely you ask."

I walk around the car, cross the street and continue on toward the diner. My body tenses, expecting to hear the sound of gunshots and feeling the sensation of hot lead piercing my back, shattering bone and shredding organs.

Instead I hear a car door slam. Then an older voice calls out to me.

"Can I have a moment?" he implores.

I turn and see a thin, well-dressed man in his sixties with graying hair slicked back and a cane in one hand—that he obviously doesn't need for walking as he lithely jogs to catch up to me.

It's Tony Vitali.

"I apologize for my associate's rudeness. Can we talk?"

"I'm meeting someone."

"Just a few minutes, come, I'll buy you a cup of coffee."

He walks past me toward the diner I'm going to anyway, so I follow.

Inside, he makes a beeline for a corner table, and sits with his back to the wall, with a clear view of the front door and the kitchen. I stand in the doorway, scanning the diner. Eddie Horne sorts through a crazy quilt of sticky notes at a table, he looks up when I enter and waves for me to join him. I catch his eye and then look toward the corner where Tony Vitali gives his order to the waitress. Eddie instantly recognizes the old man, then drills into me with an inquisitive stare. I shrug, then proceed toward the back table where the elder Vitali waves me toward a chair across from him.

The waitress sets a cup of coffee in front of me—heavy with cream and sugar, the way I like it—before I even sit down. The elder Vitali folds his hands around his cup, takes a sip, then looks up at me. He notices I haven't touched my coffee.

"Cream and sugar, no?"

"Yes," I say, then quickly pick up the cup and take a sip. It's hotter than I expect.

"I make you nervous, don't I," he states.

I nod.

"A product of my reputation. Some would say well deserved."

I take another sip from my cup.

"I wanted to talk to you because we're both fathers."

I cringe as he says that, as if we're just the same. I was a father. The father of an amazing, brilliant, funny, polite little boy.

He was the father of a monster.

"And we both lost our sons," he continues.

I remember a scene from the third Godfather movie where an assassin kills a man with his own eyeglasses. Unfortunately, Tony Vitally is not wearing glasses.

I take a long drink of the scalding liquid in my cup and fantasize about throwing it in the old man's face.

"You know, I was in the courtroom during my son's trial."

I don't remember him ever being there.

"I watched you and your wife endure the indignity of it all. I saw that shark of a lawyer tear you a new one on the stand. I saw your hearts drop when they read the verdict."

I sit still, wishing for this to be over.

"Okay," he finally concedes, "I can see I'm not getting through with this bullshit, so I'll get right to the point. Mikey thinks you whacked my son."

I stare at him, stone-faced.

"Frankly, I don't think you've got it in you, but Mikey is a pit bull when he gets an idea rattling around in that thick skull of his. He's old school. Wants to put your head in a vice, smash your hand with a ball peen hammer, shit like that."

He squints at me.

I remain frozen.

"I can certainly understand if you did kill Anthony. Can't say I wouldn't do the same if I was in your situation."

I look down, hopefully with a tinge of grief.

"The thing is, I know what it takes to kill a man. It's not an easy thing. Mikey thinks you're smart enough to have pulled it off, and he even thinks you got the balls for it, but me, I don't think you'd take the chance. I think you wanted to, I think you want to whack me right now."

I look at him again, this time with defiant determination.

He smiles. "Yeah, like I said, I'd want to do the same." He stands, pulls a money clip out of his pocket, peels off a fifty and tucks it under the saucer beneath his coffee cup.

"I'm going to tell Mikey to lay off. You don't have to worry about him stabbing you in your sleep and cutting off your toe."

I betray a hint of a shiver.

It amuses Tony Vitali to know I'm scared of him.

I wonder how amused he would be to know he's arrogantly dismissing his son's killer.

"But like I said, Mikey is—what's the word... tenacious. So don't give him no reason to do nothing stupid."

He grabs his cane and starts for the door, patting me on the shoulder as he passes. I turn and look toward the booth by the window where Eddie Horne is sitting, mouth agape, watching the notorious mobster stroll through the diner.

I walk over to Eddie's booth and join him.

"What the hell?" he asks incredulously. "Do you know who that was?"

I give him a second to realize what a stupid question that is.

"Okay, obviously you know who he is, the conversation would've been pointless if you didn't. What did he want?"

"He wanted to tell me he doesn't think I killed his son."

Eddie takes a deep breath, absorbing the entire situation. "Well at least you got that going for you."

We look at each other for a minute, then laugh.

"Yeah," I agree, "there's that."

Eddie grills me on the details of the conversation. I am happy to oblige—after all, I'm here to ask him for a favor.

I tell Eddie the story of Erica Miller. He remembers reading about it back when it happened. It's not something he would normally pick up, but he has contacts in the business, stringers who might be interested. It's just the kind of story that could gain national traction. He promises to see what he can do.

I thank him, and we order lunch, passing the time with small talk. He promises to get me a draft of his book, but first wants to add a bit to my chapter to include the scene in the diner.

five

The cast comes off revealing a shockingly white arm underneath.

"Jeez, looks like you had a serial killer's arm transplanted on," Roger jokes. I laugh, then pretend that it has a mind of its own and is reaching up to choke me.

Roger had talked me into letting his neighbor—the doctor who had replaced the cast when it got wet in the lake—have the honor of removing it. We came up Friday afternoon, taking off from work a little early for a guy's weekend. Sarah and Rebecca's idea, actually. Sarah had some showcase she was doing, and Rebecca and Amy were off to the casinos, feeding money into digital slot machines.

I twinge in pain as my muscles and joints protest being moved after weeks of immobility.

"I can give you a little something to grease the skids. May be stiff for a while yet," the doctor offers. He reaches into a drawer, pulls out a couple pain reliever samples and holds them out.

I take them with my good hand and stuff them in my pocket. "Thanks."

"Any time. My PC's been running like a dream since you worked your magic on it."

"You just needed a little spring cleaning."

"Is Roger bringing you to the game tonight?"

I glance over at Roger.

"Hadn't mentioned that yet," Roger confesses. Then to me, "We have a catch-as-we-can poker thing when enough of the wives are off doing other things. Friendly game, but the pots can get a little out of control when Doc is bluffing."

"You're always welcome to call me."

"Don't think I won't. Sarah had a very good month."

The two of them share a laugh over a private joke. I smile. Poker might be right up my alley, after all I've had quite a bit of practice lying to people's faces the last couple months.

six

I come out a little ahead after five hours of poker at Roger's friend Jeffrey's house. He's an old timer on the lake, the house he lives in was built by some dime store magnate who went bust during the depression. Jeffrey's family were the caretakers, and, being frugal people, snatched the property up for a song. Jeffrey has eight children, all waiting for him to die so they can fight over who gets the lake house, but Jeffrey tells me he's going to outlive all of them 'cause he likes his grandkids better.

Roger and I walk back to his lake house. I understand why he insisted we not drive, we're both too inebriated to operate a bicycle let alone a car. Once we get back, he offers me a nightcap.

What the hell, I think. Might as well make the most of our guys' weekend.

We watch some mixed martial arts and fantasize how we would take down the sweaty, bleeding gladiators on the giant screen.

I don't remember much after that. Somehow, I made it to the guest room because that's where I wake up with a splitting headache. The bathroom is stocked with various remedies. I remember the pain killers the doctor gave me and down one with a cup of fizzing Alka Seltzer, then manage to climb into the shower and let the steam sweat out the remnants of the alcohol.

After a long fifteen minutes, I slip into some clothes and wander through the house, searching for Roger. He's sitting on the back porch, sipping what looks like a Bloody Mary.

"The dead rise," he remarks. He doesn't seem to be under the same hangover cloud that I am.

"Can't remember the last time I was that drunk," I tell him.

"It was just last night," he offers with a smirk.

Just the thought of laughing makes my brain hurt.

"You up for some golf later?"

"Don't know how good my game'll be. Arm's still stiff."

"It'll help loosen things up. We can go hit a bucket at the range, maybe pick up a quick nine."

"Yeah, why not? Assuming I can turn off this buzzer in my head."

He nods toward his Bloody Mary. "Hair of the Dog?"

I shake my head gently, not wanting to scramble the eggs in my skull any further.

"Hey, I meant to ask," he continues, "Rebecca told Sarah something about you meeting Tony Vitali?"

"Yep. That was certainly a weird moment. Like something out of a Scorcese film. You always think those movies are all, you know, the Hollywood version, but those guys really do that crap. He sat with his back to the corner, had the silverware removed from the table—"

"No shit?"

"—it was surreal. I didn't know whether to crap my pants or laugh."

"What did he want?"

"I think he was sizing me up, to see if I was the one who knocked off his kid."

Roger laughs. "And?"

"Turns out I don't have the balls for it."

"Well, in this case that's a good thing."

"It is indeed."

I sit back, the world spins.

"I'm going to make you something that will get you back on your beam in no time," Roger proclaims. He stands and heads toward the kitchen. I lean forward slowly and lay my head out on my arms. The morning sun warms the back of my neck.

I hear a blender running inside. Then a couple minutes later Roger returns with a tall glass of a green, foamy concoction.

"Drink this," he commands, "all at once, don't sip just chug it down."

I'm too weak to challenge him, so I sit up, lift the glass to my mouth. It has a minty smell to it, and although it doesn't taste too bad going down, it finishes with a bitter punch that sends a spasmodic shiver down my spine.

"Trust me, go lie down for a half an hour and you'll be right as rain."

"What does that even mean, 'right as rain'?" I ask.

"Fuck if I know. Go. Don't make me carry you back to bed because I seriously couldn't do it. You look like you've put on a few pounds."

I push myself up out of the chair. By the time I get back to my bed, the pounding in my head subsides to a distant thunder.

seven

I wake to the ringing of my phone. It goes to voice mail before I can pick up. It's Rebecca.

I sit up amazed to find my hangover all but gone. I check the time. I've been sleeping for a little under an hour. Gotta get that remedy from Roger.

I call Rebecca right back, but it goes to her voice mail. I leave a quick message about heading out to the golf course to try out my newly unencumbered arm, then change into something more appropriate for country club golf and find Roger.

We run into another of his poker buddies from the previous night. Despite Roger's miracle smoothie, I still feel like I'm wearing a wet burlap bag, but these guys look like they've just gotten back from a spa. I wonder if that's just another Friday night for them.

My arm loosens quickly after a few swings, but my shots all slice viciously. The Pro sees my predicament, suggests an adjustment that straightens things out quite a bit.

It's an old school course, we walk it while caddies carry our bags and offer their expert advice about how to approach the next shot and how the greens are playing.

I even manage to win a couple holes in our friendly skins game, but lose back all of my poker winnings and then some on side bets.

We dine at the clubhouse, then Roger invites some of the guys back to his place, he's got baseball on the big screen.

I stick to beer for the rest of the night and in the morning, I'm "right as rain."

Roger convinces me to stay for lunch. He grills copious quantities of meat which we eat with an unhealthy side of home fries and margaritas.

It's well past five when I hit the road. I get home a couple hours later. There is no sign that Rebecca has returned from her casino trip. She and Amy have likely fallen prey to the outlet malls that lay in waiting on the route between here and there for gamblers who are either flush with slot machine winnings, or in need of a little something to soften the blow of losing.

I fire up the computer and catch up on some tech blogs I read regularly, stumble upon some stuff that might be useful for work.

I find myself falling back into my old life more and more each day, and I manage to convince myself that my life didn't end when Nick's did. It changed forever, but it's still going on. Those people who tell you, "He would have wanted you to keep on going," just might be onto something.

eight

Rebecca wakes me. Not with a gentle nudge while whispering my name in my ear like she would if I slept through my alarm. She wakes me with lustful nibbles along my neck that traverse my chest and wandered down to where she has my full attention. She teases me to the point of climax, then backs down again. She swings her body around so I can return the favor while she continues pleasing me.

I know her body well enough that I can predict almost to the moment when she loses interest in gratifying me to concentrate on her own building orgasm. She flips around and straddles my face. My hand reach around to pull her in close, then my fingers traces light lines on her skin as they wander toward her breasts, teasing her nipples as she positions herself so I can best take her closer to climax.

She pulls back, leans down and kisses me. She is voracious tonight. As she sucks my tongue into her mouth, she guides me inside her and starts sliding her body up and down along mine. There's a layer of sweat between us that amplifies the sensations as her hard nipples seem to cut grooves into my chest.

Our mouths are still joined, still hungrily devouring each other. I grab her tightly so I can roll us over. Now I'm on top and it's my turn. She lifts her hips to change the angle of my penetration slightly, and I increase the tempo, switching from shallow, slow strokes to deep, pounding thrusts.

She moans plaintively, digging her nails into my skin as her back arches and she quivers at the moment I release. I realize I've been holding my breath and take a couple of deep ones as my head swims from the rush of endorphins flooding my brain. I collapse on top of her, exhausted to the point of unconsciousness.

I'm reminded of the days when Rebecca and I were dating. When passionate sex like this was a nightly routine, rather than a once in a while thing. But even this has another dimension to it. Ever since that night at Sierra Winds Resort, and that evening after we got my arm set at the hospital, and the weekend at the lake…

I'm suddenly wide awake. I slide off Rebecca. She's still lost in bliss, her hair splayed out over the pillow, a satisfied grin gracing her lips.

Then it hits me.

"Who did you kill?"

nine

Her eyes slowly open and focus on me. I can see it there. That unrepentant sense of righteousness.

"José Lorenzo," she replies softly.

The man whose dogs attacked Erica.

I shake my head. "You promised you wouldn't kill anyone else."

"No," she replies, "*you* said *we* shouldn't kill anyone else."

My head spins as the pieces fall into place.

The guys' weekend to get me out of the way.

The girls' casino trip to serve as her alibi.

The whole thing with Eddie Horne to throw me off the track.

How could I have been so blind?

She excitedly starts telling me all about it, as if she can't hold it in any longer. "Amy and I planned every detail. We staked out his house, brought the dogs treats so they would get to know us, staged another car up near the casino so we could drive back and kill José while the casino's security camera had our car in their garage all night.

"You should be proud."

"I'm not," I reply. "This is wrong."

"I can't wait till the next group when Wendy and Yule tell us how relieved they are to know that Lorenzo is dead."

I shake my head. "We can't go back to the group now. Someone's going to start asking questions. Barb is already getting suspicious."

"It was beautiful," she continues, oblivious to my horror. "Amy and

I came up with a wonderful plan."

"What plan?"

"You remember that movie, 'Hannibal'? The one with Anthony Hopkins, where the guy had trained pigs to eat people?"

There is a look of excitement in her eyes.

"Apparently, the guys who fight dogs use strays to train them. The scent of another dog drives them nuts! So, Amy had the idea of making Lorenzo smell like a dog and then getting him into that kennel.

"Of course, we had to knock him out somehow. That was easy. The guy loves tequila, so we just sent him a spiked bottle of the most expensive stuff we could find—don't worry, we paid cash and got it at a place that sells cases of the stuff."

I sit back, transfixed. She is animated, excited. I don't know this woman.

"Anyway, we got some surplus wet suits, all black—I'm surprised you didn't think of that—parked a few blocks away and waited till it was dark. We took alleys and stayed in the shadows until we got to Lorenzo's house. The front door was unlocked, so we just walked right in and we saw him passed out on his couch. We looked around to make sure there wasn't anyone else in the house. The basement was set up for the dog fights, like one of those MMA cages. And we could see there was a ramp that led to a cellar door that connected to the kennels.

"Amy found the controls, he had those magnetic locks so that he could open the gates to the kennels, let the dogs into a kind of staging area, then open the doors to the cage so they could fight. The place smelled like stale blood and beer.

"Once we figured things out, we dragged Lorenzo down to the basement and put him in the cage. We threw in another Tequila bottle—one that wasn't spiked—so it would look like he was just drunk and careless. Then Amy took out a bottle of dog pee she had collected—don't ask me how. Anyway, we sprinkled it on him, then for good measure wrapped some raw bacon around his neck."

Rebecca revels in the details of their plan. I can see the excitement growing in her eyes as she continues.

"Amy opened the doors to the kennels. At first the dogs didn't come in. We took some bacon and slipped it through the chain-link fence. I even tried meowing, to see if that would get their attention. Eventually we got them into the staging chutes. They started going nuts once they saw us, and even started turning on each other, so Amy opened the door to the main cage, and they rushed in.

"At first, they didn't know what to make of it. Then one of them sniffed around Lorenzo, then started licking the bacon around his neck. One of the other dogs tried to get at it, too, and that's when it got fun.

"The dogs started stepping all over him, some of them must've noticed the smell of the dog urine we put on him, 'cause they started ripping at his clothes. Then they started ripping at his flesh. Once they caught the scent of blood, they just went for it. I think I saw Lorenzo's eyes open for a second, and he might've tried to scream, but the dogs had their jaws locked on his throat by that point, and he went limp.

"Once we knew he was dead, we cleaned up, you know, wiped down any fingerprints and stuff, then sneaked back out into the dark and made our way back into the alley. No one saw us. We got to the car, drove back to the Casino, then played slots the rest of the night."

She sighs smugly. "It was perfect."

I grab her by the shoulders, look her straight in the eyes. "If I've learned anything in the last couple months, it's that there's no such thing as perfect. What if Vitali's people were watching you? What if you went through a red light camera? What if someone at the Casino noticed you weren't there when you say you were?"

All of my questions bounce right off of Rebecca's steely demeanor. She dismisses my concerns with a roll of her eyes and a wave of her hand.

"You worry too much. No one has caught on to us yet, and no one is going to. We were careful, just like you taught me."

Taught her?

"Look, if it bothers you that much, I'll stop."

"Yes, it does. It bothers me that you're going around killing people after we decided it was over."

"Okay, okay. I get it. It's just that Amy and I wanted to help out Wendy. We know how she feels."

"So do I."

"It's not the same," she says, "you're not a mother."

"What's that supposed to mean?" I shoot back. "Just because I wasn't the one who was pregnant, I can't feel the same loss?"

She shakes her head in frustration. "Forget it. You wouldn't understand." She stands, wraps a sheet around her body suddenly embarrassed by her nakedness.

I can't think of a thing to say.

She walks to the bathroom, slams the door behind her.

A chill scurries down my spine.

ten

The church sanctuary is empty.

The doors are open when I walk up, so I go inside, not knowing what to expect, just needing a place to sit and think.

Maybe pray.

It is almost noon. It's Monday, and instead of sitting behind my computer or checking the servers at work, I've been wandering the streets of my neighborhood, visiting some of Nick's favorite places, the parks where he played with his friends, the candy store we went to every Saturday, the hill we used to sled down in winter.

At some point, I found myself at the church Rebecca and I had started going to a while back. We haven't been to any services since those first few—our weekends have been otherwise occupied—and whether I ended up here consciously or not, I know this is where I need to be.

I look around. The stained glass windows cast a kaleidoscope of colorful shapes across the pews. Careworn bibles and hymnals fill the nooks on the backs of the benches. The cross behind the altar is plain, unadorned.

I bow my head, trying to put into perspective the consequences of my actions. I have been directly and indirectly responsible for the death of four people. Rebecca and I both have had close shaves with death ourselves. The fact that the police—or the mob—hasn't caught up to us yet is pure luck.

I think of all the things I did wrong along the way, the most grievous of all allowing Rebecca to become a part of it. My mind replays that phone conversation when we first decided that we were going to kill Vitali. I wish now that I had just talked her out of it. Nothing we've done has brought Nick back.

And now I'm here in this church, praying for forgiveness, that if there is a heaven, I haven't completely screwed up my chance to be with Nick again.

My phone rings. I'm not sure which pocket I put it in, and it takes a few rings for me to find it.

A middle-aged woman pokes her head in from a door to the side of the altar, shoots me a curious glance.

I shrug an apology, then answer the phone.

"Hello?"

"Who is this?" the voice at the other end asks.

"Amy?" I ask.

"I was trying to reach Rebecca. Did I dial the wrong number?"

I look down at the phone, realize that I grabbed Rebecca's by mistake.

"No, we must've gotten our phones mixed up."

"Oh, well, I just wanted to see when she wanted to reschedule our girls' weekend."

"Reschedule?"

"Yes, is she feeling better? She sounded really sick when she called on Friday."

My heart skips a couple beats.

I'm relieved to know that Amy wasn't a part of another murder. But then a curtain of dread falls around me, making it difficult to breathe. Rebecca killed Lorenzo by herself. What else did she lie about?

"Yes, she's much better," I manage to say. "Try back tonight, I'll make sure we get our phones sorted out."

"Okay, thanks. Bye," she says.

"Bye."

I put the phone back into my pocket, stand and turn to leave. The Pastor is at the back of the church, a smile on his face as he makes his way toward me. "Ah, welcome my son, it's good to see you again."

"Reverend," I say simply.

"It's been a while since we've seen you and your wife."

"Ex-wife."

"Oh, right. Sorry. I guess I'm an optimist at heart, hoping you might find reconciliation amongst your salvation."

"Me, too," I offer, matching his smile.

"Were you just stopping in for a quick chat with the boss, or is there anything I can help you with?"

"I guess just the quick chat."

"Well, I hope whatever it is, it works out for you."

"Thank you."

"And we'd love to see you both again on Sunday."

"We'll definitely try," I promise.

We shake hands, and it seems as if he can see the turmoil in my mind. I must not be doing a good job of containing my fear and concern.

"God bless," he adds.

"Thank you."

I hurry out without trying to seem to be in a hurry.

Outside, the sunlight and warm air stifle me. My breathing becomes labored, the world starts to spin. I race toward some bushes just as the remnants of my breakfast force their way out, violently.

I fall to my knees, and my real prayers begin.

eleven

I find my phone back at the apartment and leave Rebecca's on the nightstand from where I had grabbed it.

There is a message waiting.

I listen.

It's from Eddie Horne. He wants to buy me lunch. Considering my breakfast had recently vacated my stomach, I call him back to accept.

The phone rings immediately after I hang up with Eddie.

It's my boss. "Are you all right? Haven't heard from you today, figured you were still sleeping off the weekend," he says.

"Yeah, I must've slept through the alarm. I meant to call, but I was finally able to get some sleep and just—"

"Don't worry about it, buddy. Call it a sick day, we'll see you tomorrow?"

"Definitely," I answer.

"Great, need to talk to you about something—nothing bad, but it is important, so make sure you get your butt in here."

"I will."

"All right. Hi to Rebecca for me."

"Will do."

I hang up without waiting for a goodbye. I really don't even want to go back to work. I feel like everything outside of killing Vitali that I've done over the last six months has been a shell, an exoskeleton I've outgrown and need to shed and discard.

I set my alarm and lie down for a nap.

Luckily, I don't dream.

twelve

Eddie is excited.

He tells me about the death of the dog fight guy.

I mention that I heard something about it on the radio—which I did. The details were thin, the newsworthiness limited to the fact that his dogs had been responsible for the death of a young girl.

"I have a source in the coroner's office," he tells me in a hushed tone. He looks around for anyone listening in. No one seems interested in our conversation. "He passed along some gruesome details."

I of course know what he's going to say. How the man's own dogs savagely ripped out his throat.

"Someone really did a number on him."

Not what I was expecting. I display my genuine surprise. "What do you mean?"

"Well, when the cops first got there, they thought he had been attacked by his pit bulls. He'd been dead a couple days, and the dogs had really gone to town on him."

"Isn't that what happened?"

"Once the medical examiner got the bastard on a slab and took a closer look, turns out the dogs had a little help."

Some bacon left in the wound. I suppose to myself.

Eddie checks his periphery again. "Someone took a razor blade or something to the guy's neck, sliced the flesh to ribbons. Like I said, at least one of the dogs was hungry enough to dig in, but some of the cuts were still evident, and there was scoring on the vertebrae. Someone killed him and wanted it to look like the dogs did it."

Eddie's words slip in and out of my consciousness, dancing with the story Rebecca told me and the revelation that Amy had not been there. I pictured Rebecca in her black wet suit, slicing at Lorenzo's neck, a fiendish grin on her face. I imagine that her description of him waking up while he was dying is something she witnessed a little more directly than she had led on.

"Hey, buddy, sorry. Didn't mean to gross you out or anything."

I return my attention back to Eddie, shake my head. "No, I'm okay. Did a little too much partying over the weekend."

"Oh." Eddie nods. "Listen, there's something else I really wanted to talk to you about, just between you and me, okay?"

I nod. "Sure."

"Well, you asked me to look into this guy on account that he got away with being responsible for the death of that little girl."

"Erica."

"Right. Well, it got me to thinking about Vitali. How someone took him out and he, too, was responsible for the death of a child."

I shrug. "They were both scum bags. Sounds like coincidence."

"Yeah, I don't believe in coincidence."

You and Mikey Manzonetti, I think to myself.

"So, I did a little digging. There have been a couple other strange deaths involving people who were involved either directly or indirectly with the deaths of children."

Damn.

"One was that woman, Sharon Dempsey."

"That was a domestic thing," I interject. "Rebecca and I were up at my boss's house on that lake around the time it happened. Murder-suicide. Something about a lover…"

"That's the official story, but I talked to some of the local cops, and there were some witnesses who say they heard a commotion on the Dempsey's dock around the time of the murder."

"Did anyone see anything?" I ask nervously.

"No, but the deputy I spoke to said the spurned lover thing just didn't feel right to him." Eddie took a sip from his coffee before continuing. "I also found a story about a guy who burned to death at his grease trap roadside diner. Turns out he was implicated in the death of a boy and his father."

I'm not sure how much more Eddie knows, maybe he's playing me, fishing for information. It wouldn't look good if I held anything back. I sit back, appearing shocked.

"Are you saying he was murdered, too?"

"Again, the local cops have their suspicions, but no proof. There were tracks from a car parked in the woods across from the diner. What were they doing there?"

He takes another sip from his coffee, letting his words hang in the air for a moment.

I sigh heavily, expressing my wonderment. "You think they're connected?"

"I don't know. I'm trying to figure out an angle on that. I already pitched the idea to a publisher. May have a bestseller on my hands—if I can link them together."

"Sounds a little far-fetched," I say.

"Yeah," he answers, "may work better as fiction. It is a good hook."

Eddie leans forward, inspiration lighting his eyes.

"Hey, don't you and Rebecca go to some survivor's support group?"

I nod.

"That could work," he mused. "I could weave a mysterious character between the chapters of the kids' deaths and their killers. He seeks out these support groups, lurks in the background, listening, learning, picking out the next target for his own private justice.

"Yeah... that could work," he ponders.

Better than you know, I think.

"I mean, it's a stretch that there's any one person actually committing these revenge killings—assuming they are murders—but if I tell the stories right, people just might buy it. They'll want to buy it."

"Still sounds a little out there to me," I say, but I can see that the idea has a hold on him, one that he won't easily let go.

thirteen

Rebecca and I sit across from each other at the dining room table, quietly eating the lasagna I cooked on my day off. She eats hurriedly, alternating checking her watch or the clock and shooting me a distracting grin.

"Are you going somewhere tonight?" I ask.

She takes another bite of lasagna before she answers, biding her time while she thinks of another lie?

"Movies with Amy," she answers, her mouth still half full while she tears off a piece of garlic bread.

She really wants to get away.

"I saw Eddie Horne today."

"You two are becoming friends?"

"He talked to someone he knows in the coroner's office about Lorenzo."

Rebecca's eating slows.

"Oh, and you forgot your phone today. Amy called to apologize to reschedule the casino trip. She hopes you're feeling better."

She drops her fork, and wipes her mouth with her napkin, a reproachful stare fixed on me. "Do you really want to talk about this? Aren't you the one who always says the fewer people who know the better?"

"You lied to me."

"I didn't tell you everything."

"You sliced his throat."

"He had it coming."

"Who are you?"

"Why don't you tell me? You're the one with all the answers."

Rebecca folds her arms across her chest.

"All I wanted was some peace," I say, "And maybe…"

"Maybe we'd fall back in love?" she asks. "Maybe I'd see you for the caring, loving man you always thought you were?"

I shake my head. "I thought we could start over."

"From where?" she asks. "I know we did what we set out to do, to kill that bastard who took our son, but that doesn't erase the fact that Nick is gone. There's no coming back from that. My life ended that day. Everything since has been…"

She looks up at me, a look of clarity crossing her face.

"I'm a ghost. A spirit, damned and stuck on Earth. Doomed to relive that pain every day."

"I feel the same way," I tell her.

"Then you know how it felt when we killed Vitali. You know the sense of purpose it gave me. For a brief moment it was like coming back to life."

"It was wrong."

"No, the only thing wrong with it was it didn't last."

My god, why is she making so much sense?

"Cooper, Dempsey, I know you felt it, too."

I did. "I also remember that I almost lost you."

"But you didn't. Nick's death transformed me. Transformed us. Can you honestly tell me we haven't left the world a better place by ridding it of those vile people?"

"It's still wrong."

"No, it's not. It's the only thing that's right."

She reaches across the table and grabs my hand.

"Do you really want to start over?"

"Of course I do."

"I need this. If you want to be with me, I need this. And I need you to be a part of it."

She pulls my hand toward her, and the look of defiance and purpose melts from her face. She looks vulnerable and afraid. It feels like the first honest thing she's said to me since we killed Vitali.

And she's right.

"We can't go on like this forever," I plead.

"I know," she admits. She lets go of my hand and sinks back in her chair. "I just need…"

"Need what?" I ask.

"Doing it alone was… there was something missing. It wasn't the same without you."

"It frightens me to think of you out there by yourself."

She takes my hand again. "I need you to help me with one more."

I start to shake my head.

"Just one more. The last one," she promises.

I want to believe her.

She gets up from her chair and comes around to my side of the table, then slips into my lap, takes my face in her hands and kisses me.

I do believe her.

"Who?"

"Justin Buermann."

I draw a blank.

"The guy who took Barb and Brian's daughter on her last joy ride."

I think back. Had they ever mentioned that name?

"If we could just give them some peace, I really think I could try."

"Try?" I ask.

"Try to start over," she finishes.

Before I can reply, she kisses me again. Her lips taste of the garlic and herbs from the sauce in the lasagna. She presses her warm, soft breasts against me as she kisses me even more deeply, running her fingers through my hair.

She reaches down to find me aroused by her unexpected seduction.

"Take me," she whispers.

I slip an arm under her legs, another around her back and stand up from the chair. She seems lighter than I remember. Her hair falls against my cheek as she buries her face in my neck, and I carry her to the bedroom.

The sex is back to the pedestrian version that marked the last months of our marriage, but even that is still satisfying and comforting.

She lies still on the bed, one hand resting on her naked belly, the other in a loose fist next to her face. I watch her sleeping, perched on the edge of the bed fearful of moving and waking her.

I've decided I will do what she wants.

How can I not?

I am a ghost, too.

BETSY

The Dead Kids Club

one

At work, I catch up on the tasks that piled up while I was "out sick."

My boss reminds me that he wants to talk to me as he rushes into a meeting, promising to catch up to me after lunch.

I find time to whip up another thumb drive virtual machine and start assembling information about Justin Buermann.

There are a few articles online about the prom night accident, and several police blotter entries that mention his name.

More digging uncovers some stories since the accident. One is about a scholarship award. Another details a charity organization's efforts to promote after-school activities for at-risk teens. A third is an engagement notice.

Naturally, I assume these are not the same Justin Buermann. I hope they are not. This is not the life of a remorseless killer, someone who got away with taking the life of a young girl before she had a chance to live it.

I dig deeper.

Buermann *is* an angel. He's engaged to the daughter of an internet mogul and active in several organizations that mentor troubled kids. He speaks to high school assemblies before prom about drinking and driving. He's a real-life Mother Teresa.

Shit. What have I gotten myself into?

I unplug my back-door workstation and return to my desk. It takes me through lunch to catch up on my reports and updates. There's a tap on my shoulder.

"Got a minute?" Roger asks.

"Sure," I reply.

"My office."

I lock my computer screen and follow Roger back to the corner where he has his office. Instead of sitting at his desk, he leads me to the informal conference area where he collapses into an armchair and directs me to the couch. He puts his feet up on the coffee table and grins.

"So, how would you like to have your own office?" he asks.

I'm surprised at first. Roger had hinted at a possible path to promotion, but an office meant manager, a big leap.

"Anderson is leaving, moving to California to work for some startup. Operations is yours if you want it."

"Hell, yeah," I reply. It means at least a fifty percent bump in salary.

"Well, we have to talk to some other candidates, but barring you committing murder or something, I'd say it's yours."

I laugh at his joke.

two

We arrive at the group meeting late. Rebecca surprised me with an after-dinner flirtation that grew into a full blown seduction. The normalcy of it is the most appealing part, it felt like we were newly-weds again.

A part of me understands that this is her way of motivating me. A promise of what our life can be if I go along with her plan for one last act of vengeance.

But I don't care.

I suspect she knows the same things about Justin Buermann that I know. It would be pointless for me to argue the possibility that he's trying to make amends for his actions and he's undergone some redemption despite the fact that the technicalities of the juvenile courts rendered the consequences of his actions minimal at best.

Barb is talking when we walk into the room. Our regular seats are empty, and we quickly and quietly sit down under a momentary glare from Barb as she kicks off the session with a story about her grandniece. She tries to hide it, but there is a tinge of sorrow in her voice that her sister has grandchildren, while she and Brian never will.

As she speaks, I glance around the room. There is a new couple, one of whom I recognize.

Eddie Horne.

He catches my eye and tips me an almost imperceptible nod.

What the hell? Is that his wife? I don't know a lot about his personal life, but I don't think he's ever lost a child. I don't think he has any children at all. He has mentioned the wife, but would she go along with posing as a grieving couple to research a book?

I lean over and whisper, "Eddie Horne is here," into Rebecca's ear. She looks at me, then follows my gaze to where the writer is sitting with his companion.

She returns her attention to Barb, giving him no more thought than she would any other newcomer to the group. I follow her lead, even though it feels like a betrayal.

I look around. Amy is there. Horne will surely recognize her from the research he's done so far. And even though Barb chased away the Portmans, Yule and Wendy are there. In fact, it is quite a full house tonight, many of the semi-regulars have pulled out extra folding chairs and made a second circle. Barb basks in the attention, speaking a little longer than she usually would.

Old Harold is parked in his corner, too, watching his fingers entwine around each other with an almost autistic single-mindedness.

I'm distracted when Barb asks the regulars if they have anything to share this week. She calls my name again.

"Uhm, well, things are going—"

"Let me tell them," Rebecca interrupts.

I look at her, questioningly.

She slips her arm through mine and turns a broad smile to the group.

"Some of you know that even though we were divorced when we lost Nick, his death has brought us closer together. We've been living together for a while, trying to get through this with each other and, well, I think due in no small measure to the support we've gotten as part of this group, we've decided that we're going to get remarried."

She doesn't say it giddily, or even with any hint of excitement. She knows just how to play this room. It's not a joyous occasion—that wouldn't be appropriate. It's a milestone, another step on the endless journey of coping with our loss.

Some people react as if this is something they've been expecting for a while.

Barb seems to adopt an air of resentment, as if Rebecca has purposefully tried to upstage the story about her grandniece.

Amy does betray a hint of excitement. She shares a conspiratorial look with Rebecca. I wonder if Amy knew she was going to be making this announcement, if this is another level of encouragement to ensure I go along with her plans for Justin Buermann.

At the point of the agenda after we've introduced ourselves and our stories to the interloping newcomers, Barb asks if Eddie or his wife would like to say anything. He begs off sharing at this point, preferring to listen and get to know everyone first.

He glances toward me.

I try to convey my disapproval, but I don't think it cuts through my efforts to hide my familiarity with him.

Barb offers the floor to one of the other newer couples in the group and they confess having a hard time dealing with the anniversary of their daughter's death to cystic fibrosis.

Rebecca plays concerned empathy, her arm wound around mine and resting her head on my shoulder as tears trickle down her cheek.

Barb casts a reproachful look our way, as if our announced reconciliation is an affront to the group.

I wonder if it's an affront to the truth.

three

I wait at the usual booth. He's late.

The delay gives me a chance to cool down the white-hot anger I feel when I think about the hubris Horne had, showing up at the group, faking his way into our confidence. I'm even angrier at myself for allowing it to happen. Why didn't I say anything? Why didn't I call him out? I have nothing to hide from those people, but my silence was a betrayal to them. I allowed a stranger—a pretender—into our midst.

Our group is very exclusive. The dead kids club. No one wants to pay the dues to get in.

While I contemplate the cream swirling in my heavily sugared coffee, Eddie sits down across from me, an expression of eager excitement playing across his face.

"Okay, you're never going to believe this."

I don't answer, but that doesn't seem to deter him. His enthusiasm blinds him from detecting my dismay.

"I was up all night researching this. I have a friend at the police department who pulled the vehicle registration info on the people at the meeting."

I break my silence. "That's a confidential group."

"I just wanted to get their names, cross reference—"

"The group is supposed to be like AA, if people don't want to share their names, addresses, what they do for a living, they don't."

He seems shocked at my dismay. "Aren't you curious about what I found? This could be big."

I'm indignant. "I know what you found. Some of them are parents of children whose killers have died."

His expression shifts. He realizes that I've been holding back on him.

"Why didn't you say anything?" he asks.

"I didn't tell you because it's none of your damn business. What the hell were you thinking? You can't just dress up as a grieving parent and show up at something like that. It took some of those people years to gather the courage to confront the feelings that haunt them day in and day out. What gives you the right to go poking around in their lives? I'm sorry I ever mentioned it to you."

The excitement drains from his face. "Okay, you're right. I did cross the line, but did you think I wouldn't dig around? Do you know how many other killers who put people in that group have died?"

I knew exactly how many. Three—besides Vitali.

"Seven," he tells me.

What?

"Four of them have been fairly recent, but I found three others in the last few years."

He pulls some photocopied microfilm newspaper articles from a folder. I didn't realize those things still existed, evidently there are enough Luddites like Eddie around to justify keeping those gigantic viewers around in some back room of a library somewhere.

"And the weird thing is, a lot of them happened in the month of July." He rearranges the articles in chronological order. "Like clockwork."

I inspect the articles. They are all quick blurbs, stories of people who died unexpectedly, and who had been associated with the death of children. I know all the families from the group, one was a malpractice case, the other two were traffic accidents. The doctor and the two drivers died in different manners, one was a stroke, one interrupted a burglary, the last drowned.

"I know my idea of a killer who picks his victims by way of grieving parents support groups was supposed to be fiction, but that got me curious, and I started checking the papers for any deaths that occurred in July that were associated in any way with people who were involved in the death of children."

He pulls out a half a dozen other stories and lays them out dramatically in front of me.

"Coincidence?" I ask.

"Maybe, but you know how I feel about coincidence. These seem to happen every year within a couple weeks. All within a fifty-mile radius of here. And all the people who died, were involved in the death of a child."

I look closer and some are merely obituaries pulled from one local paper or another, cross-referenced with articles from the incidents that tie them to a child's death. The closer I look, the more I can see that in most of the cases, the deaths are not of a suspicious nature. One is a man who was on the board of a school bus manufacturer linked to faulty vehicles who died of a heart attack. Another is a woman who succumbed to the flu who was an executive at a pharmaceutical company linked to contaminated chemotherapy drugs.

"Eddie," I begin, "some of these are a bit of a stretch."

"You can't deny there's a pattern," he responds defensively.

I shake my head. "I can't see it. My guess is that on any given day in a metropolitan area as dense as this one, that there's going to be someone who dies who can be linked tangentially to the death of a child, or children... it's just..."

He scoops all the papers into a messy pile, starts to straighten them. "You're right," he confesses. "I thought I was on to something." Frustrated, he shoves the roughly collated papers into his bag. "I had a hypothesis that there was some type of serial killer out there killing child killers, and I culled the evidence to fit. But you're right. There's nothing real here. Nothing anyone would take seriously. I'm better off sticking to fiction."

He sighs, dejectedly. "And I'm sorry," he adds. "You're right, I had no business going to your support group. That was wrong of me. My wife really read me the riot act when we got home. She thought we were going to dinner theater."

I laugh at the notion. "So, there is a Mrs. Horne."

"Ms. Kenilworth, actually," he corrects. "Do any women change their names anymore?"

"It's a dying tradition."

"Yeah, I know. Same thing's happening to journalism. That's why I have the blog and am looking for a best seller under every rock."

We sit in silence for a few moments. My anger mellows into pity.

"Eddie, thanks for apologizing. It really bothered me that you were there. It was a violation. And I felt like I was the one betraying them."

"Won't happen again. Let me make it up to you. Do you bowl?"

"What?"

"Do you go bowling?"

"Once in a while."

"There's a little six lane dive over on Forest. They make the greasiest French fries in the world, buck a line on Wednesday nights. My treat."

"Big spender," I joke.

"Come on, it'll be fun. Let's hang out without talking about..." He trails off, realizing that what he was about to say next wouldn't help the situation.

"All right," I tell him.

He smiles. "Really? That's great. Thanks."

"For what? I have to warn you, I can get very competitive."

"For at least being open to being friends."

I roll my eyes and shake my head. "Just shut up and buy me some pie."

He presses his lips together, then waves a waitress over. I order a slice of the apple pie, he signals with his fingers to make it two.

Friends. I like the sound of that.

four

I walk out of the server room and Roger calls out my name.
"Busy?" he asks.
"What's up?"
"Want you to sit in on an interview. One of the candidates that H.R. sent over for the manager vacancy."
I shoot him an inquisitive glance.
"Just a formality, I assure you. Thought you could do the technobabble song and dance. I suck at that stuff."
"Okay."
I follow him to one of the meeting rooms. A woman, tall, lean, jet-black hair tied back and wearing a smart suit is waiting. She stands when we enter, a warm smile greets us. "Hi," she says, "Dawn McAllister."
Roger makes our introductions while my brain shifts gears after hearing her name. I know that name. I just saw that name somewhere. It's so familiar.
"Why don't you tell us a bit about yourself?" He pushes her resume in front of me.
She offers a practiced recitation of her academic and professional history. Most of it goes in one ear and out the other.
I look down at the resume.
McAllister Systems.
Then it clicks. Michael McAllister, the internet mogul who has a daughter who is marrying the man responsible for the death of Betsy

Brown.

I was interviewing Justin Buermann's fiancée for the job that was promised to me.

She concludes by summarizing her experience, and my boss asks her why she wants to leave her current position and come work for us.

My mind reels. I mean, this has to be a coincidence, but does it get any weirder than this? The woman who is going to marry the man Rebecca wants me to help murder is sitting across from me, touting her impressive skills, and her desire to find a more challenging position.

The paranoid imp that lives inside my head shouts, *She caught you snooping around the internet, digging up dirt on her fiancé. She's come to check you out, find out what you're up to. She knows!*

I shrug it off. That's absurd. It is just a coincidence.

I don't believe in coincidence.

Or maybe a sign.

But a sign pointing in which direction?

"Can you fill her in on what we're running in that room you convince me to spend so much money on?"

I snap out of my daydream. "Of course." I turn to Dawn. "Actually, it's mostly video game systems, he doesn't know the difference. We have huge LAN parties when he goes home."

They both laugh.

Then I rattle off the latest hardware we're running, the state of our server OS migration and the legacy systems we've been trying unsuccessfully to get rid of for years.

She rattles off a bunch of questions.

I answer, deftly, expertly and without hesitation, and debate the pros and cons of moving our core systems to the cloud.

She turns to my boss. "One last question."

"Yes?"

"Why in the world are you interviewing me when you have someone so obviously suited for the position sitting right here?"

Roger smirks, caught.

"Never mind," she continues. "I find myself in the same position all the time. I do thank you for the opportunity to meet you both, though. I sincerely hope we do get the opportunity to work together sometime."

She gathers her things and stands.

"I'll be in touch," my boss offers, perfunctorily.

She smiles, knowing he won't.

For some reason I can't resist adding one more thing. "Ms. McAllister, I just want to say I'm very impressed with the charity work you do. It's nice to meet other professionals who actually make a difference in the real world as well as our little corner of the cyberverse."

God, did I just say, "Cyberverse?" What geeky graphic novel did that come out of?

"Thank you." She fishes a card from her bag. "If I'm not going to get a job out of this meeting, maybe I could get a chance to talk you into making a donation? We're having a gathering at my father's house next weekend. Call the foundation's office, I'll make sure you're on the list if you're interested."

"I'll check my schedule," I answer, accepting the card.

"We'd be happy to lend our support," Roger adds.

We all shake hands, and she assures us she can see herself out.

"You're engaged, and so is she," my boss reminds me.

I shake my head as if the thought had never crossed my mind. If only he knew the real reason I wanted to find out more about her charity work.

The universe is a chronic practical joker.

five

I fill Rebecca in on the interview with Dawn McAllister and the invitation to the charity event.

"We have to go!" Rebecca insists.

"It connects us to him. If you really want to do this, it has to be clean."

"And how will it look if we purposefully avoid him right before he's killed?"

"Like any other death in the state that happens every day."

"Except you just turned down his fiancée for a job. And you flirted with her."

"Nobody flirted. That part was just Roger being Roger."

"We're going," she insists, "make the call." She leaves the living room and enters the kitchen, depriving me of another protestation.

Just as well, I don't have one.

Part of me wants to believe that going there and meeting this guy will convince her that he is not like the others, he's made something of his life and tried to make other's lives better, too.

A truly repentant soul.

The scent of garlic and browning Italian sausage invades my senses. It's been a while since Rebecca made my favorite meal, the one I used to beg her for when we were dating: her homemade cheese ravioli with meat sauce, and mozzarella and garlic bruschetta. It was gourmet foreplay.

I dig the card out of my wallet and pick up the phone.

It rings only once before a friendly receptionist answers and asks what she can do for me.

I give her my name and explain that Dawn McAllister suggested I call about an invitation to her charity event.

She puts me on hold.

"You called," another voice says with a tone of surprise.

"Dawn?" I ask, "I mean, Ms. McAllister?"

"Yes, nice to speak to you again," she says, "and Dawn is fine."

"Well, when I mentioned your invitation to my…" I hesitate saying the word, "fiancée, she insisted we go. We're both big believers in your cause, and now we have a chance to be big supporters as well."

She laughs, "I know how much a 'computer guy' makes, so don't think I'll be shaking you down for some enormous check. I must confess, I do have an ulterior motive."

"Oh?"

"My father is going to be there, and he'll talk anyone's ear off about the latest technology and how he would've done it, I'm hoping you might be the designated tech geek, and keep him occupied."

"Are you kidding? It'd be an honor. I follow him online."

"Perfect. Is your fiancée in IT?"

"No, real estate."

"Well, I know I have some guests who would catch her interest, too. I'll make sure the details get emailed to you. So glad you called. See you there."

"Thank you," I say, "Goodbye."

"Bye."

I hold on till I heard the connection break.

God, I think to myself, it's a good thing Roger didn't hear that conversation. The accusations of flirting would be renewed with an elevated vigor.

Rebecca pokes her head in from the kitchen. "Are we all set?"

"Yep," I answer, "All set."

She crosses toward me, the scent of her cooking thick around her and gives me a garlic flavored kiss, then smiles lustfully and returns to the kitchen, humming.

If nothing else, doing what Rebecca wanted did kick-start our sex life.

I flip open my laptop and Google Michael McAllister, Dawn's father. I haven't really read his blog or followed him on Twitter, and was relieved to find that he did indeed have an online presence I could connect with, so my boast would not be unveiled as the little white lie that it was.

Michael McAllister had stepped down from being CEO of his namesake company several years before but maintained a high profile in the industry. I'd seen him on various talk shows, and he'd pop up as an expert on the radio opining from time to time on the latest iPhone, or changes in Facebook's Terms of Service or what went wrong with the last election. I figured if I was going to pass myself as a Michael McAllister aficionado, I would need to get up to speed on his latest proclamations and evangelisms.

I lose myself in reading his online posts. I find I agree with a great many of his positions and am growing eager with genuine excitement at the opportunity to meet him.

Sometime later, Rebecca sets the table with the feast that she knows will get me to do anything for her.

I guiltlessly sit down at the table and devour more of it than I should've been able to.

And after all that, there's a blueberry cheesecake for dessert.

I stare at it for a moment, wishing I had paced myself a little better on the ravioli and bruschetta.

"No dessert?" Rebecca asks.

I stifle a burp. "It looks delicious, but I don't know if I have room for it just now."

Rebecca gets up from her spot across the table, walks over and sits on my lap then draws a finger through the gooey blueberry topping and licks the bit that threatens to run down her hand. She demonstrates how good it tastes with an orgasmic moan, then holds her finger in front of my mouth.

I part my lips and she holds her finger a little closer, forcing me to go the rest of the way myself. I do so, and receive my sweet, fresh, juicy reward.

Rebecca pulls her finger free, then dips it into the cheesecake again, deeper this time to get a scoop of the cheesy part as well. But instead of offering it to me, she smears it between her breasts, and licks the remainder off her finger.

I don't hesitate to remove the delicious mess from her chest, then lick her neck, then nibble an earlobe, and finally share a blueberry cheesecake flavored kiss.

"Want to go in the bedroom and work up an appetite?" she asks.

I nod enthusiastically.

She slides off my lap and leads the way to the bedroom.

"Wait," I say, then turn back to the table, grab the dessert and follow Rebecca with the cheesecake in hand.

six

The pins erupt with thunder in a furious explosion of white and red as the ebony ball smashes into their midst.

Eddie spins around doing a move he must've copied from an old Michael Jackson video, then licks the tip of his finger and marks an X in the air.

I roll my eyes, having endured his "strike dance" several times already. Fortunately, he didn't have one for spares.

He slides behind the scorer's desk, pencils in the strike and tallies up the score for the previous frames. This place is perfect for his Luddite sensibilities. No fancy electronic scoring, no light shows accompanying blaring pop music, just a little six lane bowling alley tucked away between a cigar shop and a cobbler. I must've driven by this place hundreds of times and never noticed it.

"You're up," Eddie reminds me.

I nod, and cross to the lane, glancing down at the scoresheet which shows how definitively I am being beaten. I pick up the sixteen-pound ball that had holes big enough for my fat knuckles and do my best to guide it down the center of the waxed lane toward the triangle of pins. The ball quickly veers off to the side, giving them a glancing blow, but a friendly rebound knocks down more pins than I deserve.

Eddie laughs. "You need a few more beers in you, you're too tense."

"I haven't bowled in probably ten years."

"Yeah, yeah, it was five years ago last game." He signals the bartender-slash-shoe-manger-slash-cashier to bring over two more beers.

I make a half-hearted attempt at the spare and make it. I turn to Eddie, lick my finger and draw a slash in the air.

"Mathematically impossible for you to catch up at this point," he boasts.

"And I thought I was competitive."

"Yeah, I know. It's a fault. Melissa won't even play cards with me anymore."

The bartender drops the two beers into cup holders behind the seats that at some point in the past were filled with waiting bowlers, then departs without a word.

Two silent old men at the bar watch baseball on the black-and-white TV — how many of those do you see any more — and a single bowler in the far lane racks up strike after strike with a gleaming translucent ball. The embroidery on his worn shirt names him, "Freddy."

The bell hanging from the front door tinkles.

Two men in dark suit jackets enter. They look around and their heavy-lidded eyes settle on me and Eddie for a moment, then they move to the bar and drop onto the stools.

Eddie glances over his shoulder and watches them for a moment, then gives his ball a half-hearted toss down the alley, creating a split.

I tease him for his uncharacteristically poor attempt.

He takes a seat next to me and tightens his laces while he speaks in a low whisper. "Did you see those two guys who just walked in?"

I reach behind me for my beer, catching a glance at the newcomers.

"Friends of yours?"

"They're from Vitali's crew."

I cast a quick, hopefully inconspicuous glance in their direction.

"You sure?"

"I've got their mug shots tacked up on my office wall."

"What are they doing here?"

"I don't know. It's not the typical place they'd shake down."

"Maybe they like to bowl."

"In suits? Maybe they're following you. You did catch Tony Vitali's interest. Maybe Mikey Manzonetti changed his mind about you having the balls to take out his kid."

"Yeah, sixteen pounders."

Horne doesn't laugh.

"Should I be scared?"

"Maybe I should be. They could just as easily have taken offense at something on my website."

"You know, I've been meaning to ask you. You don't seem very tech savvy—"

"The same college kid who set up my email address to print messages on my fax machine has it so I can send typewritten pages directly to a blog post."

The system he describes catches my interest for a moment, and I want to dig further, but my focus returns to the members of Tony Vitali's crew who decided to drop in for a beer at the bowling alley Eddie and I just happened to be killing a few hours at. "You really think he had a change of heart?" I ask nervously.

"No, you'd be dead if that was the case."

"Good to know. So, what do we do?"

"Well, we can finish our line and pretend they're not there, or we can just call it a night." Eddie suggests.

I think about it. Vitali's goons make me nervous. "Let's get out of here," I say. I pull out a twenty-dollar bill and clip it to the score sheet, then hurriedly change my shoes and flee with Eddie under the watchful eye of the mobsters.

seven

I drop off Eddie at his apartment building, then continue on to my place.

A large, menacing SUV follows me.

Even in the dark, I can recognize the driver and passenger in my rearview mirror as the two goons that were in the bowling alley.

No doubt that they were there on my behalf now.

I arrive at my apartment building and pull into the parking garage.

The SUV takes up a position across the street.

It is certainly going to be interesting trying to kill Buermann under the watchful eye of the Mob.

eight

Rebecca listens intently as I tell her about my run in with Vitali's men.

"So," she begins, "what does it mean? They can't follow us the rest of our lives, they'll give up after a while. And if they don't, we'll find a way around it."

"Maybe Mikey's convinced Tony Vitali to give us another look."

Maybe Rebecca was more careless than she thought with Lorenzo.

"Jeez, paranoid much?" she asks mockingly.

"It's not paranoia if the mob is actually following you," I reply.

"Whatever. I'm not going to live my life like everything I do is going to tip off Manzonetti, or the police, or Vitali, or heaven forbid upset Barb Brown." She grabs her phone and jacket and heads for the door. "I'm going to Amy's. She's picking out nursery stuff. And I need a distraction from your drama." She looks at me fiercely. "And don't think you're going to use this as an excuse to let Buermann off the hook. You can think of a way to get around Vitali's guys, and we're going to that charity thing!"

She leaves abruptly, stealing any chance for me to respond.

nine

Barb is not at the group meeting.

Brian does his best to follow the format. There are no new members, so that makes things easier for him, and some of the other regulars help things move along.

Everyone is eager to wrap things up, and they break into smaller groups.

Brian ends up on his own, rearranging things at the refreshments table.

I approach him. "Need a hand?"

He smiles when he sees it's me.

"Yeah, I'm kinda lost here. I'm not used to doing this without her."

"I hope she's feeling better soon."

"I'm not sure about that."

"What do you mean?"

"We've been arguing a lot lately. It's like the last ten years have all come crashing down on us at once. I really bought into this whole thing at the beginning. Sharing feelings, unloading grief, remembering the good stuff…"

"You guys do a lot of good," I remind him.

"Yeah, well, nothing is as therapeutic as a seeing your child's killer get what they deserve, huh?"

There is a disturbing tone to his voice. A man on the edge.

"I'm sorry."

"It's not your fault," he says. "I'm happy for you and Rebecca. I really am. For you guys and all the other parents who have gotten some resolution over the years. I'm also jealous as hell. And to be honest, it's been driving a wedge between me and Barb."

"If there's anything—"

He cuts me off, "—Anything you can do?" He chuckles. "Yeah, how about knocking off Justin Buermann?"

The words hang in the air between us.

Brian wipes a tear from his cheek. "I shouldn't be dumping this on you."

"Brian," I put a hand on his shoulder, "that is exactly what you should be doing. That's what you and Barb have created here, an outlet that we all need."

He nods. "I know. I know."

"I can't imagine going on for as long as you guys have."

Brian shrugs. "Well, if you want to see how it wears you down you just look at Old Harold." And he does just that.

I do, too.

Old Harold sits in his corner, knitting his fingers together as if weaving his unspoken grief into an invisible shroud.

"What is his story?" I ask.

Brian shrugs. "I've heard stories about his story, but nothing actually from him," he confesses. "You up for a drink?"

ten

I give the car keys to Rebecca and tell her that I'm going to get a drink with Brian. She's curious, but just accepts the keys and warns me not to stay out too late, knowing I'll fill her in when I get home.

We go to a little neighborhood place, where the jukebox isn't too loud, and no one complains if someone lights up a cigar.

Brian and the barkeeper are on a first name basis, and Brian's first drink is delivered without him even ordering it. The bartender looks to me, and I tell him I'll have the same.

Brian empties his glass before he starts the story.

"Harold has us all beat," he begins, "he not only lost a son, but a daughter-in-law and two grandchildren.

"They were getting ready to go on a summer vacation, a young family, the son and his wife were in their mid-twenties, and the kids were a year apart, but both still in preschool. The second-hand minivan they had broke down, blown transmission or something. It would've taken more than a week to fix—even if they had the money for it—so instead, Harold offered them the use of his car, one of those big old Mercurys. Not quite as family friendly, but it'd get them to the lakeside cottage they had rented, and they could enjoy their trip.

"They never made it to their destination. I don't know the exact details of what happened except that there was some sort of accident on the tollway, and the car caught on fire. The gas tank exploded, the car was filled with a fireball that killed them all."

Brian downs his second drink in one swallow and waves to the bartender for another.

"When was this?"

"Over twenty years ago, I think. Like I said, Harold is an old timer. Before Barb and I started this group, we attended another one, quite a distance away. Unfortunately, there were enough parents in this area that it made sense to start a local group. Harold was one of members that made the move."

"Did they ever determine whose fault it was?"

"I don't know. I heard the story from the leader of that old group. I don't know if it was a sleep-deprived trucker, or a wrong-way driver, or just a horrible accident.

"When I think about Betsy, and the way she died, I thank God that she was killed quickly. I can't imagine how hard it would be to know that her last moments were spent in such agony."

Cooper's last moments were like that. But he deserved it.

"And you can understand why Harold never shares. He must blame himself to some degree. It was all a series of unfortunate events, wrong place, wrong time—"

Just like Nick on that part of the sidewalk when Vitali ran him down.

"—But I get it. He must tell himself that if he hadn't loaned them his car, or if he had driven them himself, or if he had rented them a safer vehicle, or any of a hundred things that would've changed what happened. He'll never be able to forgive himself. In one moment, he lost two generations, the future of his family."

"Is he married? Is there a Mrs. Old Harold?" I ask.

"He's a widower. She passed away before the accident."

"What does he do for a living?"

Brian shrugs. "I suspect he's retired now, before that I have no idea."

We sit in silence for a while, I nurse my drink while Brian starts on his fourth.

"Thanks," he says patting my wrist. "It helps to tell that story out loud for some reason. I guess it reminds me that as deep in Hell as I am, you can always go deeper."

"If there is a Hell, you know Vitali and the others are burning in torment a hundred times worse than what we're going through."

Brian lets out a short laugh. "Right." He raises his glass in a toast, "To Hell, may it forever torment the monsters who took our children."

Then he adds, "And may Justin Buermann join them before I die."

eleven

I sit at the police station on a hard wooden bench, exchanging glances with a bored desk sergeant.

Detective Kort asked to meet me after work. He didn't say why he wanted to meet, I assumed it had something to do with the message I left after my run in with Mikey Manzonetti's guys several nights before.

The desk sergeant's phone rings. He answers, listens, then hangs up. "You can go back," he tells me.

I push myself up off the bench, then wait for him to buzz me past the reinforced door leading to the detectives' area.

Kort is poking away at his computer keyboard when I approach, using the eraser end of a pencil to laboriously type out something that he immediately loses interest in when he catches sight of me.

He waves me to the chair next to his desk that I sat in the last time.

"Thanks for coming in," he starts.

"Whatever I can do to help," I answer.

"Well, I'm afraid I have some more questions about the Vitali case."

I react shocked and confused—because I am. "What about it?"

"Well, we might have a suspect and I just want to ask you a few follow-up questions—in light of your recent encounters with members of the Vitali Family."

"I'm not sure I understand."

"Well, it's obvious that Tony Vitali has taken an interest in you since his son's death, but I'm wondering if there was anything you noticed before that maybe didn't seem relevant at the time, but now in retrospect might be important."

"Like what?"

"Like people following you. Strangers in strange places. The same faces in unrelated locations."

Before Anthony's death? Why would the Vitali's have been following me then? "Why?"

"Well," he continues, "we have reason to believe that whoever killed him wanted to implicate you."

"I'm confused."

"Well, for example, there was a witness who says they saw a suspicious couple casing Anthony Vitali's house some weeks before the murder."

"Suspicious?"

"The same car driving up and down the block. No make and model, but you do have a dark sedan?"

I nod, dumbfounded. What's going on? How did this turn around on us?

"See, that's the kind of thing that defense attorneys seize on during a trial. 'Why didn't you follow up on this lead or that lead?'" he remarks. "I just need to cross all my T's."

"I'm sorry, are my ex-wife and I your new suspects?"

"No, no, not at all. You guys have an alibi. The clerk at that resort verified that you guys came in before the time of death and didn't leave again until the next morning."

Except that we both did leave and come back that night, I thought. I wonder if he's playing a game with me. If he has some red light camera footage of me or Rebecca racing to or from Vitali's house.

"The woman who found the body also claims that she saw a couple walking away from Anthony Vitali's house between the time of the murder and her return. But since you and your ex-wife were nowhere near there... just another one of those loose ends a lawyer could try to weave reasonable doubt around."

"Of course," I say agreeably.

"Personally, I think for whatever reason Mikey Manzonetti has a hard-on for you, he's going all out to scare up any evidence he can, getting witnesses to come up with little things here and there to throw suspicion your way."

"Who is the suspect?"

"Well, I can't really talk about it. Ongoing investigation and all."

"Oh." Is he lying?

"One more thing that came up. I understand that you're part of a support group?"

Shades of Eddie Horne's violation of that corner of my life raise my blood pressure. "That's kind of a private thing," I insist.

"Yes, of course, I don't want you to breach any kind of confidentiality—although legally, it's not technically a privileged communication."

"What does our group have to do with anything?"

"I understand that some of the other parents have had recent turns of fortune similar to your own."

I remain silent.

"I know you probably wouldn't answer this question even if you could, but I'm afraid I have to ask. Is there anyone in the group who you think might be capable of going vigilante, you know, like in those old Charles Bronson movies?"

I shake my head.

"'Death Wish.'"

"Excuse me?"

"The movie. You ever see it?"

"Sure, long time ago. What does that have to do with—"

"Nothing." He shuffles some papers, "Okay, sorry, really, I hate that I have to ask these questions, but if you'll bear with me for a moment longer."

What else can he want to know?

"Do you know Brian Brown?"

"You must know that I do."

"Yes, of course, he and his wife Barbara run the group. Do you think he might be capable of doing something like that?"

"Like Charles Bronson?" I ask with genuine incredulity.

"Well, yes."

"Not a chance," I reply, almost laughing at the thought.

That was his suspect? Brian?

"Well, if you think of anything else, you have my number. And of course, I'm still very interested if Mr. Manzonetti continues to harass you in any way."

"Thank you."

I get up to leave.

"One more thing…"

Who does this guy think he is, Columbo?

"Congratulations. I understand you and your ex are getting remarried."

I cock my head, wondering who might have told him that.

"She seemed very excited about it. Best of luck."

I obscure my alarm with a smile. "Thanks."

I turn around and head for the door, check my watch and then quicken my pace as if I just remembered an appointment I was late for.

twelve

I bring Rebecca into the bathroom and turn on the shower.

"Why didn't you tell me you spoke to Detective Kort?"

"Don't yell at me," Rebecca retorts, her usual defense for avoiding a conversation she doesn't want to happen.

I take a breath and calm down. "How could you not tell me about that?"

"You didn't tell me you were going to see him."

"I thought it was about the Manzonetti stuff."

"It wasn't a big deal."

"What if we contradicted each other about something?"

"About what?"

"Anything."

"I didn't tell him anything new."

"Did he ask you about people in the group?"

"I told him that was private."

"What about that night at the resort?"

"I told him that we fucked like there was no tomorrow. What do you think I told him? That we slipped out and killed that monster? Do you honestly think I'm that stupid?"

"No," I say out loud.

"Then stop treating me that way."

"I'm sorry. I'm just worried about—"

"What?"

"This whole Buermann thing. Maybe we shouldn't—"

"I knew it. You are such a pussy."

"I'm trying to protect us. There's too much attention. From the police, from Manzonetti, Vitali's goons, from Horne, the group. We're tempting fate."

"Fuck you. If you don't want to do it, I'll do it myself."

"Rebecca—"

"We had an agreement! You said you would do this with me."

"Look, we can do it, but just not now. There's too much we don't know. The way Manzonetti's been digging stuff up on me, I wouldn't be surprised if he has us bugged. And I'm not buying that sheepish, by-the-book act Detective Kort is trying to pass off. He tried to play us off each other. He's got a scent of something, and he's not going to let go."

She folds her arms and leans against the vanity, pouting.

"I know this is important to you, but that's all the more reason we need to be careful. I told you when we started, it doesn't work if we sacrifice ourselves in the name of revenge. It doesn't make sense if we get caught and they get the justice we were denied."

"What does it matter?" she asks, looking away from me, dejected.

"Right now, it's all that matters."

I see tears welling in her eyes.

"I thought you understood. I thought you felt the same way I did."

"I do," I reassure her. "You know I miss him just as much as you do."

She shakes her head. "Not the missing."

"What?"

"Didn't you feel, I mean..." she gathers her thoughts, "at first there was pain, that ache, that spot inside me that was the rest of his life that was suddenly nothing. It was just empty—no, worse than that, it was dead." She shakes her head. "Maybe you don't know. How could you?"

"What are you talking about?"

"I'm the one. I'm the one who carried Nick, who had him grow inside me, felt the first time he kicked, I did that. You contributed your part, but it was inside me that his life began, it was at my breasts that he was nourished and grew."

There's nothing I can say to that. I feel like a giant, selfish penis.

"He left something behind inside me. And now it's dead. But I'm not. And it's so heavy." The tears roll down her cheeks.

I do my best to just listen, to let her know I'm at least hearing her, even if I can never know anything about how she feels.

"Killing Vitali helped, and Cooper and Dempsey and Lorenzo. And doing it with you was wonderful. It truly felt like it did when we first met, when I couldn't wait to see you next, when being with you was electric."

I take a breath. "I don't know that I want that if it means we have to keep on killing to keep us going."

"We just need to finish."

"And how do we know when we're finished?"

She puts a hand to her belly, then looks at me hard, fighting back tears. "When this feeling, this black hole of pain inside me is gone. That's when we're finished. All I know is if we stop now, I won't be able to take it. I won't be able to go on."

I don't know what to say. A moment ago, I was dead set on convincing Rebecca that we needed to stop. We need to find another way to move on. Now she's telling me that if I don't, she has no reason to live.

She reaches out and takes my hand, places it against her belly.

"I still need you," she tells me, stepping closer. "I still want you." She presses her forehead against mine.

I close my eyes. I know there's a question coming next, and I know how I'm going to answer it.

"Do you still want me?"

She kisses me lightly.

"Yes," I tell her, "I do."

thirteen

Lunch with Eddie is a regular event, now. Sometimes we talk about his work, sometimes I befuddle him with all the technology I deal with in my work.

Today, I have a favor.

"There's something I'm hoping you can help me with."

"Shoot," Eddie offers.

"You're gonna think I'm a hypocrite."

"I think everyone's a hypocrite, what makes you so special?"

I laugh. "Well, I need your help to look into something that happened to some family members of someone in the group."

Eddie nods. "Yep, you're a special type of hypocrite."

I shake my head, "Never mind."

"No, no, I'm just jerking your chain," Eddie assures me. "Happy to help. What can I do?"

"Well, I'm looking for information about a family who died in a car accident on the tollway twenty years or so ago."

"Ah," he says smiling, "before the age of your precious internet."

"Yes," I admit, "it's been a while since I've done the library thing, and I was hoping you could give me some tips, point me in the right direction."

He pulls out a pad. "It'd be quicker if you just give me the details and let me work my magic."

I hesitate.

"Don't worry, just between us. I promise. I dropped that serial killer novel I was toying with. Turns out my agent is getting some interest for a hardcover printing of my Vitali Family book."

I feed him the details that Brian had shared with me.

He stops writing and looks up at me.

"You say this was twenty years ago?"

"Or so."

"Young family, two kids, both boys under five?"

"Yes."

"Car explosion on the tollway."

"Well, there was an explosion."

"This is weird," he tells me, "I know all about this."

"You do?" I ask, puzzled.

"Old Harold must be Harry 'The Shark' Finn."

"Sounds like a mob nickname."

"Yeah, and not a very original one at that."

I start putting it together. "Old Harold was in the mob?"

"He was one of Vitali's lieutenants. A brutal enforcer. Allegedly, one of Vitali's rivals, Bruno Batone, put out a hit on him. Apparently, some young hitman looking to make a name for himself planted a bomb in Finn's car."

"Holy shit."

"Yeah. Only he screwed up the wiring. Finn drove around with it under his car for days, but it never went off."

"And then he loaned that car to his son's family," I deduce.

"Civilians," Eddie added. "They had the misfortune to hit a pothole or something in just the right way that whatever connection was loose on the bomb set it off."

"No wonder he blames himself." Brian had it all wrong. He wasn't blaming himself out of misguided guilt, he was blaming himself because the bomb was meant for him, and he handed his son the keys.

"The incident started a war between the families. Finn supposedly killed the guy responsible, then dropped out of sight. Apparently Batone dropped the contract. Everyone thought he moved to Ireland or something. This is amazing…"

I look up at Horne, "Eddie, you can't—"

"Don't worry," he assures me, "I told you this was between us. I won't tell another soul. I owe you that much at least."

"Thanks."

"But lunch is on you."

fourteen

We drive up to the McAllister estate. I'd seen photos on the internet but seeing it in person adds a whole new dimension. Extravagant is an understatement.

An usher greets us at the gate, checks our names against the guest list, then waves us through. The pair of Vitali's goons that are tracking us today stay on the main road.

A valet takes our car—it's out of place among the Audis, Benzes and Teslas lining the driveway.

We walk up to the door and are escorted through the house to the back yard where tents and tables are set up, a band plays on a stage in front of a dance floor and, myriad waiters and waitresses mingle amongst the cast of a J.Crew catalog with various hors d'oeuvres and glasses of Champagne. I'm relieved it's not a black-tie affair, I feel enough out of place.

"Wow, she really has a crush on you for her to let us in here with that paltry donation we made," Rebecca observes.

"Knock it off," I tell her. "She's just a nice person."

"Uh huh..." she chides back. "So, this is how the one percent lives. How come we don't have a house like this?"

"Sorry, I forgot to invent a key piece of technology that every device that connects to the internet uses."

She shakes her head, "Should've married the lawyer."

"Well, it's not too late..."

She squeezes my arm and gives me a kiss on the cheek.

Dawn McAllister spots us, sets down her half empty Champagne glass on a passing tray and approaches.

"So glad you could make it!" she says with a smile.

"Dawn, this is my fiancée, Rebecca," I say, bypassing the ex-wife part.

Rebecca smiles back, "Thank you for the invitation. I have to ask, why are you looking for shitty management jobs in I.T. if you—"

"—have a billionaire for a Dad? Well, he's a bit old school. Most of this will go to charities like this one when he dies, and the small percentage that he'll allow me to enjoy is in a trust. It will only be released to me once I make my first million dollars."

"Wow, that's harsh," Rebecca says.

Dawn laughs. "Yes, I guess so. I mean, it's not like I grew up a pauper, but I can appreciate my father wanting me to earn the right to be rich. I have enough friends who are spoiled rich kids to realize he has a point. So, I'm getting whatever experience I can, wherever I can get it while I kick around some startup ideas."

"Well," Rebecca says confidentially, "I know a great engineer who could use some ground floor stock options in a hot startup."

"Rebecca!" I admonish.

Dawn laughs it off, "Don't worry, I've got my eye on him." Something catches her attention, "Wait right here, I'll be right back."

Rebecca leans in to whisper in my ear, "Told you she had a crush on you."

"You know she meant that professionally."

Dawn returns with a familiar face hidden behind a pair of wraparound sun glasses. She introduces us to her father, Michael McAllister.

"Well, Dawn promised me there would be someone here who knew more about CPUs than IPOs." He puts an arm around my shoulder and starts to walk me toward a buffet table. "First question, though, iPhone or Android—or are you one of the ten people who bought into Windows Phone."

Dawn steers Rebecca toward a different crowd of people, likely a selection of idle rich who she can pass out her Realtor's business card to.

My conversation with McAllister is mostly one-sided. True to his reputation, he is opinionated, and loquacious.

I enjoy the interaction, knowing I'll get dozens of jealous looks from the guys at work when I tell them about it.

Eventually, a familiar face drifts by and McAllister snags him by the arm. "Justin!" he exclaims, "come meet my new friend."

Justin Buermann puts on a charming smile and offers a firm handshake along with friendly eye contact as his future father-in-law introduces us.

"Justin here is another one of those sheeple who swallow up the latest and greatest gadgets they dream up in Cupertino—whether he needs it or not."

Justin grins. "What can I say, I'm not the tech genius my fiancée is."

"Still don't get what she sees in you."

"Well, Dawn's mother wasn't a computer whiz, and you still loved her."

"True, true. You do have a point there."

"I need to go inside and light a fire under the caterer. We're running out of scallops," Justin says. "Nice to meet you," He adds, shaking my hand once again, then heads toward the house.

"Good kid," McAllister offers, "troubled youth, but he really seems to have tried to make amends."

Let's hope he's not quite that angelic, I think to myself.

"Excuse me, but where would I find the restrooms?" I ask, seeing an opportunity to get some one-on-one time with Buermann.

"In the house, make a right down the hall, second or third door on the left—I can never remember."

"I'm sure I'll find it."

"And then you're coming back. You're the one person here who is making this afternoon bearable for me."

"I'll be back," I promise, then head on into the house.

fifteen

Once inside, I follow the stream of waiters carrying in empty trays, hoping they'll lead me to the caterer Justin is discussing the scallop shortage with.

I end up in an enormous kitchen that is filled with activity, but minus any sign of Buermann. Instead, I try to retrace my steps and locate the bathroom McAllister gave me directions to.

Somehow, I get turned around, and whichever way right and left were when I entered the house are completely obscured by the architectural complexity of the mansion. I start opening doors, hoping to find the bathroom behind one. Instead I find a closet, a library and another closet.

I approach the fourth door but pause before opening it. There are voices inside. Voices and moans? I smile at the notion of a couple of the guests—or even the staff—getting it on in McAllister's mansion and make a note to run the idea past Rebecca. Not quite the level of excitement of killing someone, but it might be enough to spark her wild side.

Against my better judgment, I find myself slowly twisting the doorknob and pushing the door gently open. It's a study, and across the room, on a desk, a couple is engaging in exactly what I speculated they were doing. I slowly pull back until I recognize something. The shirt the man is wearing is the same one that Justin Buermann was wearing.

He must've run into Dawn on his way to talk to the caterer. I'm suddenly embarrassed that I'm spying on my hostess and her fiancé.

The copulation comes to a sudden and dramatic end. And the woman's face—which was previously blocked by Justin's body—comes into view.

It's not Dawn.

It's a blonde, wearing a waitress uniform.

He backs away from her and pulls his pants back up.

She buttons up her shirt and straightens her skirt. "Well...?" she asks, "you're not holding out on me, are you?"

Justin smiles and fishes a small vial out of his pocket and tosses it to her. She unscrews the top and uses the small spoon attached to it to lift a tiny mound of white powder to her nostril and quickly snorts it up.

"Hey, save some for me!" he says, then snatches the vial from her and snorts two scoops himself.

Some powder ends up on his upper lip. "You have a mess," she tells him. The waitress pulls his face toward hers and licks it off. "Don't want that pretty girlfriend of yours to know you're misbehaving."

Justin snickers. "She's so clueless, she buys anything I tell her."

"Is she as good a fuck as me?"

"Not even close. But the bitch is rich and gonna get richer. Stick around after the party, we'll do round two."

"Sex or coke?"

"Both, baby."

I quickly close the door before he decides it's time to return to the party and catches me spying on him. I dash down the hall, turning in the direction of the sound of the band. My heart is pounding, my breathing is heavy. I burst into the fresh air, find the nearest tray of Champagne and down a glass.

"Careful, you'll get the hiccups if you drink it that fast."

I turn to see Rebecca. She sees me flushed and her face shifts to a look of concern.

"Are you all right?" she asks.

I take a deep breath, smile and tell her the good news.

"Buermann is an asshole."

She smiles as well, takes my arm in hers and leads me back to the party as I give her the blow-by-blow of Buermann's drug-fueled infidelity.

sixteen

It's a rough day at work. We're installing a new system for managing our warehouse, and it's not going well to say the least. I work till after ten, overseeing the process, making sure all the boxes on our deployment checklist are ticked off and all the related systems and services are tested.

Roger calls me several times, reminding me that this is our primary business system, if it looks like there are any problems, we have to roll back to the old system until we can get it right. I assure him that despite some anticipated issues, everything is going as planned.

It's fairly boring for me. I'm not doing any of the actual work, just coordinating the hand-off of tasks, so I take advantage of the downtime to do some more research into Justin Buermann, and manage to discover an apartment he keeps near the airport. He shares his current address with Dawn McAllister, but I discover—via some shady services that look up semi-public information on anyone for a fee—that it appears that he has a bachelor pad that Dawn may not know about. From the behavior I witnessed at the charity event, I could well imagine what kind of quality time he spends there.

In between running some perfunctory tests on the system cutover, I do some digital surveillance of the apartment via Google maps and start to formulate a plan to do some surreptitious on-site investigating as well. This seems like the perfect place to take him down as it will shatter the illusion he has crafted around himself to be found in such a neighborhood.

The deployment concludes, all the assigned tasks and tests are complete. I phone Roger to give him the good news and send out the all clear email to let the rest of the company know we can resume distributing sporting goods.

I give Rebecca a call to let her know I'm on my way home. It goes to voice mail. She's likely over at Amy's, again, the two of them have been spending a lot of time together, planning for Amy's baby.

Out in the parking lot, I notice something is missing.

My shadow.

The ever-present goons who have been trailing me night and day are gone. Hopefully, Vitali has reconsidered his reconsideration, or just gave up as Rebecca predicted.

I get in my car, start it up, shift into reverse and look up to find Mikey Manzonetti's dark eyes filling my rearview mirror.

"Bet you're wondering where your babysitters are," he says.

I sit still, silent.

"Don't worry, they just got the night off."

I wasn't worried about them, more about myself. Then about Rebecca and the fact that she didn't answer her phone.

"And I haven't done anything to the misses, either. Oh, sorry, forgot you're not married. Yet."

"What do you want?"

"Well, it has occurred to me that I've been sweating the wrong bereaved parent. I mean—and follow me here—if you are the guy who killed Anthony, then your ex must've at least known about it."

"We had nothing to do with it."

"Yeah, that's what you keep saying. And I don't have anything to prove to my boss what I know to be true." He leans forward. "What I know," he repeats slowly and purposefully, "to be true." He leans back. "But I will. 'Cause now I know that there's more than one nut I can crack. And from what I've seen that lady of yours is a little unstable. And I don't think she's as clever as you."

"If you touch her—"

"What?" Mikey asks, "You'll stick an ice pick in my head?"

I stay quiet.

"I'm a very patient man. And I'm not going anywhere."

And with that, he opens the car door and slides out.

I realize that the car is still in reverse, and my foot is pressed against the brake pedal all the way to the floor. I slip it back into park and take some deep breaths as I watch Mikey walk toward a dark SUV that slows to pick him up, then speeds off.

seventeen

Rebecca is asleep when I get home.

I breathe a sigh of relief, then get ready for bed myself as quietly as possible.

I take a peek out our living room window. A black SUV is parked across the street. They're back.

I notice some baby catalogs she must've collected for Amy on the nightstand with some of the page corners folded over. I'm glad there's something positive going on in her life.

The idea of Mikey confronting Rebecca the same way he's done to me haunts my thoughts. I see the scene play out in my mind.

Rebecca is at Babies R Us with Amy, picking out furniture. They split up, and Mikey approaches her.

"We haven't met," he begins, "but your ex-husband and I go back a ways."

Rebecca sizes him up and tries to ignore him.

He persists. "You see, he's done a good job of convincing people—including my boss—that he didn't kill my friend. I mean, I will concede he had a pretty good reason. Anthony was careless and irresponsible in the accident that took your son—"

Rebecca laughs. "Are you for real? The 'accident' that took my son? That stupid bastard murdered him. And he got everything that was coming to him."

"You see, this is why I have the notion that your ex-husband, and maybe even you, have a motive."

Rebecca shrugs. "I don't know what you're talking about." She turns her back on him and starts browsing through crib bedding.

Mikey, undaunted, continues. "I think you do know what I'm talking about, and I think you know that I know and are trying to figure out how to convince me that what I know I know isn't what I think it is."

Rebecca turns around, a smirk on her face. "Well, don't think too hard, you'll strain that tiny little brain of yours."

Mikey's expression shifts from one of professional detachment, to personal insult. "Are you patronizing me?"

Rebecca shrugs. "I don't think I can be patronizing if you don't even know what patronizing means."

Mikey grabs her arm. "I think you owe me an apology."

"Fuck you," she offers instead.

"I don't think you know who you're dealing with, Missy."

"You obviously don't know who you're dealing with, moron."

Mikey squints into her eyes. Wondering if he needs to push any harder.

Rebecca leans in, speaking in a hushed tone. "You think you won't wake up with an ice pick in your thick skull? You think we can't find out where you live, who you fuck? You think you're any smarter than your dead friend?"

Mikey smiles, and grabs her by the arm.

"Get your grimy meat hooks off me, you asshole," she demands.

Mikey lets go, still smiling. He reaches into his coat and pulls out a micro cassette recorder. "Gotcha," he says.

"You got shit."

"I got enough to collect the bounty on your head."

"Oh, really?" She reaches into her purse and pulls out a gun.

Mikey's grin disappears.

Rebecca lifts the gun and aims at his head. She pulls the trigger and Mikey's head snaps back as a red dot appears on his forehead. He falls over like a felled tree, crashing into a crib behind him.

Rebecca tucks the gun back into her purse.

A crowd gathers.

Amy returns, sees the body lying on the ground. "Who's that?" she asks casually.

"Some dumb fuck," Rebecca answers. "Did you find anything you like?"

"No," she answers.

"Well, we can try that place downtown. They had cute stuff on their website."

"Okay."

They start for the door, winding their way through the furniture displays and racks of baby clothing.

Sirens blare from outside.

A SWAT team bursts into the store.

"Get down!" a gruff, armored officer screams at Rebecca and Amy.

"He's over there," Rebecca informs them.

"I said, on the ground. Face down, hands behind your head."

"Listen, the guy you want is back there." She reaches into her purse.

All the SWAT teams' rifles swing toward her.

She pulls her gun out. "I already took care of him for you."

"Drop the gun!" the officer screams.

Rebecca rolls her eyes, and points with the gun toward the area of the store where she shot Mikey. "He's right back—"

Before she can finish her sentence, shots ring out. Her body twists and her blouse blooms red flowers as each bullet enters her body.

She drops the gun, then looks down at the blood oozing out of her wounds. "Come on guys, look what you did."

She falls to her knees, then onto her face.

Rebecca lies face down on the bed.

I crawl in next to her and stare at the ceiling, wondering how all of this is not going to end very badly.

eighteen

At breakfast, I tell Rebecca about Mikey.
She brushes it off. "He won't get to me," she insists. "Don't worry."
Easy for her to say.
"I know what you're trying to do," Rebecca says plainly.
"What's that?" I ask.
"Trying to get me to back off killing Buermann."
"I keep thinking there's too much attention on us."
"Look," she says, "I know you already have a way around Vitali's guys and Manzonetti."
She's right. I have thought of something that might work. "Well, just because there may be a way doesn't mean—"
"Come on," she interrupts, "you know that's just an excuse. He's been deserving it longer than any of them. You told me yourself that Barb and Brian are going through a real rough patch, and you know—despite all the touchy-feely stuff Barb spews—that they need this. God, over ten years. Can you imagine?"
I can't.
What I can imagine is the million and one things that can go wrong, all the eyes that are on us for one reason or another. Perhaps Eddie Horne stumbling across the missing piece of the puzzle that will tie Rebecca and me to all these murders.
Hell, do we really believe that the other parents in the group haven't put it all together? And that Brian, at least, after baring his soul to me won't realize that we are the ones responsible when Buermann is

killed?

This is a bad idea, getting worse by the minute.

Rebecca smiles. "You worry too much," she tells me, then gives me a kiss on the cheek. "See you later, I'm going out baby shopping with Amy."

She's out the door before I can check her purse for a small handgun.

nineteen

I pull into the movie theater parking lot, checking my rearview mirror for the ever-present goon squad. They follow me into the lot, parking where they can see my car and the entrance to the theater.

I pretend that I don't know that they're there, imagining that they are living under the delusion that they're just that good. I leave my keys on top of the front wheel, hidden by the fender and head into the theater.

They don't follow me in, instead, taking up a position to watch my car—which is what I was hoping for.

I left my phone and wallet at home, walking out with just a handful of cash. With my keys hidden, there's nothing on me that can be tracked.

I choose a long running movie, one that according to the display behind the cashier has already started and pay with cash.

I skip the concessions, tuck my stub into a back pocket and make my way to the far end of the building where there is an emergency exit. Typically, there is an usher there who keeps high school kids from letting their friends in. But at this time of day, the very first matinees are starting, and the theaters are mostly empty.

I duck out into the bright sunlight and cut through an alley. As I walk, I change out the reversible jacket I'm wearing, don sunglasses and a plain baseball cap I had tucked inside, and head toward the train station down the street.

Once I'm at the station, I locate the bicycle I had stashed there a few days earlier, unlock it and started peddling toward the address of Justin Buermann's secret apartment.

It takes me nearly half an hour. Halfway through, I take off the jacket and tie it around my waist. I'm working up a bit of sweat—the route is mostly uphill. Fortunately, that means the return trip will be easier.

The apartment is in a low-rent neighborhood. I try to make myself as inconspicuous as possible and search for a spot I can stash the bike. I circle the apartment building and find a gate that is out of view from the street, chain the bicycle to it, then circle around to the front.

There is no security on the building. The door to the atrium where the mailboxes hang on one wall is unlocked. I check the box for the apartment number Buermann leases. There is no name.

There also are no security cameras, and the phone that at one time acted as an intercom to ring tenants from the atrium is missing its handset and half of the buttons.

Buermann's place is on the first floor. I walk down the hall and find his apartment at the far end. Some of the other apartments are obviously abandoned, the doors are missing.

His door is locked. I jiggle the knob anyway and test the strength of the door with my shoulder, but despite the disrepair of the rest of the building, the door is unyielding.

There is a back door to the building, it too is unlocked. I walk out into the meager yard that is a few feet of gravel and weeds demarcated by a chain-link fence which has several gaps in it.

I walk around the perimeter of the building, locating the windows that look into Buermann's apartment. They are dirty, but I can see inside. One window opens into a kitchen, another into a bedroom, and a smaller one into what I assume is the bathroom. All of them are covered with rusted iron grates.

The bathroom window is higher than the others and looks like it is open a crack. I grab the grate and try to pull myself up. My weight pulls the upper mounts of the grate away from the wall and I realize that the whole thing is not really attached at all. The screws that hold it in place have long since been stripped from the exterior of the building, and it's likely that Buermann himself has used it to gain entry when he's forgotten his keys, or wanted to come and go unnoticed.

I lift and pull and the grate comes free. I set it against the wall and use it as a miniature ladder to boost myself up. The window swings open, and I gain purchase with my elbows, then wriggle my way in.

There is a sink below the window. I hold on to it so I can ease myself in without damaging the fixtures, the window or myself.

I pause for a moment, making sure there is no one in the apartment who heard my illicit entry, then I slowly step out of the bathroom into the bedroom.

There is an actual bed in the corner, the bedding is surprisingly clean. For some reason I had pictured a ratty mattress on the floor with vomit stained sheets, but obviously Buermann wanted some place nice enough to entertain his hook-ups.

I pass through the living area—which is home only to a chair pointed at a television—and enter the kitchen. There is a table paired with a couple chairs. It's fairly clean, though sparse. I open the fridge and am not surprised to find it chilling a couple cases of beer. The freezer is home to a bottle of vodka.

I begin searching the cabinets, the closets, looking for anything incriminating or anything to verify that I was in the right place. There are a couple utility bills with Buermann's name on them.

Under the bed there's a stash of condoms and a pair of handcuffs along with some other sex toys that likely come in handy on the occasion he's not able to perform himself.

In the bathroom, I check the cabinets, medicine chest and linen closet. Nothing but the bare necessities.

I lift the lid on the toilet tank and find a bag taped to its underside. No one could accuse him of being original. There looked to be enough white power inside to garner a felony conviction.

I take it and start searching for an alternate hiding place. There is a wall heater that has a little flap that opens to tend to the pilot light. It's been painted shut, but a little scoring from a kitchen knife loosens it enough for me to open it and stuff the bag up and out of the way of the tiny blue flame. It's summer, and unlikely that Buermann will be using the heater, but I turn off the gas, regardless.

A plan formulates in my mind—just as Rebecca predicted. I imagine Buermann coming to his illicit bachelor pad, hoping to score a hit from his stash, and instead finding only the clean underside of the toilet tank lid.

He furiously starts tearing the place apart.

Rebecca and I are watching from outside. As he makes his way through the house, and starts emptying drawers and cabinets in the kitchen, we sneak into the bathroom through the window, then lay in waiting in the bedroom.

He storms back into the bedroom, and from behind I bash him over the head with the same toilet tank lid. Hopefully, he's at least stunned if not unconscious.

We use the handcuffs to bind him to the bed. I retrieve the stash of drugs and pour it directly into his mouth. I imagine its ingestion will be enough for a fatal overdose. To make sure, we'll smother him with a pillow. Obviously, it will be seen as a murder, but in this part of town, and considering the circumstances, that will only serve to bring attention to Buermann's covert activities.

I take a towel from the kitchen and wipe down every surface— even ones I know I didn't touch. I brush away the paint chips I left from loosening the heater hatch, then put the bathroom back the way I found it. I take the towel with me as I wriggle back out the window and use it to wipe down the glass and the grate after I place it up against the wall and push the screws back into place.

I check my watch. There's plenty of time for my downhill bike ride back to the movie theater.

I walk back into the alley to where I left the bike locked and find only the cleaved chain in a heap on the ground.

twenty

I look around and see a couple kids down the alley, snickering at me.

I smile at them, then curse myself for being so careless.

The bike could conceivably be traced back to me, but I can't think of that now. Obviously, I'm not going to confront them. Instead, I offer a friendly wave which they return with a chorus of middle fingers, and I turn and retreat down the other end of the alley.

Shit. What was going to be a leisurely bike ride, is now going to be a run.

I need to cover almost six miles. If I was in shape, I could do that easily in under an hour, but I haven't been running since that day Rebecca and I first decided we were going to kill Vitali.

Fortunately, the downhill grade I was counting on to make my return ride a breeze will help with the run.

I start off at an easy jog, then settle into a pace that I feel I can keep up for a while. I barely make it a block when the kids from the alley appear, riding bikes—one of them mine.

"Hey, lose something?" they chide.

I try to ignore them and keep running.

"Are you lost, old man?" one asks.

Another one of them rides the front tire of his bike into my calf. I stumble, and almost take a spill, but regain my footing and continue on.

The assorted delinquents laugh and urge their friend to try to do it again.

I'm able to leap quickly to the side and avoid his assault.

"Hey," another one calls out, "you look like you can use a vacation."

I smile at him, hoping they'll tire of me soon.

"Or at least a short trip," he adds.

I don't see the miscreant who has biked up on my other side. He sticks out a foot from his bike and catches my ankle.

This time, I don't recover and hit the ground, hard.

I manage to break most of my fall by putting my hands out, but my palms take a major scraping along the pavement which also happens to be littered with tiny rocks and broken glass.

Then I roll onto my shoulder and bang the back of my head against the curb. Momentum carries my body forward, and I feel the tip of my nose scrape along the rough cement, and my knees take a beating as well. Finally, the elbow that had recently been freed from its cast bangs against a metal signpost.

At first, shock prevents me from feeling the full effects of the fall, but after a moment the pain sets in. First in my palms. They feel as if they are on fire. Then my knees and elbows ring in pain, and then a throbbing begins where my head banged against the curb.

The kids who orchestrated my literal downfall exchange fist bumps and hoot and holler as one of them searches my pockets for anything of value.

Fortunately, since I had left my wallet and phone at home. The only thing they find is the change from my movie ticket and my fifty dollar watch—which they take from my wrist and then ride away.

I lie still for a moment, my eyes closed, half expecting a barrage of kicks or taunts to add insult and additional injury to my injury. But none is forthcoming.

I manage to sit up and take in my surroundings. A few people across the street see me stir and then continue on their way.

No one offers to help—which is just as well. I don't want to have to explain myself to anyone about why I'm in this part of town with no wallet or phone.

I struggle to my feet, careful not to press my palms against anything. They are raw and oozing blood. Ragged pieces of skin hang in shreds, and dirt, rocks and glass are embedded in the wound. I pick out the larger pieces, but I'm going to need to clean them. I don't see any establishments nearby that would offer public restrooms. I consider heading back to Buermann's place to use his bathroom, but I'm not sure I'd be able to manage reentry.

After a few deep breaths to try to lessen the pounding in the back of my head, I take a step and nearly buckle. My right knee took a harder hit than I thought. Putting weight on it is almost unbearable, but I force myself to take another step, and then another, until the movement loosens my swollen joint enough to resume a quick walk.

Without my watch, I'm uncertain of my pace or how long I have before Vitali's goons might start to suspect I've given them the slip.

I press on, managing a slow jog, then find a gate that favors my left leg in a sort of skip-run.

Six miles, I tell myself.

After the first mile, I try to calculate how long I'd been running, how fast, and parcel out a portion of my remaining energy to the next mile.

At what I guess is the three-mile point, my mantra shifts to a recurring assurance that I'm halfway there. But I'm taken by thirst. The day is getting hotter, and I'm starting to feel a little lightheaded. I know from my running days, that I'll be susceptible to cramps if I don't get some water in me, but my route is not runner friendly. There are no public drinking fountains, and the dingy shops I pass are useless to me without any money.

I trudge on, and soon the railroad tracks are in sight which means I'm less than a mile from the station. I look up at the sun, trying to get an idea of which side of noon I'm on, and guess the hour, but in truth I have no idea if I've been running for one hour or three. At least I'm heading in the right direction.

When the station is in sight, I allow myself to slow to a walk. I'm drenched in sweat, and the inside of my mouth feels like cotton.

I pull open the door to the station with my fingertips, and limp over to the men's room.

It's locked.

I look over at the ticket window, and there's a sign letting passengers know they can buy their tickets on the train.

I try the drinking fountain, but it offers only a weak trickle. I try to collect some water with the corner of my mouth, but only manage a few drops before I give up.

The movie theater is another block and a half away. I make my way down the alley toward the back door. There is an usher standing guard. I smile at him and open the door.

"Sorry sir, you need to go around front and get a ticket."

"I have a ticket," I tell him, then reach around to my back pocket and find my stub tucked safely there. Thankfully, the kids who mugged me didn't take it as well. I liberate it with my fingers and hand it to him. He examines it, then takes a look at me.

"Just stepped out to get some air," I say.

He hands me the ticket with a bewildered look and then holds the door open as I limp in.

I head for the restrooms and straight for one of the sinks. It has an automatic sensor that operates when your hands are under the faucet, so I hold my damaged palms under it, waiting for the stream to begin.

Nothing happens.

I try the next sink, then the next one. Finally, I get a stream of hot water to flow. When it hits my hands, they scream in pain. I force myself to let the water flood the wounds until I see the dirt rinsed away from the raw flesh.

I take my hands away, and stick my mouth under the faucet, but am rewarded with just a sip of hot water. I try holding my hand in a way that will trip the sensor while my mouth is in position, and manage to get a couple swallows of the near steaming water, enough to quench my thirst for a bit.

I douse my hands with soap from the dispenser, hoping it's the anti-bacterial variety. It stings, but I force myself to rub my palms gently together until it foams and seeps into every open cut, then rinse them once again.

There are paper towels, so I grab a few and use them as makeshift bandages. Spots of blood seep through, but for the most part, I think I'm past the worst of it.

In the mirror is a sweat soaked, dirty man with a finely striated scrape across the tip of his nose. I wet a paper towel and dab at it. That's going to be an unavoidable scab for a week or so.

Then I feel a bead of sweat trickle down the back of my neck. I grab another paper towel and wipe at it. It's not sweat, it's blood. I press the towel against the growing lump on the back of my head, and it comes back soaked red.

I pray that the back-door usher didn't take it upon himself to call the police or an ambulance, or even a manager, but I suspect I would know if he had by now.

I apply pressure until the parade of towels I press against the back of my head comes back with only a few spots of blood. It's then that I realize I have lost my hat and glasses somewhere along the way. And the jacket that I had tied around my waist is also missing.

Fortunately, the t-shirt I'm wearing is dark and hides the blood.

I look at my elbow in the mirror. It isn't bleeding, but I can see signs of swelling when I compare it to my other elbow.

I lift up my pant legs to check on my knees. The right one is bloodied, and there is a tear in my pant leg. The left looks okay but is tender to the touch.

Someone enters the bathroom. They eye the pile of bloody paper towels I've accrued on the counter as they pass.

I clean up after myself as a few more patrons trickle in. A movie must be letting out. Seems like a good time to go myself.

In the parking lot, I spy Vitali's men where I left them, and walk as best I can, trying to hide my limp, back to my car. I grab the keys from atop the tire where I hid them and open it. Once inside, I take a moment to settle my nerves. I look at the clock in the car. It's almost four. I've been away for nearly three hours.

I start the car and drive directly home.

twenty one

Back at the apartment, I chug a cold bottle of water from the fridge, then head straight for the bathroom, and carefully peel off my clothes. I stand under a hot shower for what seems like an hour.

Then I slip into my robe, fill four bags with ice, and lie down on the bed with one each on my knees, my elbow and the back of my head.

I hear Rebecca enter. She calls out my name.

"In the bedroom," I answer, weakly.

She appears at the door, just as puzzled by my condition as the usher at the back entrance of the theater was.

"It's a long story," I say.

"Where is your phone? Sally called, she says Roger's been trying to reach you all day. There's something wrong at the office."

I sit up and look around. My phone is on the night table where I left it, but when I pick it up, it's dead. I find the charging cord, plug it in, then swing out of bed to my feet and limp out into the living room where I left my laptop.

"What happened?" she asks.

I turn on my computer and wait for it to boot up. "I went to Buermann's place."

"Was he there? Did he do that to you?" she asks.

"No, this happened on the way back. I had a little run-in with some local kids."

"What did you do, challenge them to a game of rugby?"

I'm too sore to laugh. The computer comes to life, and I open my email. There is a flood of messages from Roger and most of my coworkers. They've been scrambling all morning to figure out why incorrect orders have been flowing out of the warehouse. Stores are complaining, the CEO has been breathing down Roger's neck, and everyone is looking to me for answers, and I've been missing in action planning a murder.

"Shit!" I mutter, Then, in a loud, primal scream, "Shit! Shit! Shit!"

"What is it?" Rebecca asks.

"I fucked up," I answer. "Somehow, I missed something."

My phone rings in the bedroom. I race to answer it before it goes to voicemail. Roger's name and picture are on my screen. I answer.

"Yes, I just saw the emails," I say in reply to the barrage of questions on the other end. "I can be there in fifteen minutes."

I listen for a moment. The weight of the situation grows heavier as I hear the anger and disappointment in Roger's voice.

"I understand. I'm on my way."

I end the call and close my eyes.

Rebecca sits next to me. "What is going on?"

"The new system we lit up last night. There's something wrong. Stores are getting stuff they didn't order, and nothing that they did order. There is a million dollars of inventory in the wrong place. And it's all my fault."

"You can fix it, right?" she says.

"I don't know. I don't know what's wrong."

"What can I do to help?"

"Can you drive me to the office? I want to get working on this in the car if I can."

"Of course," she says. "Let me help you get dressed."

I silently accept her offer, knowing full well that I'm in no position to manage it myself.

She redresses the bandages on my hands, helps me into pants and a shirt and even puts on my socks and shoes. In an odd way, I welcome the attention. It's coming out of love and concern, not violence and death.

That's a nice change.

twenty two

By the time I get to the office, I think I've figured out what's wrong.

I had been using our staging environment to test the deployment of the new system, and when we switched it on live, I neglected to verify that the data was coming from the production ordering system, rather than the database of test orders.

Orders were going out that were essentially randomly created to try to simulate peak load conditions. Unfortunately, they in no way reflected reality, but it took two shifts of warehouse workers filling bad orders before the complaints started rolling in from our customers.

I present Roger with my findings and a plan of action.

It means recalling all the orders that went out, restocking the inventory in the warehouse, and then reprocessing the actual orders. It will take two days to recover fully.

Roger stands silently behind his desk, shaking his head.

"Do it," he orders.

"It's already in motion," I assure him.

He looks up at me, the disappointment on his face makes me want to cringe.

"You know that this will sink your promotion," he says.

I nod. Not exactly a news flash.

"And my neck is on the chopping block as well," he adds.

"It was all my fault. I'll take the hit. Just tell me who I have to explain it to."

"Shit flows uphill," Roger says. Then, his expression changes to one of concern, "What the hell happened to you?" he asks, waving at my visible injuries.

"Running accident. Took a bad spill."

"Was that before or after you slipped up on the deployment?"

"After," I admit. "I can't tell you how sorry I am, Roger. If I need to quit to take the heat off of you, I will. I'll write up my resignation right now."

"No way," he answers, "you're not getting off that easy. You're going to live in this office until you get this straightened out, then you and I are going to call every one of our store managers and apologize and explain why this is never going to happen again. Then, we'll see if the board still wants blood. If we're lucky, we'll both come out of this with our jobs."

"I'm sorry," is all I can think to say.

He shakes his head. "Just fix it." He collapses into his chair and casts his gaze up at the ceiling.

I back out of the office and return to my desk. There is a queue of admins and developers waiting to ask me questions and show me reports. They all look at me with a mixture of pity and relief.

Relief that it wasn't their fault.

twenty three

By the time I have things sorted out at work, the constant pain in my knees and elbow had diminished to an occasional twinge, and the palms of my hands have scabbed over. Liberal applications of antibacterial ointment have prevented any infection, but my hands are useless for anything besides some light typing and nose picking.

Rebecca is of course furious when I tell her this puts off our plans for Buermann. "Just until I'm healed," I assure her.

"You're just stalling," she insists.

I hold up my hands. "No, I'm not!"

She dismisses my dramatic gesture with a wave of her own hand. "Whatever."

"Rebecca," I implore, "what do you want me to do? I nearly lost my job—hell, I nearly lost my life—and you're questioning me?"

She spins around with a look of adamant defiance. "Are you saying it's my fault? I'm not the one who decided it was best to case Buermann's apartment alone. I'm not the one who fucked up his job because he was Googling how to kill a cheating junkie. If you would've included me, if you would've trusted me, none of this would've happened."

I realize she's right. In trying to prevent any unnecessary risk and exposure, I ended up achieving just the opposite. I bow my head, accepting whatever additional berating she has in store for me.

Instead, she places a hand on my arm. "It is a good plan, though. I'm very proud of you."

I lap up her praise. *Good serial killer, good boy!*

"I'll make you a deal," she offers, "we'll wait one more week, but if your hands aren't ready by then, I'm the one who'll whack him on the head with the toilet tank lid."

What a perfectly reasonable proposition, I think to myself.

"Of course," I tell her. "In a week."

"Good." She gives me a peck on the cheek, then picks up her purse and grabs her phone. "I'll be at Amy's. Her crib arrived, and she needs help to put it together."

I start to offer my assistance, but Rebecca casts a reminding glance down at my bandaged hands, and then smiles.

"You just get better. I won't be late." And she leaves.

I tell myself, the quicker we get this last killing over with, the quicker Rebecca and I can resume our lives.

Whatever that turns out to be.

twenty four

Barb is back at the head of the group this week. She seems rejuvenated, and the meeting goes according to her plan as she asserts her will over the proceedings.

It's nice. Brian appears to be back to his jovial self as well, but there are cracks in his facade, like he's just playing a role.

I know how that goes.

There are no new members, so no sharing of stories, just affirmations and reminiscences.

As the meeting is winding down, I catch Old Harold—or should I say, Harry "The Shark" Finn—looking at me. I can't remember anytime he's looked at anyone except for when he encouraged us to celebrate the death of Nick's killer and allow ourselves to accept the relief it brought.

This time, he's not speaking, just looking at me inquisitively. Not that I'm not interesting to look at. I still have a scab on my nose and bandages on my hands.

But he doesn't seem to be curious about my injuries, he's looking deeper than that. He notices me matching his stare, and we lock eyes for a moment. I imagine I can see the cold-blooded killer he used to be under the emotionally beaten exterior he's worn for more than two decades. Is "The Shark" still in there?

I remember what Eddie had told me, about how Old Harold had exacted his revenge on the man responsible for killing his son's family. Yet he was still damaged. Empty. Sitting in the corner, listening to people relive the horror of losing their own children, and the ongoing pain of life without them.

I'm the one who breaks eye contact, shifting my focus to the young woman relating how difficult it has been for her remaining children after the oldest died of a neuromuscular disease.

I look back and he's still staring at me. But it's not accusatory, or pitying, or annoyed. It's like he's trying to send me a mental message. Shouting at me with his eyes.

But I can't hear what he's trying to tell me. I can't make out the words.

What are you trying to say?

He just nods, as if he's already told me the answer.

"Are you all right?" Rebecca whispers in my ear?

I turn to look at her and realize that I've been staring at Harold longer than I thought I was. The others are breaking up into the post-sharing gatherings around the coffee and cookies.

"I'm fine," I tell her and offer a reassuring pat on her hand.

"I'm going to talk to Amy."

"Okay."

She gives my arm a squeeze, smiles, and gets up to make her way toward the corner Amy has staked out with a cup of coffee cradled in her hands.

I look back toward Old Harold, but he's gone. I look around and catch a glimpse of the tattered tales of his overcoat slipping out the door. I stand to follow, but a hand on my shoulder stops me.

It's Brian. "Got a minute?" he asks.

I look back toward the door, then offer Brian a friendly smile and a small white lie. "Sure, but I've got this nagging feeling that I left my headlights on. Just going to run out and check."

"Sure, sure," he says, and takes his hand away.

I nod clumsily, and wind my way through the group to the door Harold left by. Outside, I scan the parking lot. Looking for any of the cars that have their lights on or are starting their engines. It occurs to me that I don't even know if Harold even has a car. I run to the corner and look down each street, first one direction, then the next. I spot him in the halo of a dim streetlamp a half a block away and jog toward him.

He hears my footsteps and turns. At first, he seems alarmed, but not afraid—more wary, as if daring trouble to find him, poised almost like a predator. When he sees it's me, his stance relaxes to that of a harmless old man. He waits for me to catch up, and I slow to a walk.

"Harold—Mr. Finn," I begin without any clear idea of what I want to say to him. I look to him for some help, hoping that he'll say out loud what he was trying to silently convey to me back in the meeting room. But there's only an inquisitive look.

"Is there... is there something you wanted to say to me?" I ask.

He stares at me blankly.

"I just got the feeling, that you were trying to tell me something, and I don't know what it is."

He nods.

I sigh, exasperated. "See, that's the thing. Why did you just nod? Are you telling me there is something you want to tell me? Or confirming that I don't know what it is? Or do you just nod at random moments."

He lowers his head, then turns to walk away.

I head him off.

"No. No, you can't just walk away from me. I know about you. I know who you were, and what happened to your son and his family. What is it? What do you want to say?"

He looks at me with an air of compassion this time. For a moment I think he's on the verge of tears, but instead he takes a deep breath, then swallows, as if he's fighting back words trying to push their way out of him.

Then, he stands a bit taller, and reaches out and puts a firm hand on my shoulder. The frailty is gone from his face, there is an intensity behind his eyes that frightens me. It reminds me of Mikey Manzonetti. It reminds me of the killer I sometimes see in the mirror.

"Look, kid, you know how it is with this group. We all can say to each other, 'I know how you feel' and mean it. You and me more than any of the others."

He knows.

"You say you know me. You say you know my story. I believe you know part of it, and have guessed more of it, but I promise, you don't know it all."

He pauses, gathering his thoughts. "Their names, they stay with you. The people you lose. The people you…"

The people you kill, I think.

He nods.

"I've killed more people than I can count. Men, women, rich, poor, people in the prime of their lives, and some already on their deathbeds. I remember all their faces.

"They haunt me," he adds, then he looks around him, as if staring down unseen apparitions. "All of them. All the time." Then he looks back at me. "But it's not too late for you."

Too late for what?

His grip on my shoulder softens, and he pats it in a slow rhythm like a feeble heartbeat. "You have so much life left," he says, "you've done enough, you can stop now."

He lets go, then his posture droops again and the light behind his eyes dims as he turns and walks away.

I watch him go, giving in to the futility of my quest for any further understanding. His final, cryptic words hang in front of me.

A black SUV creeps along the street across from me. I recognize it as the one Vitali's goons used to follow me to the movie theater.

I stop and stare at the faces hidden behind tinted windows.

It doesn't move.

I continue back toward the meeting, and they follow me.

I stop once more, take a breath, then walk into the street straight toward the SUV.

Its engine revs and it races away with a brief squeal of rubber and a quickly dissipating cloud of engine exhaust.

I put my hands in my pockets to keep them from shaking, but that just inflames their unhealed wounds and sends lightning bolts of pains up my arms. I realize that I was hoping there would be a confrontation, that something would occur to stop the runaway train I find myself on.

But it seems there is no other course but onward. Despite my own misgivings, despite Old Harold's cryptic warnings, and despite common sense.

I walk back to the meeting, thinking up a second white lie to tell Brian as to why it took so long to check my headlights, but by the time I get back, the meeting has broken up, and Brian is gone.

twenty five

"Figure it out!" Rebecca demands. She hasn't taken my latest attempt to call off killing Justin Buermann very well.

I shake my head. "Look, we don't know when exactly he's going to be at his hideout, and if we did, we'd have Vitali's men on our tail. We can't do it. At least not now. We have to lie low."

"For how long?" she asks.

"A few months," I tell her, "a year at the most."

She slams her hands down on the dining room table, then stands and turns her back to me.

"There's too much that can go wrong. We have to wait for Manzonetti to back off."

She faces me, a determined look in her eyes. "So, you think we should allow Justin Buermann to go on with the farce he's perpetrating? Let him marry Dawn McAllister? Sleep in her bed while he fucks drug whores on the side?"

"Rebecca—"

"Is that what we've become?"

"We can't be responsible—"

"We are responsible! Once we found out that he's a monster, that he always has been, how can we let him... it's Vitali all over again."

I shrug. "I know it's hard. But there's nothing we can do right now without risking ourselves."

"If you knew how hard it was, you would be coming up with a way to make it work, not excuses."

"They're not excuses. They're reasons. And good ones."

"We can't wait."

I stand to make my point once more. "We have to. There's no way we can—"

"I'm pregnant."

I fall back into the dining room chair behind me, the room spinning as I process her revelation. I almost forget to breathe.

Pregnant?

Am I happy? Mad? How am I supposed to feel?

"Well?" she asks. "Don't you have anything to say?"

"I…" *Say something, you idiot!* "That's fantastic."

She raises her eyebrows at me in that way that means I should reconsider what I just said and come up with something better.

"It's just unexpected—in a good way. I mean, a baby." I smile, but I know she sees the fear behind it. "How do you feel about it?"

She shrugs and sits back down. "I'm keeping it."

"Of course."

"I've been thinking about it, ever since…"

She doesn't need to say the name, she doesn't need to say, "Nick," I know exactly what she means.

I reach out for her hand. "We've done what we started out to do. We've done more than we ever meant to. And now… now we have a chance to start over."

"What, like he never existed?"

"No, no. I just meant… I thought my life was over. That there was no reason to go on. And now…"

She takes my outstretched hand into hers. "And now we have that reason."

"Right."

She lets go, closes her eyes and takes a deep breath. "It just doesn't feel right. How can we bring a child into a world where people like Justin Buermann get to do whatever they want, take advantage of whomever they want, destroy lives and keep on living themselves?

"If you want this, if you want our child and a life with me, there's only one way we can do it. We have to finish this."

"It is finished."

"No." She sits back, fierce determination on her face.

I realize that if the mere possibility of being with her again was enough for me before, the prospect of being a father again, of having that unconditional love in my life once more…

"How?" I ask.

"*We* can find a way," she insists.

She puts a hand to her belly.

And I nod.

twenty six

I come in early to the office so that I can clear out the day's work and make sure the recovery from my deployment screw-up is on track.

Then I hide myself in the server room and spin up my virtual terminal.

I start by looking up everything I can find on the McAllister Foundation, particularly the outreach programs featuring Justin Buermann. There are videos on the website of his presentations. There are touching testimonials of people whose lives he turned around.

There is a schedule of upcoming events.

I scroll through the dates and locations noting a series of local high school programs next week featuring Buermann.

He will be in town.

And chances are that that means he'll want to escape the hypocrisy of his life by filling his veins or nostrils with whatever drugs he can buy with his fiancée's money, and—as Rebecca eloquently put it— fuck some drug whores.

But when? Does he ever spend the night there?

Right about this time I regret having destroyed the surveillance cameras we used to track Anthony Vitali's comings and goings. But then I realize that with him, we were spying on someone who followed a schedule. Someone who had a regular Saturday night routine.

Getting video on Buermann would be an exercise in futility. I wouldn't learn anything about him. He was all over the place. He traveled. A lot. And his little hideaway was a situation of opportunity, not a lifestyle.

I had no idea how he got there. How long he stayed. How often he brought someone with him.

My initial plan was based on being able to watch his place in person. But with Vitali's goons on my tail, that would be next to impossible.

I start looking into cellular based GPS tracking devices like the one we planted on Vitali, but with live tracking. But then I realize a simple ride in an Uber could circumvent that.

"Got kids?" a voice asks me.

I look up, startled to see the smiling face of a short, squat blond man peeking at my screen.

"Uhm, can I help you?" I say, as I check my screen for anything incriminating or inappropriate. The only thing visible are the search results for GPS trackers.

"Oh, sorry, we haven't been introduced. Sam West." He extends his hand and I automatically shake it. "I just started this week, it's been kinda crazy."

"Yeah," I say, and raise a hand singling myself out. "That would be 'cause of me."

"I heard. This isn't the best way to tell you, but I'm your new boss."

"Oh." The realization sinks in. Of course, Roger needed to fill the spot that I was supposed to take. I guess I'm grateful he didn't hire Dawn McAllister. "Congratulations," I offer.

"Yeah, awkward. I know you were supposed to get the job."

"I'm just grateful for the opportunity to make things right." I indicate the screen. "Sorry about the non-work activity, I'm just—"

"Aah, don't worry about it," he says reassuringly. "As long as you get the work done, I think it's perfectly all right. It's all about balance. Just as long as it's nothing NSFW or, you know, selling trade secrets to the competition."

I laugh along with Sam. "No, nothing like that." I quickly think of a reason why I would be looking at GPS tracking gadgets. "My wife—

well, my ex-wife, but we're working it out—she's in real estate. Never takes a mileage deduction because she can't be bothered with filling out the IRS compliant logs, so I thought—"

"Smart." He says. "I got this thing that plugs into the on-board diagnostics port, does the GPS thing with a phone, but also tracks hard accelerations and hard braking—I have a teenager just starting to drive. He hates it. He tells me he gets graded at school all day long, he doesn't want to be graded while he's hanging out with his friends, but, that's the price of being a new driver in the digital age."

"Yeah, my parents would've had a whole different opinion of me if they could've tracked all the things I did when I was in high school."

"You and me both!" He laughs again. "Well, just wanted to say hi, and thanks for everything you're doing. I'm glad you're sticking around."

"Well, I'm sorry you had to start off in the middle of a shit storm like this."

He ignores my self-deprecating apology. "Listen, when things settle down, let's do lunch. I'm sure you have a lot of ideas for what we should be doing better or differently around here."

"Sure."

He smacks me on the arm. "I'll send you a link for that thing I got for my son. I'm pretty sure they have a business mileage logging feature, too."

"Thanks."

He nods and winds his way back out of the server room. I can't help thinking it should have been me on his end of that conversation, but that path is gone, and I wonder how long I can remain on this new one.

twenty seven

I subtly point out the black SUV parked across the street.

Eddie squints into the afternoon sun as he sits in what I'm coming to think of as "our booth" in the diner down the street from my apartment.

"They're still following you?"

"Since the bowling alley. These are different guys. Do you recognize them?"

The windows are rolled down on the SUV, Eddie takes another look.

"The driver I know, Freddy Federico. The other guy… I need a better look."

"Are they waiting to, you know…" I leave the question hanging, hoping Eddie gets my drift without my broadcasting it to any curious passersby.

"Kill you?" Eddie shakes his head. "If they were, you wouldn't see them coming. No, this is just a message."

"What's the message?" I ask.

Eddie points his thumb in the direction of the SUV. "They're watching you."

"Oh, thanks, I never would've figured that out without your keen insight into the world of organized crime," I respond, sarcastically.

He raises his hands in a mock defensive gesture. "Hey, I don't pretend to know everything about how these guys think."

"Best guess," I counter.

"Hmm, well, maybe they're trying to frighten you."

"Jeez. It's working."

"You could go back to the police."

That's all I need. Cops keeping an eye out for me while the mob shakes me down while I'm trying to plan an impossible murder, I think to myself.

"What could they do?"

"Well, it's just a thought."

"What else is there? I'm thinking trying to find Vitali and asking him would be difficult?"

Eddie scratches his head. "Well, I can think of a few places you go to find him. But you're not going to be able to talk to him unless he wants to talk to you. And if he wants to talk to you, well, you know how that goes."

I nod.

"So, the only way to figure out what is going on, is to just let it play out. Wait for the other shoe to drop," Eddie says.

"I don't even know exactly why the first shoe dropped."

He shrugs.

The waitress brings us pie and tops off our coffees.

Eddie stirs in an excessive amount of sugar, then starts poking at his pie. "Listen," he says, "I wanted to apologize again. For the thing with the group."

I let his apology hang in the air for a while. It was still a bit of a sore subject, one I discover I have not completely let go of.

"I crossed the line. I know that. Sometimes I forget that there are real people behind the words of a story."

"It's okay," I reassure him. "I understand—well, I don't completely, but I'm willing to try to get past it."

"Thanks. I only bring it up because of Harry Finn."

"Old Harold?" I ask, my curiosity now piqued.

"Yeah, I did some more digging around on him."

"What did you find?"

"I know you're going to think I'm crazy, but I think he's the one."

"The one what?"

"The one killing the child killers."

I raise my eyebrows in surprise. Doesn't this guy let go of anything?

"Look, I know you can write off some of the deaths to coincidence. But there's a pattern. Almost every July, starting a few years after Finn's family was killed, there's been a death."

Okay, at least he's narrowing his suspicions—away from the murders that can be traced to me. "That's kind of thin," I suggest.

He sighs, almost despondent. "You're right. But there's something about it. And now that I add a retired mob hitman to the mix, the anniversary of his son's death, the profile of the victims…"

"You want my honest opinion?"

"Of course."

Suddenly, some of the things that Old Harold said to me on the street make sense. Is that what he was getting at? He knew what I was doing, because… because that's what he was doing, too?

"Sounds like you're reaching," I say to him. "Sounds like you want that bestseller."

Eddie taps the table with his fingers for a moment, thinking.

"Well, it is a good story. And there's something about it. My gut is telling me, there's something there…"

"My gut is telling me it wants some pie," I say, hoping to change the subject. And we both dig into generous slices of French Silk.

twenty eight

I check the mailbox when I get home, but it's empty. Rebecca must be back from work already.

I climb the stairs and walk down the hall to the apartment. I've been practicing what I'm going to say to her for the last couple of days. All of my research, the constant watchfulness of Vitali's men, and now Eddie Horne's relentless journalistic intuition.

There's no way we can pull this off. There's just no way I can think of that we can find out when Buermann is going to be at his secret place. Anything I can think of to shake the mob goons would make it nearly impossible to get in and out of there successfully—considering my last encounter with the locals.

She's got to see that. She has to understand that this is not the right time. We have to walk away from this one. We can tip off the McAllister's about the drugs, derail his plans to marry Dawn, maybe even get him arrested. That would be enough, wouldn't it? Take away the nice, comfortable life he's conned his way into? She has to see that it's the only thing that makes sense.

I enter the apartment. The living room is empty.

"Rebecca? You home?"

"In the dining room," she says.

I turn the corner and see her sitting at the table with Amy.

I smile a greeting to Amy who clearly has a pregnancy glow about her even though she's barely showing.

"I had an idea," Rebecca says.

"I see," I respond, nodding a hello to Amy.

"Hi," Amy says back.

"Sit," Rebecca invites.

I round the table and sit across from Rebecca and Amy.

"You told her," I say.

Rebecca nods, then smiles.

"So, is that your idea? We get a single soon-to-be-mother involved as an accessory to murder?"

"Just listen," she says. "I was thinking about what you've been saying, how it would be difficult to find out when Justin is going to be at his apartment, how we avoid the guys in the Black SUV, how we get away with it all so that we're around to raise our baby."

"It's not possible, Rebecca, I've been trying, honest I have, but there's just no way, not now at least."

"But there is," she insists.

I shake my head. "Even with Amy, there's just no way. We can't—"

There's a knock at the door.

Rebecca starts to rise from her chair.

"I'll get it," I say, and get up myself and head for the door. I press my eye against the peephole. There's a couple outside our door. Familiar faces.

It's Tina and Larry. Jeremy's parents.

I stand back from the door. Rebecca walks past me, shoots me a reproachful stare, then opens the door.

"Come on in," she says.

They walk inside and Rebecca closes the door behind them. She escorts them to the dining room.

"Hi Tina, Larry," Amy says.

"Oh my goodness," Tina exclaims, "Look at you! When is your due date?"

"End of October," Amy answers.

I pull Rebecca aside. "What's going on?"

"You're right. We can't do this with just Amy's help."

"You told them, too?"

"Yes, of course I did. We need them." She slips out of my grasp and goes into the dining room. "Can I get you anything?" she asks our newly arrived guests. "Coffee? Wine? I think I have some beer."

"I'll take a beer," Larry replies.

"Make it two," Tina adds.

I'm frozen. I feel naked and exposed. What did she tell them? What do they know?

"Can you give me a hand?" Rebecca asks me as she crosses to the kitchen.

I follow, and once we're out of view, whisper into her ear, "What are they doing here?"

"Helping, of course," she answers.

There's another knock at the door.

"I'll get it," Amy shouts from the other room.

Rebecca grabs a couple of beers from the refrigerator, hands them to me along with the bottle opener from a drawer, and then picks out a couple ginger ales from the fridge before closing it. "Come on, they're waiting."

I follow her back to the dining room, where Amy is orchestrating a reunion with our two newest guests, Yule and Wendy.

Erica's parents.

When I walk in the room, they all fall silent. Rebecca walks past me, hands one of the ginger ales to Amy, then takes the beers from me and hands them to Tina and Larry.

"Well, everyone, we're almost all here."

Almost?

Larry stands up. He crosses to me and grabs my hand and pumps it firmly.

I wince as my palm is still rather tender.

"Sorry," he says. "Tina and I, we don't have the words to tell you how much what you did made a difference in our lives."

Wendy takes a step toward me, starts to say something, but then takes another step and throws her arms around me. I can feel her tears running down my neck. Yule pats me on the shoulder.

I had nothing to do with Lorenzo's killing. But obviously, Rebecca gave me credit for relieving their agony as well.

Rebecca steps up between Yule and Wendy. "I'm glad you could come."

"Anything you need," Yule says. "Just ask."

I step back. This is too much. This is wrong.

"Do you people understand what we've done? What we want to do?"

"Of course they do," Rebecca answers.

I look to her, then to all the faces in the room. They aren't the same faces I saw at the support group. These aren't just grieving parents.

There is another aspect to their presence, a purpose that has managed to ensnare them into its dark clutches.

Do they know who they are now?

This is the real Dead Kids Club.

There's another knock.

I sigh, weary. Who is it now?

I sink into a chair and bow my head, afraid to see who it is, who else Rebecca has sucked into our conspiracy.

"Hello, everyone, sorry we're late," a familiar voice says.

I feel a hand squeeze my shoulder and look up to find Brian's eyes smiling down on me.

We're late?

Rebecca ushers our final guest of the evening into the dining room.

Everyone makes way for her, Larry pulls out a chair at the head of the table, and Barbara Brown takes her seat.

The meeting can now come to order.

twenty nine

Rebecca brings in a couple folding chairs from the living room closet to accommodate everyone at the table. They all look to me, even Barb.

Brian is the first one to speak. "Rebecca told us you didn't know we were coming, that this would be a surprise to you. But I want you to know, it wasn't a surprise to us when she told us what you two have been doing.

"I think we all knew, in the backs of our minds, deep in our hearts, that the people who took our children didn't just happen to die. But we also didn't want to ask any questions. When a prayer gets answered, you don't ask God why, you just say thank you."

"Thank you," says Amy.

The rest of them join in the chorus. "Thank you."

Rebecca takes my hand. I look over to her. She's smiling.

I shake my head. "You should all go home. Forget about this. You shouldn't be involved."

"You shouldn't have to bear this alone," Wendy replies. "We all owe you so much."

"Is it true?" Barb asks.

All eyes turn to her.

Barb's usual veneer of compassion and forgiveness has given way to an intensity I've never seen in her before, even when she was upset when things slipped out of her control at group. "Is Justin Buermann the monster who Rebecca says he is. Has all of it been a lie?"

There's no point in keeping anything in anymore. I nod. "I saw it myself. He was unfaithful to his fiancée, he does drugs, he has an apartment he keeps secret from her where I found more drugs and evidence of habitual infidelities. His community outreach is a farce. He's not who he pretends to be. There is no remorse, no repentance, no redeemable aspects to his character whatsoever.

"He's as close to evil as I've ever seen," I conclude.

"Then..." she pauses before going on, determination setting into her face, "then we want to help."

I stand to speak to all of them. "Look, I know how all of you feel. I know. But it's not possible. There are too many things that can go wrong, and with more people involved... I can't ask any of you—"

"You don't have to ask," Brian interrupts. "Just tell us what you need."

I look at them, at their eager faces staring back at me, waiting for me to tell them what to do. How they can help me kill a man.

And Barb. Barb! How could the woman who preached forgiveness and acceptance for all those years... how could she be here? How could she be a part of this?

And while my mind tries to reconcile the Browns' involvement, how Rebecca managed to persuade them to help us do the one thing they had worked so hard to remove the need from us to do, I was also pulling together elements of a new plan. A way to actually pull this off.

We aren't just two anymore. There are nine. Nine people, nine sets of eyes and ears... nine ways things can go wrong.

Rebecca squeezes my hand, and my doubts and fears evaporate.

"All right," I say with a tone of acceptance, "If we're going to do this, there are a couple rules. One, we come up with a plan and follow it exactly. And two, if anything goes wrong, if anyone is compromised, we walk away from it. This only works if we can get away with it."

I see a smile on Rebecca's face. This is what she wanted. The part of me that was capable of planning a murder.

I sit back down in my chair.

"Listen carefully," I begin. "We don't write anything down. Tomorrow, I want all of you to go individually to the first place you can think of that sells those pay as you go phones, get the smart kind with the touch screen. You pay cash and bring them to me. I'll activate them under false names and emails and then I'll give you back a phone other than the one you bought."

Everyone nods. It's a bit of a risk to have everything go through me, but that's the only way I can think of to make sure it gets done correctly and securely.

"I'll load them up with an app so we can chat with each other, one where the messages self-destruct after they're read. It will be completely anonymous and untraceable, but we'll still use code words in all of our communications. We only communicate via the app, no phone to phone calls—unless it's a call you would make amongst yourselves normally on your own lines. Keep your regular routine as much as you can."

I can see the intense concentration of everyone in the room, their keen attention is focused on me. No one is interrupting with questions or making their own suggestions. More and more I'm convincing myself that this can actually work.

"As I see it," I explain, "there are three major obstacles we need to overcome. One, we need to find out when Buermann is heading toward his drug pad. I know he's going to be local next week, he has several high school outreach dates scheduled, so we should be able to keep track of him and determine when he's heading in the direction of his hideaway.

"Two, I—and likely Rebecca as well—have a tail, some guys who seem to be intent on following us. They are connected to some local mob figures, so if that bothers anyone to cross their paths..."

No one speaks up, no one even betrays any indication of hesitation or reconsideration.

I continue. "And three, we need airtight alibis and an escape plan for me."

"For us," Rebecca interjects. "I'm doing this with you. Just like the others."

From past experience, I know this is an argument I cannot win, so I nod.

"For us. This is what I'm thinking…"

And for the next hour and twenty minutes, I explain to my attentive pupils exactly how we're going to kill Justin Buermann.

thirty

Rebecca and Amy start clearing the table as the group breaks up. I see Barb in the living room, standing at the window by herself.

"Barb."

She turns to me.

"I have to ask..."

She nods, then pulls me as far away from the others and Brian as she can.

"Brian has a gun," she explains. "He's had it for years, used to go shooting with his dad. I never liked it, and when his father passed, I thought he got rid of it.

"Lately, he's been... I caught him just sitting with it, staring at it, and I knew, I just knew, that he was trying to work up the nerve to kill himself."

"I don't think he would do that," I say.

"I've been married to him for over twenty-five years. I know that's what he was thinking.

"I can't lose him, too," she says. "When Rebecca came to us and explained what you were planning to do, he came back to life... he came back to me.

"I can't go on without Betsy *and* Brian. Whatever I need to do to keep him in my life, I'll do it.

"I can't lose them both."

I nod, understanding her reasons, now.

They're not too different from my own.

thirty one

Justin Buermann's schedule during the days he conducts his outreaches to local high schools is fairly consistent. What I think of now as my team has him covered everywhere he might go. Of those of us who work, some have called in sick, others have taken vacation and personal days, or scheduled imaginary afternoon dentist or doctors' appointments to make sure we're available during the critical hours when Justin is on his own.

We work in pairs, rotating locations from day to day. One couple covers the McAllister residence. Another stakes out the high school where he's speaking that day. And a third drives through the neighborhood where his drug pad is, taking note of any police or gang activity that could interfere with our operation, and another tracks the guys in the black SUV.

Rebecca has been putting in half days. She's shared her good news about the baby with her coworkers and is using morning sickness as an excuse to come and go as she needs.

I've been working overnights, having convinced my new supervisor, Sam, that I can get more done while the systems are relatively quiet from the day's noise.

Vitali's goons reliably follow me back and forth. I note that they are using at least two different vehicles, and perhaps as many as three or more different teams—one of which Rebecca reports is following her as well. Evading them is going to be the biggest challenge, but we have a plan for that.

During the day, I sit in front of a jigsaw puzzle spread out on the coffee table in our living room. I've designated certain quadrants of it to represent the various locations we're monitoring, and the way the pieces are arranged and assembled serve as visual mnemonics to help me track Buermann's movements. I'm doing well keeping it all in my head, but with all the moving parts I want to make sure I don't miss anything, so the puzzle is my way of keeping track. To the casual observer, it looks like a puzzle being worked by someone who is in no hurry to complete it. To me, it's a map of Justin Buermann's life. With a swipe of my hand, any semblance of order that anyone might chance to perceive would be erased.

I'm surprised to find myself feeling proud. Everyone is doing exactly what they're told. They're following the rules I set down for them, the ephemeral messages we send back and forth are brief and use the code words we had agreed upon.

The first two days of surveillance are practice. I'm very confident that Justin won't indulge in his private, illicit rituals until Dawn is out of town. According to the foundation website, she is scheduled to address a session of the state legislature today regarding a bill that would support the foundation's work.

Today will be the day.

After weeks on the road, and three days at home wearing the mask of a reformed, repentant sinner seeking penance and absolution, I'm confident that instead of returning to the empty house Justin shares with his fiancée, he'll run as fast as he can to his personal drug den and engulf himself in the sweet bliss of his sins.

I can feel it.

I send a message to the group. "Be ready. The purple egret is hungry."

Okay, as codes go, it's a bit corny. Rather than assigning a specific code word to Buermann, I've instructed the group to use a combination of a random color and bird name. So far, he's been the yellow goose, white dove, brown pigeon, blue duck and mauve hummingbird.

A reference to any retail store is his home.

The schools use random university or college names.

And for the drug pad, we use restaurants.

I hope my reference to the "purple egret" being hungry is not lost on the others.

Today is the day he gives in to his demons, and the day I unleash my own.

Today is the day he dies.

thirty two

Rebecca comes home around lunch time.

We make sandwiches and eat in the living room, my burner smartphone is on the coffee table amid the puzzle pieces, and we watch as updates trickle in, and then ten seconds later are automatically purged.

I add or connect puzzle pieces with each missive.

Rebecca rolls her eyes at my ridiculous spycraft, but I don't want to miss anything.

She finishes her sandwich, gets up and crosses to the window to check on our minders.

"Still there," she reports. She glances in a different direction. "Both of them." Then she turns to me, a hand over her lips as if she's said something she shouldn't have. "Oops, I mean, 'the moles are in their burrow.'"

I grimace. She's mocking me—rodents refer to the mob goons in my code—but I know it's just to lighten the tension.

"You only have to use the code words when you're messaging."

"Well, you can't be too careful," she taunts as she sits back down beside me and gives me a warm, lingering kiss.

Her teasing and her kiss work. I smile appreciatively.

"So," she says, "now we just wait?"

I nod. "His outreach program for today is scheduled as an after-school assembly, so he'll likely be tied up with that until around five. He left his house about an hour ago and stopped at Denny's for lunch."

"Denny's?" she asks.

"Yes, an actual 'Denny's,' not his drug pad. Larry uses a specific location, so that means—"

"I know," she says, offering a quick peck on the lips. "Just teasing. You really think this is the day?"

"I do."

"Well, I have to drop off some brochures for that house on Grand, but I have a couple hours to kill."

The way she traces the inseam of my pant leg sends a clear message as to how she wants to fill those hours, but as tempted as I am, now is not the time.

"You know we can't."

She takes away her hand and gives me another kiss, this time lingering close. "I know," she whispers. "Being pregnant just makes me so horny."

"I remember," I say with a smile. "After," I promise.

"After," she agrees, then punctuates it by gently biting my lower lip and tugging on it until it pulls free.

My phone dings with the alert of a new message.

We both shift our attention to screen, reading the text before it vanishes.

"*The olive ostrich is at Ole Miss.*"

"Must be Yule, he's so alliterative."

"Yeah."

Rebecca picks up the TV remote and finds a mindless afternoon judge show to pass the time, then kicks off her shoes and nestles next to me.

I set a puzzle piece that indicates that Buermann is at the school, then put an arm around Rebecca and let the rhythm of her breathing, and the soft pressure of her body against mine provide a welcome distraction from the waiting.

thirty three

I am alone in the apartment, watching Judge Judy berate a young girl for "loaning" her boyfriend thousands of dollars when he had no means to pay her back.

Rebecca left a couple hours ago to drop off brochures and help a coworker prepare for an open house. We have several rendezvous points depending on Buermann's actions, but for now, we're just waiting.

A message lights up the smartphone's screen.

"*The Sienna Sparrow has graduated from Stanford.*"

This is it.

I tap my own message into the screen. "*Off to the movies.*" Which is my very clever code for me going to the movie theater where I'll sneak out the back and make my way to the train station and meet up with Rebecca. From there, Amy will take us to Buermann's place.

"*Springing the rat trap,*" Brian messages, indicating that he and Yule will meet Rebecca at a predetermined location where they will help Rebecca lose the mobsters in the SUV following her. This is the trickiest part of my plan. I thought about having Rebecca meet me at the movie theater, but that would give them the opportunity to have an extra set of eyes, and I couldn't predict with any confidence that both sets of goons would wait in the parking lot.

I grab my backpack which is stuffed with surgical suits and rubber gloves and paper booties. We'll suit up when we get to the spot between the buildings where I had previously sneaked into his ground-floor apartment.

A message dings.

"See you at Thomas' place," is the message form Rebecca.

Thomas the Tank Engine was one of Nick's favorite TV shows, his place is the train station.

thirty four

I arrive at the movie theater, park, grab my freshly charged smartphone and my backpack and head for the entrance.

A new message appears as I cross the parking lot.

"Rats caught in the trap."

I let out a sigh. The plan was to have Rebecca drive down a narrow alley, and then, once through, Brian and Barb would drive down the same alley in the opposite direction hopefully blocking the Mob goons from following her.

The message indicates it was a success. She only needed a few minutes to double back and elude any chance they could pick up her trail, and the Brown's would play the confused, older couple who are afraid to back up in a tight alley.

I buy my movie ticket, and glance over my shoulder at where my own SUV shadow is parked.

One of my followers slams the door of the passenger side and heads for the theater.

Shit! He's following me inside.

I head into the theater I bought a ticket for and take a seat a few rows back from the screen where I can keep an eye on the entrance. Maybe he just needed to use the men's room?

Then the leather-jacketed man enters the theater. He casts a passing glance in my direction, as if he's looking for an empty seat in the sparsely populated auditorium, and climbs the stairs to take a vantage point where he can see me.

Damn!

I think fast, check my watch as the pre-movie presentation plays on the big screen. I get up, head for the exit and then cross back toward the concession stand. While I wait for my popcorn and coke, I catch a glimpse of my tail peeking around the corner. He spots me at the concession stand and then ducks back into the theater.

I pay for my snacks, then return to my seat in the now dark theater, setting my drink into the cup holder, and then start nibbling at the plain popcorn.

A message dings on my smartphone, and I rush to pull it out of my pocket before the ten seconds elapse and it vanishes forever.

"The Lavender Huron is heading for Arby's."

Buermann is on his way to the apartment.

I make a show of being uncomfortable in my seat, shifting and fidgeting.

Then I stand, stuff my popcorn in the adjacent seat and inspect the chair I was sitting in as if searching for something mechanically wrong with it.

I angrily flap the seat down, swearing under my breath. Then I give up, grab my soda out of the cup holder and move a couple seats down. When I reach over to retrieve my popcorn, my fingertips graze the top of the box and I spill the entire contents onto the ground.

The movie is just starting.

I grab the empty container, leave my soda and other belongings behind and exit the theater hopefully giving my unwanted guardian the impression that I'm heading back to the concession stand for a refill and will be back shortly.

Instead, I dump the container in the nearest garbage bin and stride confidently toward the rear exit, not daring to look back.

I step out into the afternoon sun and quicken my stride till I'm around the corner and on my way to the nearby train station. Only then do I cast a glance behind me.

There is no one following.

But it won't take long for the goon to realize he's been duped and collect his partner and start searching for me. If they're in contact with their counterparts following Rebecca, they'll know that she also escaped their scrutiny and realize something is up.

By then, hopefully, we'll be safely tucked away in the back of Amy's minivan and on our way to Justin Buermann's apartment.

The backpack.

I left it in the theater.

I grab the smartphone and am about to key in the abort code when I realize I'm a hundred yards from a drug store. I know Rebecca will demand we proceed even without the crime scene countermeasures. There are alternatives, we can carefully wipe down our fingerprints like I did on my first visit and burn our clothes and shoes. But the drug store is an opportunity to resupply, and I have enough cash with me for just such a contingency.

Whatever deity looks over revenge seeking vigilantes has got my back today.

thirty five

"*The silver seagull is sitting down to eat.*"

Yule and Wendy have successfully tracked Buermann to the apartment.

He's there.

I'm at the train station with a plastic bag filled with rubber gloves, paper booties, a couple over-sized T-shirts and a half dozen other sundries to make it look like a more typical visit to the drug store.

Rebecca should be here by now, but she's not.

Amy pulls up in her minivan.

I get in, slide into the back.

"Where's Rebecca?" she asks.

"I don't know, she got away from her tail, but I haven't heard anything since."

I pull out the smartphone and tap in a message.

"*Waiting at Thomas', are you close?*"

"Maybe she hit traffic, or there was an accident."

I shake my head. "No, something's wrong. She wanted to do this with me."

The phone dings.

"*Just barfed up lunch. You'll have to deal with that crazy crow without me.*"

Amy has the same message on her phone. "What is 'barfed up my lunch' code for?" she asks.

I shrug. "I think she actually barfed up her lunch. Maybe the morning sickness is really coming on."

"Maybe she has nerves," Amy suggests.

Not likely, I think.

"Whatever it is, I'm glad. It'll be safer with just me."

"I could—" Amy starts to suggest, but I cut her off with a look. "Or we can get one of the others to help?"

"No," I answer resolutely. "I've gotten them involved as much as I want to. All of you can walk away from this clean. I want to keep it that way. We have a window right now, and I'm going to take it. I don't want to have to go through all of this again."

"Okay," Amy agrees.

"Let's go."

Amy puts the van in gear and drives away from the station.

I stare at the screen just in time to see Rebecca's last message fade away.

thirty six

Yule and Wendy make a pass by Buermann's apartment and give the all clear. We're back on plan.

I slip on the T-shirt that subtly proclaims my affection for a certain brand of beer, the cap and sun glasses, then stuff a couple pairs of rubber gloves and shoe covers into my pockets and step out of Amy's minivan onto the street around the corner from the apartment.

Amy drives off and I casually check the surrounding buildings for anyone who may be paying attention. The street is deserted.

I continue on to the alley that cuts behind Buermann's building, it's devoid of people as well. There's no sign of the gang that harassed and assaulted me on my previous visit, nor anyone else that could interfere or be a witness.

I start to wish Rebecca was here. But just thinking of her and knowing that she and our baby are safe gives me the resolve I need to move forward. I not only promised Rebecca, but Barb as well.

One last killing.

One last child murderer safely tucked away in his own grave and I can finally move on with my life with Rebecca.

And the baby.

I can't let those thoughts distract me. I remain vigilant as I stroll as casually and purposefully as I can down the alley to the yard behind Justin's apartment. I open the gate and proceed to the space between buildings.

Once I'm in that secluded gangway, I allow myself to let out the breath I'd been holding and go over to the window for the kitchen. I slowly peek inside and immediately duck back out of site.

Buermann is in there, talking on a cell phone. I can hear his voice faintly through the single pane glass.

"Yeah, right. I know you took my shit. You're the only one who knew about it and you got my keys... Bullshit... No, I know exactly where I left it... I don't fucking care, just bring me another stash and we'll talk about the money later... Hey, do what the fuck I tell you, you owe me... That's right, asshole..."

The call ends. A moment later, I hear the TV come on.

I move to the living room window and risk another peek. Justin sits in a chair with his back to the window. He has a six-pack of beer on the tray table next to him, two of which are already empty. He chugs one, then opens another and starts sipping it.

He's watching television, but from where he is, he has a clear view to the bathroom and bedroom doors. I could probably slip from the bathroom to the bedroom without him seeing me, and then if I can get him to come to the bedroom, I can surprise him there.

Fortunately, he's playing the television loud, so I should be able to get through the bathroom window without being detected.

I creep along the outside wall till I get to the bathroom window. I work the screws out of the security grate and place it below the window where I can use it as a step up.

The bathroom window is still open — won't need the mini glass cutter I have tucked in my back pocket — I take a quick look around to make sure I'm not being watched.

It's all clear.

I put on the rubber gloves, then slip the paper booties over my shoes. The gangway is gravel, so I'm not worried about shoe prints there.

I step up on the grate, then slip my arms through the window and worm my way through until I'm balanced with my stomach resting on the sill, my torso and legs dangling in midair on either side of the wall.

I listen, making sure I haven't alerted Buermann. I hear him switch channels on the TV, then back to the ball game.

I lean forward, reaching for the sink below me.

Then I hear a rip.

My T-shirt has caught on a corner of the window frame. I try to work my way off of it, but I only end up making the tear bigger, so I move forward.

My hands rest on the edge of the sink, and I work my hips through the window. As I do so, more of my weight is transferred to the sink, and I hear a loud crack. The caulk that was holding the sink against the wall gives way, and my weight is pulling it even further, threatening to rip it out entirely. The only thing holding it up at his point are the thin copper pipes it's connected to.

I can't go back. If I want to get out, I have to come in first.

I pull myself through and walk my hands down to the toilet. It shifts under my weight as well. I feel the sink giving way, so I shift all my weight to the toilet, but my hand there slips and slides into the bowl. My fingers wedge into the bottom drain of the toilet as the rest of my body falls through the window.

My head crashes into the floor as my shoulder slams into the edge of the toilet bowl, and the rest of me tumbles down with a thud.

Did I yell out in pain? Did I make enough noise to be heard over the sound of the baseball game playing in the next room?

My hand is still wedged in the toilet, and I have to roll myself back up to untwist my arm enough to wrench it free with a jerk that ignites a burning pain in my shoulder, like someone trying to pry my arm off with a dull knife.

I manage to get to my knees and realize that my shoulder is dislocated.

I try to get to my feet, but a dull ache at the top of my head where it hit the floor turns into a dizzying spell of vertigo and I nearly black out.

The room comes back into focus.

I have to get out of here.

I try to raise my right arm, but the pain is intolerable, and I leave it dangling by my side.

The window is out.

Make a run for it? Would I be able to sprint to his front door, get out, get to a place where I can send my pickup message and get away before he catches me?

Before I can answer my own question, I realize that the sound from the television is gone.

I reach for the toilet tank lid with my good arm, but it's too heavy. I can't get a grip on it. I scan the room for anything else that can be used as a weapon. The towel rod?

I grab it and twist it from its brackets. It's a lightweight piece of plastic, but it's something.

"What the hell?" a voice asks from the bathroom doorway.

I turn to see Justin Buermann squinting at me through the beginning of his alcohol induced buzz. I grip the curtain rod firmly and plant my feet. The bathroom is tiny, I don't have any room to outmaneuver him.

"Hey, I know you!" he says.

I look up at him. His face is even more puzzled.

"You're that guy from the party. What the fuck? What the hell are you doing in my bathroom?"

I answer by jabbing at him with the towel rod, which only serves to make him angrier.

Then, something clicks in his head. Random dots connect in his beer-muddled brain, and his eyes widen. "You must be the fucker who stole my shit!"

I swing at him with the towel rod. He grabs it before it can make contact with his face and twists it out of my grasp.

I'm going to die, I realize.

My last thoughts are of Rebecca, the baby I'll never know, and her last words to me. "*You'll have to take care of that crazy crow on your own.*"

In the split second as Buermann raises the towel rod to strike at me, I realize there's something wrong with the message. "*Crazy crow.*" Not "*red,*" or "*blue,*" or "*chartreuse,*" but "*crazy.*" That's not a color. She knows the code. I drilled her on it till she could recite it in her sleep.

That message didn't come from Rebecca. Or if it did, she was trying to tell me something. She was trying to tell me that everything had gone to shit and to call it off.

I reach in my pocket for the smartphone.

The towel rod comes down against my neck. I ignore it and switch the phone on. It comes to life with the messaging app running. I key in the abort code. "*Fly.*" Just as my finger is about to hit the send button, the towel rod comes down again, this time on my wrist.

The phone flies out of my hand.

I scream in pain.

Buermann pushes me back, and I get tangled in the shower curtain. My head bangs against the wall, and I collapse into the tub, cracking my tailbone against its edge. Buermann starts kicking at me with his hard-heeled boots. I raise my good arm to block the blows, but most of them get by my ineffective defensive posture, cracking ribs, breaking my nose, knocking teeth loose.

"You thieving motherfucker!" he screams at me, as the blows and kicks rain down. "You're a dead man," he promises, "you're fucking dead!"

I feel reality start to slip away from me. The pain is so intense now that I hardly feel it any more. I close my eyes, lower my arm, and let go.

thirty seven

Then it all stops.
I hear a heavy thud.
Then a dragging sound.
A couple minutes after that, the shower curtain is lifted off of me.
I try to open my eyes, but one of them is swollen shut. The other only sees a blurry shadow.
"Can you stand?" it asks. It's a man's voice, a familiar one.
I reach for him with my good arm, and he pulls me up and out of the tub. I grab onto him, trying to steady myself. He wraps my arm around his shoulder and guides me out of the bathroom into the bedroom and seats me on the bed.
"Lie back," he instructs me.
I do so, and full consciousness starts to return.
He runs his hand over my right shoulder. I wince. I feel him place a foot against my side, then grab hold of my arm by the elbow and wrist.
"This is going to hurt. Try not to scream."
He pulls on my arm while pushing against my body with his foot. Just as I'm about to howl from the pain, the joint pops back into place and the agony is replaced with relief.
He turns his attention to my face, probing the wounds with his fingers.
"You have some fractures, and you're never going to be as pretty as you were before, but you'll live."

You'll live.

The words energize me, and I muster up enough energy to direct my attention to my savior.

"Harold?" I ask, not quite believing my still blurry vision.

No, it's not Old Harold standing over me. It's Harry "The Shark" Finn.

"Can you sit up?"

I push myself to a sitting position with my good arm and look around the room.

Justin Buermann is on the floor next to the bed. I lean over and see an ice pick sticking out the side of his head, and another one planted in his chest.

Harold sees me eying the body. "Don't worry, he's dead." He crosses over, retrieves the two ice picks and slips them into a plastic bag and then tucks them into an inside jacket pocket. "Smart of you to wear gloves. The booties are a nice touch, too."

I notice that he has on gloves of his own but is wearing canvas moccasins.

"How did you know I was here?"

"I followed you, thought you would do something stupid. I guess I underestimated you."

"I don't understand."

"No time to explain, we have to get you out of here."

I push myself to my feet. "My phone," I say, "in the bathroom."

He nods, then crosses into the bathroom, and comes back with the phone, dripping wet. "It fell in the toilet."

I take it from him and try the power button. Nothing.

"Anything else?" he asks.

"He caught me as I came in."

I wipe some blood from my mouth. "DNA," I respond, suddenly worried.

"As long as you're not in any databases, you should have nothing to worry about. You got lucky. If I hadn't come along…"

"I know. Thank you."

"You can thank me once we're out of here."

I suddenly remember something. "There's a dealer on his way."

"What?"

"I heard him on the phone a few minutes ago. Some guy is coming over with drugs."

"Then let's get going." He hands me my cap which has my sunglasses inside of it. I slide them painfully onto my face, then put on the cap and limp behind him toward the front door.

The pain is returning in spades. Every step tweaks my tailbone, and my face feels like someone took my head off and went bowling with it.

He takes a peek through the peep hole, then takes one last look around the room before asking me if I'm ready.

I nod.

Harold opens the door and the open space in the hallway is immediately filled with three dark shapes. Even with my diminished senses, I recognize the one in the middle.

Mikey Manzonetti.

thirty eight

"Who's this? Your grandpa?" Mikey asks.

Mikey's associates have their guns pointed at us, and they back us into the apartment. Mikey closes the door behind them.

"So, what have you boys been up to?"

Harold and I stand silent. I'm too weak and scared to say anything, but Harold watches Mikey with keen senses, taking in everything, somehow watching all three men at once.

"Search them," Mikey instructs his goons, as he takes a tour of the apartment.

One of them keeps his gun trained on us while the other holsters his and pats us down. He finds the ice picks and gloves in Harold's jacket, along with a pocketknife.

On me, they find only the multi-tool, glass cutter and about forty bucks in cash.

Mikey returns, a grin on his face. "Nice work in there. Killed him just like you did Anthony, huh?"

Neither of us say a word.

"I must say, I found your wife much more talkative."

My hands ball into fists.

"Ah, don't worry. She's okay. Didn't have to hurt her much to get her to spill the beans on you."

I start to lean forward. Harold holds out his arm in front of me, gently holding me back.

"Hey, I told you I would catch you. Didn't you believe me?"

There's a knock at the door.

Mikey's arrogance turns to concern. He glares at Harrold and me. "Who's that?" he asks in a low whisper.

The drug dealer, I think to myself. Buermann's resupply.

I shrug.

Mikey nods to his goons, and the one who searched us, walks up to the door, redraws his gun as he checks the peephole. He turns to Mikey and holds up a single finger.

Another knock. "J.B., you in there? I got your stuff."

The doorknob twists and the door swings open.

The drug dealer freezes when he sees the room full of people, none of whom are "J.B." He has a paper bag in one hand which falls to the floor. Suddenly, he turns and runs.

The goon closest to the door steps out into the hallway and fires a single shot.

There's a crashing sound as the drug dealer falls dead in a heap.

"All right, time to go. We'll do this back at the warehouse," Mikey says, then to Harold and me, "I don't have to tell you guys what'll happen if you try to get away or anything, do I?"

They escort us out of the apartment. We step over the body of the drug dealer, half of his head spread over a nearby wall, and out through the back doors of the apartment building. No one appears to have heard the shot—or if they have, they know better than to poke their heads into the hallway to see what's going on.

There is a black SUV parked in the alley. We're shoved into the back seat. Mikey takes the wheel as his goons keep us covered with their guns. "Hoods," he instructs, and the one in the back seat reaches into the cargo area and grabs a couple black sacks which he tosses to us.

I look to Harold. He gives me a slight nod, and we put the hoods over our heads.

The one I'm wearing smells of Rebecca's lavender scented soap.

In the blackness, the pain is vivid. I see images of Rebecca, beaten and bloody, and start thinking of how I'm going to kill Mikey Manzonetti.

thirty nine

We drive for nearly ten minutes.

When we stop, I hear the rattle of a motorized garage door opener.

The hood is yanked off my head, setting off a fresh wave of pain through my bruises, lacerations and fractures.

I blink with the one eye I can open and look around. We're in a small warehouse, part of which looks like it's dedicated to a machine shop. It's dimly lit, but I can see that there is an area in one corner where there's a folding table littered with bottles and cans and pizza boxes, and several folding chairs.

Tied to one of them is Rebecca, her back to me.

Harold and I are yanked out of the back of the SUV and escorted to where Rebecca is bound. As we approach, she lifts her head.

Her nose is crusted with dried blood, and one eye has a shiner. Her lip is cut and tears run down her cheeks. She smiles when she finally recognizes me. "You're alive!" she exclaims, relieved.

I nod. "Are you okay?"

"I'm fine," she says, "I'm so sorry. The baby," she explains.

"I know," I reassure her, "it's okay."

"All right, enough with the touching reunion," Mikey says. He positions a chair across from Rebecca, and motions for me to sit in it. Harold is left bookended by the two goons.

"So, this is how it's going to work. In a little while, Tony Vitali is going to come here. I'm going to tell him what I found in that poor fella's apartment and what you were doing there, and then he's going to give me the okay to pay you back for what you did to Anthony."

"What makes you think he'll believe anything you say after you beat him to a pulp?" Rebecca asks, nodding at my bruised face.

"Me?" Mikey says, amused, "Honey, that's the way I found him. Along with this old geezer."

She looks to me, silently inquiring what happened. Then she looks back at Old Harold. The confident, strong, purposeful man who rescued me has been replaced by his feeble, quiet, introverted alter ego.

"You're mistaken," she insists, then turns her gaze back to me. "He had nothing to do with your child murdering friend's death."

Mikey nods, considering, "An eloquent defense. A little thin on facts, but heartfelt. But I'm afraid it's not enough. You see, once I explain to Mr. Vitali that I found him at the scene of another killing, and that that guy was killed exactly the same way that Anthony was, I think the jury's gonna come back quick on that one."

I stare across at Rebecca, then flick my gaze to Old Harold.

She hasn't quite pieced it together yet. I never told her about Eddie Horne's theory about Harry Finn. She hasn't seen him in action, so, like Mikey, she sees only the little old man, the pathetic, worn out, bereaved shell of who he used to be.

The garage door rattles open.

A familiar limousine rolls in and parks next to Mikey's SUV.

The overhead door closes again.

A new set of goons step out from each door of the limo, and then Tony Vitali emerges, a stern and angry expression on his face.

"What the hell is this, Mikey?"

He strides over, his cane clacking against the concrete floor until he reaches Mikey's side, then looks at Rebecca and me. "I told you to leave these two alone."

Mikey starts to respond, but Tony cuts him off with a look. Then he turns and addresses his own bodyguards. "And I told you guys to protect them. How the hell did you let him get a hold of both of them."

The goons don't reply, they merely bow their heads shamefully.

Protect us?

Did I do this? Did I have it all wrong? I had assumed the SUVs were Mikey's guys waiting for a reason to snatch us, but were they really protecting us from him?

"Mr. Vitali," Mikey says, in a much less cocky tone, "if I could just explain. I know he killed Anthony. I can prove it. I caught him doing another guy the same way."

"Oh, really?" Vitali asks.

Old Harold starts to laugh. Just a chuckle at first, then louder and stronger, until Harry Finn returns with a deep throated guffaw.

All eyes turn to him.

Vitali squints with recognition. "Harry?"

"Hi, Tony. This is the goombah you replaced me with? You coulda done better."

"Shut up, old man," Mikey orders.

"You shut up," Vitali tells Mikey without taking his eyes off Harold. "Unless you're going to explain to me why you brought Harry Finn here."

Mikey's expression changes as a note of recognition and surprise takes over his face. "The Shark? This old man is The Shark?"

Vitali ignores him. "What gives, Harry?"

Harry nods toward me. "Come on, you really think that civilian could take down anyone, let alone your son?"

"No, of course not."

Mikey is getting frustrated. "Then who killed that junkie at the apartment?"

"I did," confesses Harold. He nods back toward me. "You really thought a guy who can barely see out of one eye, with a dislocated shoulder, a concussion and who knows what else could take out someone with such precision?"

"Then what the hell was he doing there?" Mikey asks.

"He followed me there."

"Bullshit. How did she know where he was?"

"He told her once he knew what I was up to."

Mikey shakes his head. He turns to Vitali, "This don't make no sense." He points a meaty finger at me. "That's Anthony's killer."

Harold ignores Mikey and speaks directly to Vitali. "We belong to the same grieving parents group. I've been going ever since Benjamin and his family were killed.

"At the last meeting, he confronted me, said he had figured out who I was, and what I've been doing."

Vitali is confused. "What do you mean, what you've been doing?"

"I took out that amateur after he missed me and killed Ben."

"I figured as much."

"And then, ever since, I've been doing the same for other parents, for those whose killers have escaped justice. Guess I wasn't as careful as I thought."

Rebecca shifts her attention from Harold to me, wondering how much of this I actually knew, and why I didn't tell her.

"He told me he knew what I was doing and begged me to stop. Your guys saw me talking to him on the street the other night."

Vitali looks to his men for confirmation, and one of them nods.

"He must've enlisted his wife, and I suspect some of the other members of the group to keep an eye on me. And when I went to make my move, he tried to stop me. And in the process, nearly got himself killed."

Vitali nods, "So, this junkie made the fatal mistake of underestimating you."

Harold nods.

Vitali takes a deep breath. "And what about Anthony?"

There is a long silence.

"I killed Anthony," Old Harold confesses. "I killed Anthony because he took away this couple's son, and I killed him because you were the one who gave the order that took away my son."

Vitali quietly stares Old Harold down.

"I've always known it was you, Tony. You shouldn't have let me live. You felt sorry for me, didn't you?" Old Harold smiles, a man confident that, in the end, the scales were balanced.

Vitali nods. "I was soft. But that's a mistake I can correct." He nods to his bodyguards. "Kill him."

The four men standing behind Vitali all draw their guns simultaneously and aim at Harold.

He just stands there and smiles, ready for whatever comes next.

A door explodes open.

Two bright flashes are accompanied by deafening bangs.

Everyone's attention is diverted to the source of the noise.

Harold snatches a gun from one of the bodyguards and fires it into the man's surprised face.

"Police! Everyone, on the ground!"

Another of the bodyguards fires at the incoming SWAT team.

They return fire.

I rush over to Rebecca. I try to release her from the chair, but she's taped to it, so I just drag her along with the chair into a corner and push her behind a file cabinet, then shield her with my body. The gunfire rages for what seems like a few minutes.

Then it stops.

I stay where I am, my arms wrapped around Rebecca. In the quiet of the aftermath, I can hear her breathing. "Is it over?" she asks.

"I think so," I whisper back. "We're fine now. Go with the story Harold told, okay?"

"Okay."

"Clear!" a voice yells.

"Clear!" another one adds.

"Freeze! Hands behind your head! Behind your head!"

I move my hands behind my head.

"On your knees!"

I obey.

"Face on the floor."

I sit back, then lean forward and wriggle myself to a prone position.

"Ma'am, are you all right?"

"I'm fine. He's with me."

"Just sit tight, we'll get it all sorted out in a minute."

The SWAT guy who commanded me to the floor pats me down. "Put your hands behind your back, one at a time."

I swing my left hand behind my back and feel the cold grip of a handcuff tighten around my wrist. Then I work my right hand back, my shoulder twinges from its recent dislocation. The cop grabs it and slaps the other cuff on. He turns me onto my back with his boot.

"I told you," Rebecca says, now free from the chair, "He's with me. He's my fiancé."

I glance across the floor. Harold stares back blankly, the life gone from his eyes.

forty

They lock me in a stark room with a stainless steel table, matching chairs and a flickering fluorescent light.

A paramedic tapes some butterfly stitches across the worst of my cuts and gives me a little white pill that takes the edge off my pain.

Detective Kort and another policeman question me. They tell me they just want to know what happened, and the sooner they get a statement, the sooner I can go home.

I give them a version of Old Harold's story.

They write it down, offer to get me whatever I might need. I ask for coffee, it's been a long day and I'm starting to feel it.

They bring me the coffee, then promise it will be just another few minutes.

Two hours later they return.

Kort now has a folder, with printed photos from the warehouse, and—he makes sure I see—Buermann's apartment.

They ask me to tell them the story once more.

I ask for a lawyer.

"You only need a lawyer if you have something to hide," Kort suggests. "Mikey's talking…"

I ask again for a lawyer.

Kort leaves.

An hour after that, Larry enters.

"What are you doing here?"

"I'm your lawyer."
"Don't you have to *be* a lawyer?"
"I am." He sits across from me. "So, what did you tell them?"
"The Old Harold story. Did you talk to Rebecca?"
Larry nods.
"That's it," I tell him.
"All right. Then I think we can go."

forty one

On the way out, I see Eddie Horne bent over the desk of one of the detectives. He spots me and winds his way through the desks as Larry escorts me out through the station.

He calls out my name.

"Hey, Eddie," I answer.

"You look awful."

"Nice to see you, too, but I can't chat just now. I just want to get home."

"Yeah, I'll bet. Listen, is it true what happened in there?"

"Is what true?"

"Harry Finn killed Tony Vitali and Mikey Manzonetti before the SWAT team shot him dead."

"Mikey's dead?" I ask.

"Yeah."

"Kort's an asshole."

"Yeah, he can be," Eddie concedes. "So, I was right? It was Harry Finn all along?"

I nod.

"And you thought you could stop him?"

I shrug. "To me he was just Old Harold, another hurting parent, lost in the world of the living."

"Jeez." Eddie sighs. "I know this is a lot to ask, but—"

"I'll tell you everything I know," I assure him, "but I gotta go see

Rebecca. We'll talk. I promise."

"Okay," he says and backs away out of my path.

I let Larry guide me toward the exit but turn back to Eddie. "Looks like you've got your bestseller," I tell him.

forty two

Larry walks me to my apartment.

Rebecca opens the door as we approach. "Thanks, Larry," she says as he hands me off to her.

The touch of her arm around my back is soothing.

She guides me into the apartment, through the living room and into the bedroom. "What can I get you?" she asks.

"A new face," I joke.

She smiles and instead gets me some Tylenol and a glass of water.

I swallow four of the tablets, then lie down.

Rebecca crawls into bed next to me.

"What went wrong?" I ask. "How did you end up in that place?"

Rebecca explains what happened after she eluded Vitali's men. "I saw another SUV behind me, only they weren't just following, they were chasing me.

"They managed to cut me off, then pulled a gun on me and made me get in their car and put on a hood.

"They tied me up at the warehouse, and Mikey started telling me that you had told him everything—but, he was willing to let me go if I told Vitali what we had done.

"I told him he was a liar. That you would never confess to something you didn't do.

"Then your message came in. And I knew you were okay. But he knew about the baby. He threatened to stab me in the belly, so I tried to warn you. I tried."

"I know," I tell her, and then fill her in on what happened to me from the time Amy dropped me off and Mikey brought me and Old Harold to the warehouse.

"It's over," I say.

"I can't believe Old Harold was doing the exact same thing we were."

"Only he'd been doing it for a lot longer and was a professional killer."

She snuggles up against me. "We weren't so bad ourselves."

"We were lucky."

She kisses me on the one part of my face that isn't bruised, broken or cut. "We were a great team, weren't we? I mean all of us. I think Old Harold would be proud."

"You might be right," I agree, as fatigue and Tylenol start to carry me away. "Thank goodness we don't have wake up tomorrow and do that again."

I close my eyes, finally ready to rest.

"Yes," Rebecca agrees. "We should wait until after the baby is born."

Author's Note

If you are a reader like me, you appreciate when a writer gives you a little glimpse behind the pages of a book in the form of an author's note. If you're a writer yourself, it's always interesting to get some insight into another author's process. And if you just enjoy reading a good book, it's nice to hear directly from the writer, rather than only through the words of his or her story.

So, dear reader, thank you for indulging with me in this short postscript.

The clichéd question writers are often asked is, "Where do you get your ideas?"

I'm not sure every writer in each case can precisely answer that. Often ideas are flashes of inspiration or come from thoughts that percolate over months or even years. In the case of *The Dead Kids Club*, it came to me in a dream.

Dreams are funny things. I don't often remember them very clearly, but on the occasion that I do, I'm often amazed at the way my mind constructs them. Sometimes the architecture of my dreams is reminiscent of the movie, *Inception*. Sometimes I find myself in a situation where I've achieved professional success, or I check my investment accounts and discover I'm a millionaire.

Other times, the dream turns out to be a nightmare.

The nocturnal hallucination that inspired this story, as you might have guessed, is one in which my son was killed. It was very disturbing, and it makes me uneasy to even write about it here. In the dream, much like the protagonist in this *The Dead Kids Club*, I decided I would kill the person who had taken his life.

I woke at that point, still overtaken by the emotions engendered by the dream. For a brief moment, I wondered if it was real, but that feeling quickly passed and I returned to full wakefulness, assured that my son was fine, and it had all been just a bad nightmare.

But a question remained. Would I actually do that? If I found myself in that situation, my child taken and his killer somehow escaping justice, what would I do?

Almost instantly, the story for a novel came to me.

Up until that point in my life, I had obtained some modest success writing for television (you can look up my credits at RichHosek.com or on IMDB.com) and had started a few books along the way, but had never finished one. It's a whole different process crafting a half hour teleplay, than writing a full-length novel.

My Hollywood days were behind me, and in between working full time and being a dad, I decided this was the time to write a book and this was the book I was going to write.

The first three-quarters came out easily, without an outline or anything other than the notion that my protagonist started from the same nightmare that was only a dream for me, and that I was going to use a character that had been kicking around in my head for a while named Eddie Horne, the Luddite crime writer. But then I hit a wall. I thought I thought I knew how it was going to end, but suddenly the days of writing several thousand words at a time ceased. I was lucky to be able to craft a single paragraph when I could write anything at all.

While I was stalled, I showed the first part to a friend, and based on the feedback, went back and started rewriting what I had so far.

And there he was. (Spoiler alert if you peaked ahead to the author's note before reading the book.)

Old Harold.

I didn't really know who he was when I first mentioned him in the chapter where my protagonist and his ex-wife go to the support group. He was just background, a part of the scenery. Why had I put him there? Was it really just random? Or was there a subconscious element at work?

I remembered how those first chapters flowed out of me, how the members of the support group seemed to tell me their stories instead of me having to write them.

"So, Old Harold, what's your story?" I asked.

And then he told me.

Suddenly, the ending I thought I was writing toward became an exit I missed on my way toward where the story really wanted to go. Once Old Harold revealed himself, I found other elements coming together in unexpected ways—at least unexpected to my conscious mind. The Dead Kids Club had their first real meeting in Rebecca's apartment and the last line of the book—which was something I was sure of from the start—became more than just an idea and was now a destination within sight.

Everything fell in place. I was on a roll.

Once I was finished, I immediately started writing another book as I tried to figure out what to do with *The Dead Kids Club*. Eddie Horne makes an appearance in that one as well, and the idea of creating a series of what I had come to think of as everyman thrillers—ordinary people in extraordinary circumstances—came to being.

Although *The Dead Kids Club* is the first book I finished, my debut novel is a paranormal mystery based on a screenplay I had written years ago with my television writing partner, Arnold Rudnick, and parapsychologist Loyd Auerbach. It falls into many categories, so if you like mysteries, thrillers, detective stories or novels about the paranormal, you'll find something in our book, *Near Death,* that will captivate you. Visit @RaneyAndDaye on Facebook, or RaneyAndDaye.com to find out more about *Near Death: A Raney/Daye Investigation.*

The next installment of my everyman thriller series, "From the Files of Eddie Horne," is a story called *The Tenth Ride.* Make sure to like my Facebook page, @WrittenByRichHosek, or join my email list at RichHosek.com to find out when it will be available.

And if you're a fan of Eddie Horne—as many of my early readers

have been—he'll be getting his own book soon as well.
Thank you for reading *The Dead Kids Club*.
And… pleasant dreams.

Rich Hosek
January 15, 2021

Acknowledgments

I have to extend a special thank you to Kathryn Rudnick, my friend of more than thirty-five years and wife to my television writing partner, Arnold Rudnick. Kathy was the first person to read *The Dead Kids Club* and told me the original beginning—where I was trying to do something cute with the timeline of the story—was too confusing. Her comments and insights have always made me a better writer. Thanks, Kath.

I also have to thank J.D. Meir (who needs to get busy and finish her novel!) for providing early feedback and editorial comments and recruiting other readers as I got closer to publishing this book.

Thanks to Isabel Espinoza and Danielle Pepa for their editorial efforts, and Jade N., whom I consider my first fan—someone who knows me only through my writing—for her comments and encouragement.

And of course I am eternally grateful to Arnold Rudnick, for his friendship and partnership during our early days making student films and cable TV productions at the University of Illinois at Urbana-Champaign, through our adventures in Hollywood, and for urging me to finally get this book out there. Although we are separated by half a continent these days, you are still my best friend, confidant and adviser.

Finally, and always, thank you to my family and friends. You mean more to me than I will ever be able to express.

Made in the USA
Monee, IL
26 January 2021